GW00361811

# MAX QUADRANT – SPACE DETECTIVE

# MAX QUADRANT – SPACE DETECTIVE

Adrian Smith

Book Guild Publishing
Sussex, England

First published in Great Britain in 2010 by
The Book Guild Ltd
Pavilion View
19 New Road
Brighton, BN1 1UF

Typesetting in Baskerville by
Nat-Type, Cheshire

Printed in Great Britain by
CPI Antony Rowe

A catalogue record for this book is available from
The British Library.

ISBN 978 1 84624 385 1

# PROLOGUE

The crucial point in our evolution, when humanity irrevocably distanced itself from all other species on earth, was the moment when the first human being became conscious of the idea of past, present and future. Not just his own, as in 'I have just killed this animal, I am now eating it and when I have done so my stomach will be full,' but the awareness that he was a small link in a chain of development. That beings now dead and turned to dust had made advances of which he was now the beneficiary, and that the collective human species was now developing ideas and methods that would benefit those yet to come. There can have been few thinking people since that time who have not been conscious of this and been frustrated by the fact that they will never know. What will life be like in a hundred years, in a thousand years, or in ten thousand years?

Back in the 1970s and 1980s, we were offered up the year 2000 as being the time in the distant future when the world would be unrecognisable from the present. Few people would have to work, no one would starve as all dietary needs would be satisfied with a few pills, and everyone would travel around cities in the sky wearing jet-packs on their backs. For those who had, as children, believed this image of the future, the turn of the millennium was something of an anti-climax. We were actually working longer and harder than before, people in poor countries still died every day from starvation, the predicted wonder pills had been supplanted by fast food, and people were still driving slowly behind one another in cars. OK, they were slightly nicer cars, but were cars nevertheless, and despite the efforts of various teenage Ford Escort drivers on Southend sea front, they could in no way be described as jet-packs.

As the sun came up on 1st January 2000, there came with it a realisation that nothing much had changed. Yes, we now had small computers everywhere, whereas thirty years previously there had been very few and each was the size of several buses, but essentially life was the same. We went to work, we bought and sold, we loved and hated and we laughed, and we hurt each other and ourselves. If we looked back in history, the evidence was there – the tools we used to help us in our lives changed over the decades, centuries and millennia, but the way we behaved remained constant. Would things ever change? Would there ever be a Golden Age of enlightenment, or is the fundamental drive that makes humanity continually advance dependent on fear, jealousy, greed and inequality? In short, will the human world of a thousand years time be a better world, one of compassion, equality and peace, or will it be just like today only with slightly better gadgets?

# 1

Max Quadrant slowly opened his eyes. The sun was beginning its slow ascent over City One of Centrum H, and Max lay still for a moment, clearing his mind before attempting to use it to kick-start his body. He rose quietly from his bed so as not to wake Chloe, his wife, and moved to the kitchen, pouring himself a glass of orange juice from the carton in the fridge. He was a creature of habit, and always started each day in the same way, sitting in silence in his favourite chair and sipping his orange juice. It was here that he mentally arranged the day ahead and on this day, 15th April 2999, he had a morning meeting with Lars Jettessen, his boss, followed by lunch with his son Dan. He would spend the afternoon in the office and then go out to dinner with Chloe in the evening.

Max was a Space Detective, and though based on his home planet of Centrum H, the capital planet of H sector, his job did not entail the solving of domestic crime. That was the role of the Centrum H Police. The role of Space Detectives was to investigate crimes committed outside the capital planet of each sector, where there was either no permanent police force, or where the complexity of the case was such that outside assistance was required. Not only was Max Quadrant a Space Detective, he was a very good Space Detective – some said he was the best. As a result, and to fend off competition from private detective agencies for his services, he was a well-paid Space Detective, enabling him to

1

live in one of the more prosperous, centrally located areas of City One and, importantly for him, this meant that he could walk to his office rather than having to travel by the various public transport systems which he so despised. Having showered, and gelled down his somewhat unruly hair, he dressed for work, piling on the layers to repel the cold outside. When H sector was first colonised by humans, the planet now known as Centrum H was the obvious choice as capital planet, having a breathable life-sustaining atmosphere already without the need to alter by way of element bombs. It was, however, a long way from its nearest star, so the daylight was watery at best and the heat from its sun was such that outside temperatures generally hovered only a few degrees above freezing.

Max maintained a brisk pace on his walk to work and once there, quickly proceeded to remove his coat and the various outer layers of his clothing, as, in common with most buildings in the centre of City One, the temperature inside his office was maintained at a constant, balmy, almost tropical level. He turned on his Visiscreen to check any messages he had received overnight, put on his sensorglove, sat in his chair and began to scroll through his inbox. Most messages he did not even open, having long ago concluded that the man who read all of his Visiscreen messages was not only the man who never actually did any work, but was also the man who never went home, never took a holiday, and probably never slept either. Besides that, Max was of the opinion that Visiscreen messages could be divided into four main categories:

(1)  Mass distribution messages, sent by people you had never met (and never would meet) or even heard of, concerning things about which you had no idea and which would not in any way affect you.
(2)  Messages sent by people who contributed nothing,

but spent all their time composing vast and overly-elaborate prose, usually liberally punctuated with the latest buzz-words and buzz-phrases which they had overheard in the lift that morning, and distributed to the widest possible audience of senior people within the organisation, pointing out where the middle and junior people were going wrong and how things would have been so much better had they been consulted first, all in the belief that this behaviour would result in their being identified as dynamic taskmasters and innovative thinkers and first to be considered when the next round of promotions came along. What Max found most depressing was that this belief usually turned out to be true.

(3)   Messages inviting him to do things he didn't want to do, go places he didn't want to go, or meet people he didn't want to meet. Sometimes all three at once.

(4)   Interesting Stuff.

It was for the fourth category that he scanned the list of messages, gently flicking his index finger sheathed in the sensorglove to scroll down. Suddenly, his finger stopped still, and the moving list on the Visiscreen froze instantly, highlighting a red (urgent) message from Lars Jettessen. Lars was Head of the Space Detective Division for H Sector, with whom he was shortly due to have a routine meeting. Why was he sending him an urgent message now? He flicked his finger to open the message, which instantly displayed itself on the Visiscreen. It simply said, 'Max. My Office. Urgent. Don't wait. LJ'.

# 2

Lars Jettessen gave the appearance of being a big man. In truth, he was only a little over average height and, while he could be described as having a 'full figure', he was neither grossly fat nor overly muscular. What made people view him as a big man were his voice and general demeanour. Had he lived fifteen centuries earlier, he would almost certainly have been a Town Crier, as even in normal conversation his voice was loud enough to make the bones vibrate in the head of anyone in his immediate vicinity. Coupled with this was a slightly paradoxical air of quiet menace – he rarely lost his temper, but always gave the impression that he was about to at any moment. Those instances when he had were now legendary and, when related to new recruits, instilled into them an instinctive fear of the man, which only served to perpetuate and increase his aura of total dominance.

Like many people in senior management positions, Lars Jettessen had little skill in performing the tasks assigned to those under his supervision. His skill was, largely through fear, occasionally through persuasion and motivation, getting those below him to perform as required and it was through this ability, rather than through being a great detective, that he had achieved his current position. That and being married to the daughter of the Head of the Space Detective Agency on Centrum A.

Max did not have a big problem with Lars. Max knew that Lars knew how good he was, and he knew that Lars was aware of the number of private agencies who were constantly trying to tempt Max away to work for them. As a result, they had a peaceful, although somewhat strained relationship. Lars liked people who worked for him to be afraid of him, as this made his job, in his mind, much easier. Also, like many aggressive managers before him, he had a vague fear and mistrust of people who were more intelligent than himself, and comparing his brainpower to that of Max Quadrant was like comparing a fish to a giraffe as entrants in a long neck competition. These factors meant that the power balance between Max and his boss was not as heavily stacked in his own favour as Lars would have liked it, but ultimately the Head of Space Detectives was judged on results, and results were what Max always provided. For his part, Max was rather indifferent to Lars. He had no real respect for the man's miniscule intellect but, provided he didn't interfere too much (which he didn't), then Max was content with their relationship. In no way did he covet his boss's position, having little by way of traditional career ambition. His ambitions related solely to his chosen path of crime solving, and his slightly odd hope was that he would one day be faced with the perfect crime – one where he knew for certain by whom, where, and how it had been committed but which even he, Max Quadrant, was unable to prove.

'What I am about to tell you,' said Lars, 'is and must remain highly confidential.' This statement was in itself tinged with irony given Lars' habit of high decibel narrative.

'Ever heard of a planet called Solauric?'

'Of course,' replied Max. 'It's the most expensive LRP there is – supposedly the nearest thing to paradise.'

'Not for one Professor Quark,' said Lars, 'he's just been found dead on Solauric. Laser pistol blast through the head. Ever heard of him?'

Max was tempted to say, 'Of course, you idiot, where do you think I've been the last twenty years?' but for the sake of harmony contented himself with a simple 'yes'. He continued, 'Professor Samuel Quark – reputedly the cleverest man in the universe. The leading authority on space, planets and the locating and identification of alien life forms. The last part purely theoretical of course.'

Lars looked up. 'Theoretical? What about the Thorians?' Max tried desperately to avoid addressing his boss as an inbred, overly-promoted numbskull, which was difficult because he was.

'Lars, the existence of the Thorian empire is a theory. No one has ever actually seen a Thorian or established any conclusive evidence that they exist.'

'Nonsense – it may be a theory, but it is a theory accepted throughout the human world. That is, apparently, by everyone apart from you. Anyway, the evidence is over-whelming – space vessels destroyed, planets annihilated. What more proof do you need? The fact that the Thorians have never shown themselves is all part of their plan. They know that they are too weak to beat us in an all-out war, so content themselves with raids and isolated attacks while they develop new weapons. You can bet your life that the moment they think they are militarily stronger than us they will attack.'

'Maybe,' said Max, quietly. 'Anyway – Professor Quark?'

'Dead,' said Lars, as if revealing some new gem of information. 'A shame we can't say the same about the Thorians.' Max realised he was going to have to change tack to get away from the issue of the Thorians. Too late. Lars went on, "Peace Through Strength". That's what it's all about. Not my words. Straight from the mouth of President Shrube.' Straight from the mouth of the President's speechwriters, thought Max to himself.

'Lars,' said Max, 'in the true spirit of my profession, I'm going to make a few elementary deductions. Please correct me if I'm wrong. Professor Quark has been killed by a blast through the head from a laser pistol. If he had killed himself, or if he had been killed by someone else whose identity were known, then I would not be sitting here in your office. This leads me to conclude that you want me to go to Solauric and find the killer.'

'That's mostly true.'

'Which part of it isn't true?'

'None of it.'

An awkward pause ensued, before Lars launched another high volume salvo. 'Basically, it's like this. The Professor is dead. Killed. Don't know who did it. I want you to go to Solauric and find out. It's a small planet, an LRP, as you know. Just a few guests and a handful of staff. Since the murder, no one is allowed in. No one is allowed out. But that's where the problem is – most of the guests are either very important public figures or are immensely rich, in some cases both. There is a limit to how long we can hold them there.'

'But we have the authority to hold them until we have investigated the crime,' said Max, 'at least until we have interviewed them.'

'Authority and political will are very different animals,' intoned Lars, leaning back in his chair in admiration of his own statesmanship. 'So I need you to go as soon as possible. There's a supply ship leaving Centrum H on the 20th. We'll get you on that. It's a three month journey to Solauric so you'll get there on 20th July. We can hold the people on Solauric till then, but once you get there you will have to get some quick results. All the people there will have long journeys ahead and they will all have places they need to be for the Millennium night. My guess is that by the time you arrive they will all be getting very twitchy to depart.' As Lars paused for breath, Max interjected. 'Especially the murderer.'

'Yes. Quite.' said Lars. 'Anyway, the 20th is in five days.

Suggest you use that time to research on the Solauric guests. Not much information on the staff, but most of the guests are well known figures and there is more information available on them than you could absorb in several lifetimes.' Most of it made up, thought Max. His ears were starting to resonate painfully with every hammer-blow word that was emanating from Lars' mouth, so he diplomatically brought the meeting to a swift close and retired to his office to consider what lay ahead.

# 3

Max Quadrant was no stranger to the subject of murder. To him, any crime was simply a puzzle. All the clues, even if cryptic, were there, you just had to put them into the framework in the right places and the solution was there before your eyes. No, finding the solution did not concern him. He would identify the murderer. He always did. What concerned him here was the people he was dealing with. In his experience, if you were questioning ten people, the nine who were not guilty would take an instant dislike to you on the grounds that in their view you should have immediately discounted them as suspects – based entirely upon their own knowledge of their own innocence. The guilty person would, of course, hate you even more but that, thought Max, was probably unavoidable.

So, one of the people currently on Solauric was a murderer, and in trying to identify this person Max was going to run the risk of making some of the most influential people in the universe his enemies. To a man of career-minded ambition like Lars Jettessen, this would indeed have been staring into the abyss. To Max, it was a more minor concern, but a concern nevertheless. For now, he had four days to get to know all he could about those from whom he must identify the killer of Professor Quark. Then, before arriving on the planet Solauric, he would spend three months in Spacesleep.

# 4

When the colonisation of other planets by earth humans began, one of the biggest early problems encountered was not, as you would be forgiven for thinking, how to survive in these strange new worlds, as this had largely been considered and addressed prior to the process taking place. Most of the planets chosen for settlement had, or could be made to have, with the explosion of the right kind of element bomb, roughly the right kind of atmosphere to sustain human life. Due to the varying distances of stars from these settlement planets, most were either too hot or too cold, but this could be endured as the amount of time most people would be required to spend outside unsheltered by man-made constructions was limited. A few planets were settled on where the atmosphere was unable to be sufficiently altered to become life-sustaining, but these were mainly occupied for the mining of mineral resources and the small mining populations could easily be accommodated within various living-dome structures. The only other use of hostile atmosphere planets was for LRPs, Luxury Resort Planets. These were usually selected for the reason of either being relatively cheap to buy or being in the vicinity of some beautiful or interesting space phenomena.

Planet Solauric was unique as an LRP in that it had a breathable atmosphere, but was used solely as a resort planet. It had originally been planned for settlement but was purchased at huge expense by Solauric Holdings and an extravagantly luxurious hotel erected thereon. A very small hotel, very discreet, and as a result unbelievably expensive.

Anyway, to get back to the point, the biggest problem in the early days of space colonisation was that of the time it took to get from one planet to another: if a journey was to take three years the queue of people lining up to undertake such a journey tended to be very short indeed. This problem was eventually solved by the development of a harmless form of suspended animation, which became known as Spacesleep and made it possible for people to travel vast distances, often in fully automated spacecraft, and be revived at their point of destination. The attraction of Spacesleep was two-fold. Firstly, the passenger did not have to endure the abject boredom of a prolonged space flight over several months or, in some cases, years. Secondly, a person in Spacesleep aged at only one thirtieth of the normal human ageing rate, so space travel became that much more attractive because par-ticipants were not, in effect, using up their life span in travel. However, as so often happens, the solving of one problem creates another, and the differing rates of ageing being experienced by different people lead to the development of SAA, or Space Adjusted Age, as opposed to AFB, Age from Birth. Take Max Quadrant as an example. When Max married his wife Chloe, they had both spent their whole lives on Centrum H and were both aged 22. Some 40 years later, and due to his extensive inter-planetary travel as a Space Detective (including one trip to a planet in the T sector, which took 10 years each way in real time), Max had an SAA of 34 years old, whereas Chloe, having never left Centrum H, was 62.

The primary reason behind SAA was to protect pension funds. In the early years of lengthy space travel, astronauts had blasted off into space in their early twenties, spent many years in Spacesleep, and returned fifty years later with the physical attributes of healthy men in their late twenties but actually being in their seventies and entitled to a full pension for the rest of their lives. Their employers, be they governments or private sector, were a bit miffed at having to pay out pensions for fifty-odd years to people who had spent most of their working lives asleep and therefore relatively unproductive. This caused such a drain on pension fund finances that the pension trustees took to hiring hit-men to eliminate those who were expected to prove a financial burden, as the cost of the assassin plus the Death Benefit payable to the dependents (who, having stayed behind, were getting on a bit anyway) were usually considerably less than the cost of funding fifty years of windsurfing and golf. Faced with potential bankruptcy of the pension system and an alarming murder rate, governments introduced the SAA system, primarily to measure pensionable age. The legislation was applied retrospectively, meaning that all those people with AFBs of under 70 on pensions had their benefits frozen until they reached an SAA of 70, forcing huge numbers of men and women who had had nothing but a life of leisure for many years, and before that had spent most of their time in Spacesleep, to look for work. Such people were, of course, hopelessly out of touch with the world of work, and in most cases with their particular world in general, and found it impossible to gain employment, meaning that governments then had to incur the huge expense of providing unemployment benefit. It did, however, lead to a significant drop in the murder rate, even though the basic rules of supply and demand meant that there was a sudden glut of professional assassins chasing a limited number of clients, culminating in the infamous spate of 'Murder one, kill one free' offers.

# 5

Max sat in the bar of Crazy Maggie's Restaurant, waiting for Dan to join him for lunch. The restaurant was, it was reputed, named after a woman who had been a country President way back in history on Centrum A. She had been lauded during her time in power as a visionary, but several hundred years later historical psychologists had examined her actions, images of her and the text of her speeches, and had come to the unanimous conclusion that she had been stark raving bonkers all the time.

As Max took a sip of his fruit juice cocktail, he looked through the bar-room throng of lunchers and spotted the slightly shambolic figure of Dan coming through the doors. Due to the amount of his life spent in Spacesleep, and the fact that Dan had only been away from Centrum H once in his life, Max Quadrant was, in terms of Space Adjusted Age at least, some five years younger than his own son. This, and the fact that Max had in effect slept through most of Dan's childhood and early adulthood, could have made their relationship strained, but in truth neither had ever known anything different and, while they were not especially close, there was no animosity between them. To the best of Max's knowledge and judgement, his son held no deep feelings of patriarchal rejection or neglect. Whilst Dan Quadrant always presented an appearance leaning very much on the unkempt side of the neatness barometer, and had certainly not gone round twice when the clown's big floppy shoes and squirty flowers were being handed out, he had a good job as an arbitrage trader at the Universal Savings Bank which enabled him, should he have so desired, to live a reasonably affluent lifestyle. Being of a cautious disposition, he chose to live a moderate, almost frugal existence, but this was through choice rather than necessity. Dan lived alone, and Max was convinced that this was also by choice, as his income was more than sufficient to overcome any physical shortcomings or character deficiencies that may have otherwise presented themselves in the marital courtship ritual. Max knew that some of Dan's work colleagues at USB suspected him of being, in their words, a 'shirt elevation specialist', due to his conspicuous lack of female companionship. On one level Max was totally indifferent to his son's preferred entrance to the pleasure emporium – or whether he just preferred to give the whole building a wide berth and continue walking down the street – but he was acutely aware that, even after many centuries of legislation, prosecution and compensation, such prejudices were still a concealed reality.

After a few minutes of small talk covering the usual family agenda of mutual enquiries regarding health and work, the conversation turned to the subject of the impending year-end festivities to celebrate the passage into the fourth millennium. In a radical departure from his normal financial restraint, Dan had decided that this was such a momentous occasion that not only was he going to push the boat out, but he was also going to get on board and do his best to sink it, as he had booked a table for three at Uranium, City One's fantastically expensive 'restaurant-of-the-moment', owned by celebrity chef Cane Mogai, famous for his use of nuclear fusion in cooking. (He was allegedly desperate to also adopt nuclear fission for culinary use in order to launch a 'fission chips' range of ready meals, but his scientists had so far let him down on this one.) Max decided he had better put his celebratory cards on the millennium table.

'I have to go away,' he said, detecting an instant flicker of emotion in his son's face which echoed similar occasions in Dan's childhood years.

'OK,' said Dan after the briefest of pauses, 'I'll just go with Mum. It's not a big issue.'

Quite clearly it was a big issue.

'Look,' said Max, 'I'm not saying I can't make it … but I'm not saying I can make it either … but what I am saying is that if it's humanly possible then I'll be there. Logic dictates that I can't do more than that. It's just that I have a long way to go, and again logic dictates that if I have a long way to go I also have a long way to come back. I can't tell you where I'm going, but I go in five days' time, and if I can sort things out in a reasonable timeframe I can make it back in time for the millennium. It's just that at this stage I don't really know what I'm dealing with or how difficult it's going to be.'

'Why can't you tell me where you're going?'

'Difficult to give an answer to that one. If I tell you why I can't tell you where I'm going then I might as well tell you where I'm going.'

'So tell me where you're going.'

'I can't.'

Max wondered for a split second whether or not to tell Dan that he was going to Solauric and the names of those being held on the planet pending his arrival and ensuing investigation. Max was not a man routinely in the habit of breaching confidentiality but, given the wealth of the individuals on Solauric and his son's position as a senior trader within USB, he thought Dan might possibly be in a position to provide certain information and insights relative to the more gilded members of society that might prove useful in his investigations. However, he decided almost instantaneously that this would be premature, and that he would make a fuller assessment of the situation once he had arrived on Solauric before deciding whether or not to involve Dan.

15

After lunch, Max walked back to his office, painfully aware that he was going to have to have a similar conversation with Chloe at dinner that evening. Long periods of travel were a necessary and inevitable part of being a Space Detective, and just because Chloe had always accepted this and had never complained, it didn't mean that she didn't have feelings of sorrow that their marriage had been a union based on separation. For Max's part, the unease of leaving a child behind had now been replaced by feelings akin to deserting an elderly relative, given their Space Adjusted Age difference of nearly 30 years. As expected, dinner with Chloe ran along the same lines as lunch with Dan. His impending departure revealed, Max made a series of heavily caveated promises to be back on Centrum H for the family millennium dinner at Uranium.

Having got these conversations out of the way, Max spent the next four days researching those currently being detained following the demise of Samuel Quark and, by the time he arrived at City One's spaceport to take up his berth on the cargo ship bound for Solauric, he had compiled a brief summary of the history and characteristics of each of them, which he had stored on his Visiport machine:

*Professor Samuel Quark (deceased)*

Almost universally accepted as being the greatest scientific mind of his generation, and of many preceding generations, Samuel Quark had, until his recent gruesome demise, been head of the Presidential Committee on research into alien life. He established his reputation some twenty years ago with his theories on the infinite nature of space and the somewhat inevitable conclusion that, if space, and therefore the number of planets contained therein (if indeed an infinite space could be said to 'contain' anything) was infinite, then even if, for argument's sake, the chances of life developing

16

on a planet was one in a billion trillion gazillion, then, due to the curious nature of infinity in relation to mathematics, the number of planets upon which life had evolved must also be infinite.

He was not the first scientist to espouse this theory. In fact the scientific world had, over the past thousand years, lurched wildly between belief and non-belief in the infinity of space and the existence of alien life forms. The simple fact was that, for all the theories and counter-theories, for every hypothesis and antithesis, no one actually knew the answer. Quark's early theories had conclusively disproved the then prevailing theories and been accepted as the truth, and would be held up as such until someone else would come along with a new theory which trashed the Quark view, or of course, until space was proved to be finite or infinite or alien life forms were conclusively proved to exist.

What had given further credence to the Quark theories was the widely-held belief in the existence of the Thorian empire. No one was sure exactly where the Thorians lived. There were wildly differing opinions on what they looked like. No one knew what language they spoke, or even whether they spoke at all. The only thing that most people agreed on was the fact that they were a bad thing. Very bad. It was generally held that a homicidal, patricidal, matricidal, fratricidal, psychopathic human serial killer with a really bad toothache was still a much more pleasant and rounded individual than the most charitable, gregarious and kindly Thorian. Whilst no Thorian had ever been taken alive or dead, and no images of themselves or their spacecraft had been captured, the manifest evidence of their wrongdoing was everywhere. Entire populations of outlying planets had been slaughtered and numerous spacecraft destroyed at the hands of the evil Thorians. A few people doubted the vile intentions of the Thorians, but they were usually scorned by the majority. 'How could their intentions be honourable,' went the arguments, 'when they destroy everything in their path and never leave survivors to bear witness to their atrocities?'

Popular belief was that the Thorians were content to raid isolated colonies and spaceships, but otherwise conceal themselves, on the grounds that their military capability was ultimately inferior to that of the human race, but that if ever they gained the martial upper hand they would launch all-out war and human civilisation would be annihilated. Fortunately for mankind, the brilliance of its scientific brains combined with massive expenditure ensured that they were always a few steps ahead of the Thorians in this particular game, enabling the populace to sleep safely, although maybe a little uneasily, in the knowledge that as long as the lead in this arms race was maintained, the Thorians would never attack. This feeling was encapsulated and kept alive in people's thoughts by means of President Shrube's 'Peace Through Strength' slogan, one of the more dramatic points of his election campaign three years previously. Samuel Quark was as indifferent to President Shrube as he was to all politicians, but President Shrube was almost reverent in his endorsement of Professor Quark as the absolute authority on all things scientific. The Professor had been one of the few people with almost instant access to the President's ear, and the whole relationship had afforded mutual benefits to both parties. President Shrube had gained intellectual kudos by his association with Quark, which served in a small way to repudiate the perception that perhaps if human settlements were powered at night by the brain power of the President then all books would have to be printed in Braille. Quark, for his part, was perceived, through his presidential access, to have influence, which led to many a businessman offering significant financial inducement for the Professor to lend his scientific approval to various potentially lucrative projects. To be fair, Quark was a man of unimpeachable integrity, and would never have given his backing to a project he viewed as being at all spurious or morally debateable, although he did usually wait until after he had received the money before declaring his aversion to the project in question.

## President Aldous T. Shrube

Being the President of the United Planets of Humanity was, ostensibly, the most powerful job there was. How much real power the position involved was open to debate, and many believed that real power lay far away from the public glare of the office of President. Some of those who so believed were the kind of conspiracy-obsessed crackpots who have plagued the human race ever since early man picked up a giraffe's shin bone and had the idea that it would make a good implement with which to hit other people in an attempt to get their own way. But the majority were of a more sensible disposition and simply realised that no economic and social system of such a size could function efficiently if all the power lay in the hands of a person who had firstly to ingratiate himself with all and sundry in order to be elected, and then spend five years desperately clinging to the post whilst at the same time planning his subsequent re-election bid. Aldous T. Shrube had now occupied the Presidential chair for three years, and was already very conscious that the re-electoral clock was ticking loudly. With humanity spread out across the vastness of colonised space, electoral campaigning was a serious business, and Shrube was determined to get a second term in office, for no real reason other than to gain bragging rights over his father, who had served one presidential term and seemed certain to get a second, only to be unceremoniously dumped out of office by a sudden swing of popular opinion against him.

Shrube was, in any reasonably objective assessment, an intellectual featherweight. Had he not been born into the great wealth and privilege of the fledgling Shrube political dynasty, there is no telling where he would have ended up, although Party Planner at the legendary Morrissey's Brewery on Centrum D would not have been high on the list of probabilities. Secretly, he despised any one whom he perceived as being smarter than himself, but fortunately for him his perception was not good, otherwise he would have been forced to remove himself to the remote wastelands of the R sector and live as a hermit. He publicly associated himself with the likes of the late Professor Quark on the grounds of reflected intellectual glory – he presumed that if the electorate saw that he spent a good deal of his time in the presence of such renowned brainboxes, then they would think he must be something of an intellectual giant himself. He had absolutely no idea what Quark was talking about most of the time, apart from the odd question about where the lavatory was or what time food was going to be served, but he comforted his own ego with the conviction that Quark was expected to be an expert in his own narrow field, because that was his only consideration and occupation in life, whereas he, Aldous T. Shrube, had the enormity of colonised space to run and therefore was compelled to consider the bigger picture. Quark had placed everyone into two categories – those who understood what he was talking about and those who did not. The former category consisted at most of about half a dozen of his scientific colleagues, and the latter of about thirty billion other people, of whom Shrube was simply one. Quark did not despise the thirty billion, he was just supremely indifferent towards them.

Shrube had gained residency in the Presidential hot-seat by promising tough action against the Thorian threat, in contrast to his opponent's policy of attempting peaceful co-existence. The election campaign of three years previously had been going against him until the Thorians' massacre of the entire population of Planet 7 in the M sector had led to a dramatic swing in favour of Shrube and his promises of swift and violent revenge. He had been duly elected and had at once embarked on a prolific episode of military expenditure, although the much vaunted revenge on the Thorians was, three years later, still unaccomplished and beginning to stretch the term 'swift'.

*Professor Horatio Tacitus*

Horatio Tacitus was a Professor of early Third Millennium History at Cambridge University on Centrum A. Like Samuel Quark, he was acknowledged as the leading authority in his chosen field but, unlike the great scientist, he was a warm character much disposed towards his fellow human beings. Not only was his historical knowledge beyond equal, but he also had a reputation for being a great teacher, imparting a degree of enthusiasm and enjoyment in his subject, which made it difficult for his students not to get carried along with him. Tacitus's period of expertise covered many of the seminal moments of human history, including the unification of all the major religions into the Universal Church of Belief and the momentous early years of the human colonisation of space. He could talk for hours on the seemingly smallest and most insignificant of subjects, and frequently did. Like Samuel Quark, he was a Presidential adviser, although in a much further removed and less influential role. Shrube felt that positioning himself with a scientist on one side and a historian on the other presented him to the electorate as a forward-looking, thrusting visionary of the future, but with a sage and reverential awareness of the past, although of course the majority of the under-educated people of the universe had no idea of who Tacitus or Quark were, and simply wondered why their clown of a President was so often flanked by a couple of eccentric-looking old men. Tacitus spent many an hour trying to convince the President to take heed of the lessons of the past when considering issues of future government policy, and on greater men than Shrube this would have been time well spent. Shrube, however, had no interest in history and spent much of his time with Tacitus trying, but usually failing, to stay awake, and had in more recent times taken to avoiding the man wherever possible. He simply could not see the relevance of the past. Dead men had no votes.

This recent Tacitus-avoidance policy made it all the more strange that the loquacious historian was on the Planet Solauric with the rest of the Presidential party, and this fact was not lost on Max Quadrant.

## Karl Shernman

The universal economy had created many a rich man. Few were richer, with one notable exception, and certainly none were more flamboyant, than Karl Shernman. He had built his empire up from nothing, a fact he was not reluctant to tell anyone who wanted to listen, or those who didn't, for that matter. He had begun in the armaments industry and used his early successes there to bankroll his expansion into entertainment, property, transport and finance. He was an acknowledged master of publicity, mostly self-publicity, continually promoting his self-made image as the man with the golden touch. There seemed to be no area of commerce in which Karl Shernman could not succeed, and every new business venture was launched with a crescendo of spectacular media events and the stampede of small investors eager to hand over their money to be a part of the Shernman magic. If magic is all about illusion, then magic it was. While some of his ventures appeared to be an unmitigated success, and were duly elevated to the status of business miracles in the collective eyes of the universe, some were definitely unmitigated disasters. To continue the magician analogy, when he sawed the lady in half it was not unknown to have to call for a good surgeon afterwards.

Despite these occasional setbacks, and despite the fact that he often had to indulge in some sort of reptilian tactics to conclude his deals, Shernman managed to preserve his public facade of uber-successful all round nice guy. To the average man, Karl Shernman was something of a hero, a straight-up guy who had taken on the stuffy corporate world with humour and panache and who had won. From his media image, you would think that he ran all his many companies across the universe single handed. When he launched his own Spaceline, he was pictured in his office signing the contract to lease a hundred shiny new spaceplanes, he was pictured at the check-in desk welcoming passengers, pictured in pilot's uniform on the flight deck, and then, just to show that for all his wealth he was still a great sport, he was pictured in a Spaceline stewardess's uniform serving drinks. Was there nothing this man couldn't do? Was there anything he didn't do? This was the illusion. If the spotlight were turned off and the stage curtains drawn back, the evidence was plain to see. Shernman spent so much of his time promoting his own image that he had little time to actually manage his business. To do this he employed a whole selection of ruthless, anonymous, uncharismatic and uncaring men who attempted to ensure that every ounce of profit was squeezed from each and every operation. Dissenters from the Shernman ideal were instantly dismissed and silenced by way of the hitherto unnoticed confidentiality clauses in their contracts. Ventures which seemed destined to fail were hurriedly sold on before their demise could harm the image of continual success, either to an unsuspecting third party or to one of his many subsidiary companies which had been set up especially for this purpose, and which, unlike the high profile, seemingly profitable businesses, were not branded with the name of Karl Shernman.

## *Blane Levitas*

There were actors and there were Actors, and Blane Levitas was most definitely an Actor. Famous for his immersion in character and absolute devotion to his craft, he bore an almost permanent intensity of expression normally reserved for the seriously injured or the terminally flatulent. He had a prosthetic left arm, having had his natural one surgically removed in order to provide a theatrically accurate portrayal of a historical figure who had famously had a fifty per cent deficiency arm-wise. It had been pointed out to him at the time that it would have been perfectly acceptable to follow the age-old tradition of simply sticking one arm down the inside of his shirt, but Blane Levitas would have no truck with such pretence, which was in a way ironic given that the whole basis of his profession was pretence. This huge degree of self-sacrifice for his art had instantly cemented the legend of Blane Levitas in the annals of thespian achievement and catapulted him to universal fame, although after his preparation for this performance casting directors always avoided offering him parts in which his character was to die, fearing that opening and closing night would inevitably be one and the same. Levitas's ego was as boundless as his sense of self-importance, and he had seen fit to ascribe to himself the nickname of 'The Chameleon' and insisted on being referred to as this in all of his many media releases, although it had never really been a name adopted by those who knew him. Their chosen term did begin with a 'c', but was much shorter.

## *Rose Saturn*

Rose Saturn was an actress. Not an Actress. An actress. She was also beautiful. Her beauty was such that it defied description and belief. The only thing that defied description and belief more was the fact that she was, and had been for some three years now, the girlfriend of Blane Levitas. There used to be a saying that love was blind, but this would go nowhere near enough to explain her romantic attachment to the monstrous, preening, self-obsessed egomaniac that was Blane Levitas. Even if the saying had been 'Love is blind, deaf, dumb, incredibly stupid and has had its head bashed in with a spade', it would still have barely caused a moment's flicker of doubt in people's incredulity at why Rose Saturn, who could presumably take her pick of most of the men in the universe, and probably quite a few of the women too, persisted in a relationship with a man who appeared to treat her so appallingly badly.

Rose had been a star from an early age, having come from a family that had produced some of the greatest stage and screen actors of the Thirtieth Century. Without ever attracting the status of 'superstar', she had been in the public eye for the last twenty years. Most people had watched her grow up, from her early awkward teenage appearances opposite her uncle, through to her gradual blossoming into talented actress and prominent beauty. To older women she was like a daughter, or a favourite niece. Younger women saw her as the sister or best friend they would love to have. Men just loved her and lusted after her.

*Sun Gord*

Sun Gord was styled by his promoters, of which there were many, as the Fastest Man Who Has Ever Lived. He was Universal and Olympic champion at 100 metres and 200 metres, and not only won every race he competed in, but won with considerable ease. On the track, his opponents could literally get nowhere near him, apart from a brief moment on the starting blocks. His total dominance of the sport had led to speculation in some quarters that he was no stranger to certain unspecified chemical performance enhancers, but the rigorous testing methods employed by the Universal Athletics Association had continually failed to produce even the slightest hint that Gord's extraordinary talents were anything other than entirely natural. Speculation by the ubiquitous conspiracy theorists was that Gord was not human at all, but was actually a Thorian, and that he was being used by the Thorian empire as propaganda to demonstrate to their own people the evidence of their physical superiority over the human race. These same conspiracy theorists listed many famous people as being suspected Thorians, from sports personalities, through to politicians, businessmen, writers, artists and actors. Interestingly, Blane Levitas was one of the few prominent people not to have been 'outed' as a potential Thorian, it being felt even by paranoid conspiracy theorists that no self-respecting race of people, however evil, would attempt to justify their innate superiority by holding up such a preening egomaniac as an example.

Despite being the most famous athlete alive, Sun Gord was something of a reclusive character. He trained alone, rarely gave media interviews, arrived at sporting venues with little pre-race time to spare, and disappeared as soon as the medals had been handed out. This was explained away by his management team as being due to the shy and modest nature of the man, that he loved his sport but chose to shun the associated limelight, but of course served only to pour nitro-glycerine on the fire of speculation that he had something to hide.


*Darren and Karen Farren*

Of all the current guests on Solauric, perhaps the ones most out of place were Darren and Karen Farren. It was not overly surprising that Quark and Tacitus were there with the

President, as they were his official advisers. Karl Shernman, the famous entrepreneur, was known to be an occasional confidant of Shrube, and it was not unusual for a President about to seek re-election to be seen to associate himself with the glamour of people like Blane Levitas, Rose Saturn and Sun Gord. But the Farrens were Lottery winners. Not only were they Lottery winners, but they had won the biggest jackpot in history after a series of rollovers on the Universal DNA Lottery.

The DNA Lottery had been running for almost a thousand years, having been originally introduced in the mid 21$^{st}$ century by a government in one of the regions of Centrum A as the only means it could envisage of compiling a national DNA database. In order to participate, you had to register your DNA and pay a weekly subscription. A computer would randomly generate a synthetic DNA sample each week, and if it was a match for one on the database, the owner of that DNA would win the jackpot prize. About three months before Darren and Karen Farren's big win, a malfunction in the synthetic DNA-generating computer had awarded the prize to various members of the same family of monkeys ten weeks running, but they were denied their newfound wealth on the grounds of not having paid their weekly subscriptions. Hence the massive rollover jackpot won by the Farrens, catapulting them overnight from manual workers to owners of the manual to every hi-tech gadget the universe had to offer. It was never revealed publicly which one of the couple had actually had the winning DNA, which in itself had provided ammunition, if ammunition were needed, for the conspiracy theorists to claim that the Farrens were in fact Thorian agents who had murdered the true Lottery winner in order to misappropriate the enormous prize.

Darren and Karen Farren had won more than any couple could reasonably expect to spend in a lifetime, but that did not stop them trying. They were conspicuous in their profligate purchase of anything and everything, and their ability to buy appeared to be almost exactly inversely proportionate to their sense of good taste. They were heroes to certain groups of people, being the living embodiment of the dream of instant transformation from downtrodden to fabulously wealthy without having to lift a finger, but to other people they were simply crass low-lifes whose unbridled extravagance was an insult to hard-working people everywhere. Following their win, there had been calls in some quarters for the DNA Lottery to be scrapped, or at least for the prize fund to be capped, and one law firm had even begun legal action on behalf of the monkeys to reclaim the money that was rightfully theirs. While the government had long since been taking the DNA of every child at birth and so no longer needed the Lottery to populate their database, they did take half of the weekly subscriptions in tax so were loathe to entertain the idea of abandonment or any change that may lessen its appeal. Publicly at least, they maintained that it should continue on the basis that it was one of the few truly egalitarian institutions, that everyone from the richest to the poorest had an equal chance of winning, as long as they weren't monkeys. In actual fact, the poorest man in the universe had a much greater chance of winning than his counterpart at the other end of the pecuniary scale, for the richest man in the universe, the richest man that had ever lived, did not have his DNA on any database anywhere.

There were seven other people on Solauric, but none was well known so the information available to Max at this stage was very limited. There was Hal Joyce and Edward Broillie, aides to President Shrube, plus five members of staff engaged at the Hotel Solauric. They, at least the hotel staff, would possibly be minor figures in the ensuing investigation, but one of them might nevertheless have witnessed something that could prove to be vital. There was not much else Max could do now until he arrived on Solauric, and it was with an open mind that he boarded the Cargo Spaceliner that would take him there. He made his way to the small human cargo area used for passengers (of which he was the only one), lay down on his allotted bed, and watched as the automated encasement slowly descended to cover him, simultaneously ejecting the mixture of gases that would serve to put him into Spacesleep, from which he would awake in 89 days' time.

# 6

You could not describe Jerrand D'Arqueville as well off. To do so would be like describing an electron as small, or space as being big. There was simply no term yet coined which could even begin to describe his financial resources. Rich, wealthy, cashed-up, loaded, uber-loaded, minted – all were so wide of the mark as to be irrelevant. Jerrand D'Arqueville was sometimes described as being the richest man of all time, but again this fundamentally missed the point, as making comparisons either against his contemporaries or against those that had gone before was like comparing an albatross to a tortoise in terms of single flight longevity.

D'Arqueville's wealth was so immense that he had long ago satisfied all of his material needs. He owned his own planet and lived there alone, his accommodation being fully automated to provide for his every need. The defensive security system surrounding his planet was second to none and impregnable – as having a majority ownership in all the major weapons developers and manufacturers enabled him to be always one step ahead of the government-controlled military. He was always careful not to release one generation of weaponry to anyone until he had first installed the subsequent generation into his own security system. He reputedly never left his own planet, and rarely entertained visitors. Mostly, he communicated with the outside world via his secure Visiscreen link, but on the occasions where a discussion was so sensitive that even a multi-encrypted communication platform could not be trusted, he allowed people to come to him, but this was a rare event. In fact, in the last twelve months, only one other person had physically set foot on his planet, and that person would not be doing so again.

While people such as Karl Shernman spent most of their time travelling the universe telling everyone how wealthy they were, D'Arqueville remained silent. He didn't need to tell anyone. Everyone knew that, despite the vast fortune of Shernman, D'Arqueville could probably buy his entire business empire with a single day's income and still have enough change left over to buy the entire population of Centrum H lunch at Uranium. He could, but he didn't. Acquisition had been a passion in his youth, but now would be pointless, like a man who owns the sea collecting raindrops to fill it further. Now, there was nothing else he wanted to buy, nowhere he wanted to go, no one he wanted to meet. But that didn't mean he had no purpose in his life. On the contrary, Jerrand D'Arqueville had an agenda. A very specific agenda. He knew precisely what he wanted to do, and he knew precisely how he was going to achieve it.

# 7

Being something of a veteran in the field of space travel, Max Quadrant was familiar with and accustomed to the process of being awakened from Spacesleep. It was not unusual to feel disorientated when induced out of an interplanetary slumber and many people were, for the first few hours at least, unable to remember who they were or what they were supposed to be doing. In the odd isolated case this feeling persisted for some time afterwards, although these instances often proved to involve people who weren't too sure who they were or what they were supposed to be doing before they went into Spacesleep either. Knowing he would need to be thinking clearly from the moment he arrived on Solauric, Max had set his Spacesleep device to rouse him forty-eight hours prior to his arrival, so by the time he disembarked from the cargo spaceliner he was primed, lucid and ready to begin.

As the natural atmosphere on Solauric was perfect for the human body, Max walked across the open landing strip without any artificial breathing apparatus, and was immediately struck by the sheer beauty of the LRP's environment. It had often been described as the nearest thing there was to paradise, and Max wondered what paradise could possibly have to offer that was not here. Between the landing strip and the hotel complex, he walked along a short winding path through an assembly of the most colourful plants he had ever seen. Either side of the path were huge lakes, lined with trees, and with every species of ornate birds and ducks either floating gently on the surface or gliding overhead, with occasionally one coming in to land on the water like a veteran pilot performing a perfectly practised descent onto a carrier top. Behind the lakes lay grass-covered hills in the foreground, off which flowed gently rolling waterfalls, and behind lay the snow-capped peaks of leviathan mountain ranges.

As Max entered the reception area of the hotel, a tall man with something of a square shaped head approached him rapidly.

'Detective Quadrant?'

'Yes.'

'Welcome to the Hotel Solauric. My name is Barrington Portent. I am the manager of this establishment.'

'Pleased to meet you, Mr Portent. Perhaps we can have a chat once I've checked in.'

'Checked in? My dear Detective, this is the Hotel Solauric, the greatest and most exclusive hotel in the known universe. You do not "check in" here. Everything is arranged.'

'OK,' said Max, 'in that case, can we talk now?'

'Certainly. But not here. The secret of our success, apart from our beautiful planet, the facilities of our hotel and its exceptional service, is discretion. If you would care to join me in my office?'

Max nodded his assent, and followed Barrington Portent down a short corridor to a room which was more sumptuously decorated and kitted out than any room he had been in before in his whole life. 'If this is the standard of the offices, what are the bedrooms going to be like?' thought Max. When they were seated, Portent leaned back in his chair and put his fingertips together, almost as if in prayer. Despite having had three months to prepare for this moment, the hotel manager seemed to be briefly unsure of what to say. Eventually, he moved his hands apart and placed them palms down on his desk.

'Detective Quadrant,' he began, 'whilst I will of course afford you every hospitality that any guest on Solauric would rightfully expect, I hope you don't take it too personally when I say that I would rather you had not come here at all.'

'I understand,' said Max. 'Murder is nasty work. Not what you want in any line of business. Particularly not yours.'

'Quite. Whoever said there's no such thing as bad publicity had clearly never run an exclusive hotel!' Portent placed his hands back together in the pseudo-praying pose, looking a little over-contented with his self-perceived witticism. He continued, 'What I mean is, I don't like this at all. Solauric is a legend. A legend of peace, tranquillity and luxury. And now we have had this dreadful killing. It will take years for our reputation to recover. It's the inconvenience of it all. For us, for the guests, for the owners. Especially for the guests. They were all due to leave nearly three months ago, but they are still being detained. Your people seem to forget, Detective, the type of guests we have here. These are all very very important people. They are all required at this very moment to be other places doing important things.'

'With respect, sir,' said Max, 'you seem to be forgetting the fact that, important as they may be, one of them is a murderer.'

'*May* be a murderer,' said Portent, momentarily looking slightly crestfallen.

'May?' said Max. 'Are you suggesting the killer came from somewhere else, murdered Quark and then departed?'

'It's a possibility. I'm surprised you hadn't thought of it yourself.'

This was not a good start. The last thing Max needed was opposition from inside the hotel, and this man was either over-zealously trying to guard the image of the hotel above all else, had something to hide, or was a complete imbecile. Max could not entirely discount the possibility that the first and third options were both true in equal measure. He

34

decided to close off this particular avenue of conversational conflict and try and get to the point.

'Mr Portent,' he said, 'before I start with my investigation of this incident, which I promise to conclude as soon as possible so that you can resume normal service, I would be grateful if you could briefly explain to me the organisational structure of the hotel.'

Portent leaned back in his chair again, once more adopting the lightly touching fingers pose. Again, he left an ominous pause before offering his reply. Was he being considered or cautious? Or did he just not know what to say?

'There are many ways to explain the organisational structure of this, or any other hotel,' was the retort, 'but I can't see that that's relevant to your job here, Detective.'

'OK, then perhaps you could provide me with a brief run-down on your staff – who they are and what they do.'

'There are many ways to explain who everyone is and what they do, but I have a hotel to run and some very disgruntled guests to try and keep happy. I would politely request that if you want to know anything about my staff, you ask them yourself, and please keep your interviews as short as possible. They all have jobs to do. You are perfectly welcome to use this office for all your needs. It's relatively out of the way and discreet, so if you conduct your business here it shouldn't interfere with the smooth running of the hotel.'

'Thank you,' said Max, 'that's very kind. I will of course need to speak to everyone who was here when the crime was committed. I am led to believe that no one has left?'

'Correct.'

'Good. If you don't mind, Mr Portent, I'd like to start with you, if you have a few minutes?'

'If it'll only take a few minutes, then yes, I'll be glad to get it out of the way.'

'Can you give me some details of what happened on 14th April, the day on which Professor Samuel Quark was killed?'

'There are many ways to explain what happened on that day, but ...'

'Mr Portent,' interjected Max, 'I am not asking you to explain the events, just to tell me what they were.'

'Very well. 14th April. Now, let me see if I can remember ... there was nothing particular about the day-time. Some of the guests went out exploring perhaps, some swam. I think the President was having an important meeting in our conference room. Then there was dinner. I'm not sure who was there, but I don't remember noticing that anyone in particular wasn't there. After dinner, some people went to the bar, some to their rooms, I suppose, and then late in the evening Miss Logi, the maid, took some sleeping tablets up to the Professor's room, as was customary, and found him dead. She summoned me immediately, I summoned the President's aides, Mr Joyce and Mr Broillie, and they sort of took over from there.'

'It was the President's aides who informed the law enforcement authorities?'

'No, it was Miss Saturn.'

'Rose Saturn? The actress?'

'Yes. The President's aides were doing the sort of things that aides do, I suppose. I don't know what they were doing actually, as they had asked me to leave the room. I was walking back to my office when I almost bumped into Miss Saturn. I must have looked rather perturbed as she asked me what the matter was. I was rather indiscreet, I'm afraid, and I told her what had happened to the Professor and that Mr Shrube's assistants were taking care of everything, but she insisted on going to see for herself and that I accompany her. To be truthful, I was in a bit of a state and didn't really know what I was doing, so I just did what she said and went back to the room.'

'And what were Mr Joyce and Mr Broillie doing when you returned?'

'They were taking the Professor's body out of the room.

Miss Saturn got rather angry, asked them to explain what they were doing. I suppose there are many ways to explain what they were doing, but they didn't seem overly interested in answering her questions. They just said they needed to put the body somewhere cold before it started to decompose. They took it downstairs and put it in one of our overflow refrigerators, the ones that we use as backup when we get a large consignment of fresh produce shipped in. That's where it is now. In the refrigerator. While they were doing that, Miss Saturn went to her room and contacted the authorities, shortly after which we received an instruction that everyone was to remain on Solauric, and that the planet was now under military watch and anyone attempting to leave would be apprehended, by force if necessary. I must admit, I found it all a bit heavy-handed, especially given the calibre of some of the guests here, but I am sure that there is an explanation for that somewhere.

'There are probably many ways to explain it,' said Max, the sarcasm shooting gloriously unobserved over the head of Barrington Portent. Quickly, before his last comment could circle twice around the room and come in on a lower trajectory crashing straight between the eyes of Solauric's hotel manager, Max moved on. 'I really do appreciate the temporary use of your office, Mr Portent. I wonder if you could let it be known to both the guests and the staff that I have arrived, and that I would like to speak to them individually as and when is convenient for them.'

'I don't need to let them know you're here,' snorted Portent. 'They've been talking about little else for the past month. The days preceding your arrival here have been like a countdown. The guests will all be eager to talk to you, to establish their own innocence and get off this planet. It's all been a terrible inconvenience for them. As for the staff, I shall inform them that they should make themselves available to you as their duties permit.'

# 8

As Barrington Portent left his own office, Max, seated at the manager's desk, noticed the figure of a young woman standing outside, and after exchanging a few brief words with the departing figure, she quickly entered the room and closed the door behind her. As she turned and walked the few paces to the chair in front of his desk, Max felt as if he had been zapped by a stun gun. Although the beauty of the planet outside had impressed him on his arrival, he had taken it all in his usual casual manner, but the manifold physical delights of Solauric were nothing compared to the absolute physical perfection of the woman before him now. Her form was absolutely flawless, and unusually for him, Max was slightly intimidated by it and momentarily found himself unable to speak or move. The woman was clearly used to having this effect, and accordingly was no stranger to having to initiate the conversation.

'Pleased to meet you, Detective Quadrant. I am Rose Saturn.' She held out her hand, again a specimen of total perfection. Max stared at the hand in front of him, temporarily unsure of whether he should shake it, kiss it, or cut it off and put it in a jar to take home. Coming to his senses, he shook hands with the actress, and recovered.

'Miss Saturn. Nice to meet you. Correct me if I'm wrong here, but you seemed rather anxious for this interview to take place?'

'Yes. I think I know who killed Quark.'

'I see … and that is?'

'President Shrube. You see, when Mr Portent had discovered the body, I met him in the corridor and he told me what had happened. I went up to the Professor's room and just as I got there those two creepy assistants of Shrube's were trying to get rid of the body. Who else would they be covering up for if not Shrube? They owe allegiance only to one man, and that's the President.'

'I appreciate your sentiments, Miss Saturn, but in my official capacity as Space Detective investigating the death of Professor Quark, I have to base my assumptions on slightly weightier determinants than personal association. Firstly, the movement of the body by Mr Joyce and Mr Broillie, which admittedly could be viewed as being suspicious and perhaps incriminating, could equally be viewed as simple efficiency, an attempt to preserve the physical evidence of the body quickly, knowing that the arrival of an investigating Space Detective would take some considerable time. Secondly, the mere fact that Mr Joyce and Mr Broillie are employed by President Shrube neither makes the President knowledge-able of and accountable for all of their actions, nor determines that everything they do is done on behalf of their employer. Thirdly, and perhaps most importantly, I have to consider the question of motive. Professor Quark was a close and long time associate of Mr Shrube. Why do you think the President would wish the demise of such an associate?'

Rose Saturn stared at Max. Not in a hostile way, more in the manner of a silent inquisitor, as if she were trying to read a book printed on his face.

'I don't know why he would want to kill him. Or have him killed. It just didn't seem right. They looked and acted like they had something to hide. I was positive they were trying to cover the whole thing up. Perhaps they meant to take the body out of the hotel, to drop it down the side of a mountain or something, to make it look like an accident.'

'Miss Saturn, the Professor had an SAA of 78. I don't think his death through some solo mountaineering accident would not have aroused some suspicion, especially as the post mortem examination would have revealed that at some point during his descent he had been shot through the head with a laser pistol.'

'OK. I'll give you that one, but I still maintain they are concealing something. The question is, the reason I was so eager to be the first of the guests to see you, is that I wanted to know if there is anything I can do to help you in your investigation? Anything you want me to find out? You see, I find that I can get people to tell me things that they might not tell other people.'

I don't doubt that for one moment, thought Max. He could not possibly enlist her as a partner in the investigation. For all he knew at this point, she could have killed the Professor herself, and this hurried attempt to throw shovelfuls of the dirt of suspicion in the direction of the President and his aides could be a simple and rather crude diversionary tactic. Still, she seemed to Max to be far too intelligent to adopt such obvious tactics if she were the killer, unless of course this was all part of some over elaborate double bluff, but in his experience truly intelligent killers rarely went for the double bluff option as they recognised the inherent danger that the person investigating the crime was possibly stupid enough to take the whole thing at face value and arrest them immediately. No, his initial reaction was that she could be useful to him in his investigations. If he were honest with himself, he could not say whether this feeling was based on a genuine intuition or whether it was just a subconscious way of justifying an attempt to spend time in her presence. Before Rose Saturn left the room, they reached an accord. For the time being, Max would proceed alone, but if he needed assistance, then Rose would be who he would use. As she left the room, Max tried desperately with all his might to concentrate on the Visiscreen on the desk and not on the slowly retreating body of Rose Saturn. Of course, he failed.

# 9

Max sat for a while, firstly trying to shake the physical image of Rose Saturn from his mind, and secondly deciding on who should be the first person he would call in for interview. He decided to call Professor Horatio Tacitus. Tacitus appeared to have much in common with Quark. Both eminent professors, although in different fields, both had been getting on in years, and of all those involved Tacitus was the only one who could be classed as being a contemporary of Quark. Both had been close advisers to President Shrube, members of his inner circle. Also, despite the differing areas of expertise of the two professors, Max was of the firm belief that knowledge and understanding could not be so definitively split up and compartmentalised as was so common to do in modern society, that all things were, to a large extent, interconnected. He remembered as a young boy reading a quote to the effect that without understanding the past you cannot understand the present and, although he had long ago forgotten the author of these words, their sentiment had remained with him always and he felt here and now that in order to work out why Quark had been killed it was necessary to place him and his work in the correct historical context, and there was no one better qualified to do that than Horatio Tacitus. He used the Visiscreen on Portent's desk to compose a quick message to the Professor, asking him to join him in the manager's office as soon as possible.

No sooner had he sent the message than there was a brisk rap on the office door. Surprised at the old man's remarkable response, Max shouted, 'Come in, please,' but the door opened and instead of the elderly Professor there entered a tall, thin man with short black hair and a beaming smile.

'Detective Quadrant?'

'Yes.'

'Edward Broillie. Nice to meet you.' The tall man took two giant strides across the room and clasped Max's hand in a grip that endured until the end of a forceful pumping ritual which Max was convinced had the capacity to generate enough energy to run the whole of Solauric's infrastructure for a week. While his arm was being used as a piston, Max quickly placed the individual standing before him. Edward Broillie, aide to President Shrube. Once the handshake had been broken, the two men took their seats on opposite sides of the office desk.

So, thought Max, let The Games commence.

'I am sure you are aware, Detective,' began Broillie, 'that Professor Quark was a very close adviser to, and a close personal friend of, the President. The President was absolutely devastated by the unexpected death of the Professor. It is a great personal tragedy for him, and when the news is made public we must be sure to emphasise this fact. Strongly emphasise it, in fact. The people must know. Obviously there must be limitations on what the people must know, and obviously there is no real need for them to know the precise circumstances of the Professor's untimely demise, nor the precise events surrounding it. It's simply not relevant. They must be made aware, however, that his death is felt deeply by the President, much like the death of a favourite grandfather, but that despite this heavy personal blow the President is resolved to continue his re-election campaign regardless of, in fact in some ways because of, this tragic event. It may even be said that the President will be dedicating his campaign to the memory of the late Professor, although we will need some time, after this is all concluded, to conduct some basic voter research to see if this would be, how can I say, a productive course of action?'

'Am I to assume from your remarks that you propose to keep the fact that Samuel Quark was murdered a secret?'

'A secret? Oh no, certainly not. President Shrube's government does not deal in secrets, Detective Quadrant. We are not in the business of concealing information. There is, however, a vast difference between the concealment of information and the careful management thereof. If, for example, we were to simply release the story that Professor Quark had passed away and that the President was deeply and personally saddened, but that such was his dedication to the presidential post that he had cast those feelings aside in a heroic act of public servitude in order to give full attention to his duties, we would not in fact be concealing anything. It could be argued, I suppose, that we were placing stronger emphasis on certain parts of the story as opposed to the other parts, but we can hardly be criticised for that. It is a natural part of the process of imparting information from one human being to another. As soon as information passes through the imperfect human conduit, it is, by definition, contaminated. Have you never played Chinese Whispers, Detective?'

'Yes, but I've also had plenty of Chinese takeaways,' said Max, 'and with those they told me exactly what the dishes were on the menu and I made my own mind up which ones I wanted and which ones I didn't. They didn't have a menu which said "Number 23, plain boiled rice" and when you ordered it, it turned out to be a seven course meal for six which just happened to contain plain boiled rice as a side order to course five.'

Edward Broillie smiled. It was a vaguely condescending sort of smile, and this irritated Max immensely. The Presidential aide suddenly adopted a more combative tone.

'Then may I ask, Detective Quadrant, how you propose to deal with this situation?'

'How I propose to deal with it is to do what I was sent here to do. To find out who killed Professor Quark and, if possible, why he was killed. I shall have the person I believe to be guilty arrested and I shall provide the prosecuting authorities with a full report of my findings. How, when and where the outcome of this investigation is reported to the outside world is no concern of mine. It's simply not my job.'

'That's nice to hear,' said Broillie. 'It's good to meet someone in your position who is not trying to further their own political agenda. I think we can do business together.'

'Mr Broillie, I have no "business" to do with you, unless of course you are in some way connected to the death of Professor Quark. And on that subject, perhaps you could answer a few questions of mine relative to the night of the Professor's murder?'

'Of course. Tell me what you want to know and I will do my best to answer your questions.'

Max was well aware by this point that getting a straight answer out of this man was going to prove difficult.

'How did you become aware that the Professor had been murdered?'

'I wasn't aware that it had yet been proved that he was murdered.'

'How did you become aware that the Professor had been killed?'

'When I saw his body lying on the floor with a hole through his head and he had no pulse.'

'But you didn't just happen to be in his room, surely?'

'Absolutely not, Detective. But you asked me how I became aware that he had been killed. I was aware, prior to entering his room, that Quark was dead, but it was only upon observing the body in the room that I became aware that he had been killed. Before entering the room, I had no way of knowing whether his death was as the result of natural causes or unnatural causes.'

'Ok, how did you become aware of the fact that the Professor was dead?'

'Myself and my associate Mr Joyce received a message from Mr Portent, the Hotel Manager, informing us that the Professor had died and requesting that we join him, Mr Portent that is, in the Professor's room as soon as possible. Mr Joyce and I duly obliged and made our way to the room in question. Mr Portent was there, and it was then that I noted the presence of what appeared to be a laser pistol wound in the side of Quark's head, and examining his wrist and finding no pulse there made a rudimentary assumption that the man was dead, and had probably been killed. You must understand that I speak purely as a layman on these matters. I have had no formal training in anything medical, so my assumptions should be regarded with extreme caution, and in any objective view of the case in hand, disregarded.'

'How did Mr Portent seem when you arrived in the room?'

'Distressed.'

'In what way?'

'He seemed confused. He was vague and incoherent.'

From Max's earlier conversation with the Hotel Manager, he knew that being confused and incoherent was not necessarily a sign of him being distressed. Broillie continued in his overly deliberate manner.

'I think, from a purely personal, unqualified point-of-view you understand, that it was perhaps the first time that Mr Portent had encountered such a situation as the one with which he was faced at that time. He seemed anxious to be able to offer some kind of explanation for the events that had occurred, but rightly, in my opinion, had arrived at the conclusion that there was perhaps more than one way to explain it.'

'Many ways, perhaps?' said Max.

'Indeed. Yes. Many ways. Although, of course, that was purely Mr Portent's personal interpretation of the situation and its preceding events, and whilst I might agree with the general summation thereof, I cannot discount the possibility that, had we both expanded on this general theory, then the conclusions we would have arrived at may well have been entirely different. On the other hand, they may have been similar, or in fact the same.'

'How did Mr Portent come to leave the room?'

'As I intimated earlier, Detective, he was somewhat distressed. Situations like this call for a cooler head than he was demonstrating at the time.' Max took a brief moment to consider Broillie's statements so far, then continued.

'You mentioned just now that, in your opinion, Mr Portent had not previously encountered the situation of dealing with a dead body. You then went on to state that you felt that the circumstances called for a cool head.'

'That would represent a substantially correct interpretation of my words.'

'Was this the reason why you asked Mr Portent to leave the room?'

'I do not recall stating that I had asked Mr Portent to leave the room.'

'Did you ask Mr Portent to leave the room?'

'Yes. I did.'

'And was the reason for this request the fact that you felt that Mr Portent was not possessed of sufficient coolness of head to deal correctly with the situation, whereas yourself and Mr Joyce were?'

'It was my perception that myself and Mr Joyce were of a calmer and more rational disposition at that moment in time, and accordingly, in my judgement, better able to deal correctly with the matter in hand.'

'Mr Broillie, given the circumstances which had occurred, namely the discovery of a body with a laser pistol wound through the head, it would seem to me that Mr Portent's reaction was perfectly normal. It was probably the first time in his life that he had been confronted with the lifeless body of a man who had just been subjected to a violent death. Most people, in such circumstances, would experience some feelings of distress. The reaction of yourself and Mr Joyce, on the other hand, could be viewed as being unnatural, to remain dispassionate, or "cool headed" as you put it, when faced with such a scene. Unless, of course, it was the type of incident you were used to.' Broillie said nothing, simply leaned back in his chair adopting his best poker face. To be fair, as poker faces went, it was a Royal Flush.

Max Quadrant had faced enough defence lawyers in his years as a Space Detective not to be unsettled by this approach to questioning. In one way it irritated him, as it made the whole process needlessly lengthy and laborious, but in another way he secretly enjoyed the intellectual challenge of it, the game of verbal chess between linguistic warriors.

'Mr Broillie, to frame the question slightly differently—'

'I'm sorry, Detective, but you didn't ask me a question. You merely made a statement regarding your subjective perception of the relative reaction of Mr Portent and the reaction of myself and my associate to the discovery of Professor Quark's body.'

'—the question I was heading towards,' continued Max, 'was whether yourself and your associate, as you call him, were perhaps not unduly perturbed by the situation because it was the type of situation to which you were not entirely strangers. That, in fact, yourself and Mr Joyce had been confronted with dead bodies in the past?'

'One can keep a cool head on the outside whilst suffering some degree of perturbation on the inside. Besides that, the very fact of remaining calm and rational in a given situation does not establish proof of having previously experienced the same, or a similar, situation. One could experience a death situation many times and be equally distressed each time. Equally, one could experience it for the first time and still remain calm.'

'So, was this the first time you had been faced with a corpse?'

'Certainly not. Both my father and my mother are sadly deceased. Being an only child, the duty of identification fell on my shoulders on both occasions.'

'What about bodies which have been the subject of violent death?'

'I don't see that that's relevant, Detective.' Max raised an eyebrow, but said nothing. 'The fact of whether or not I have in the past seen such a body is irrelevant to the case in hand. If you were investigating the fraudulent sale of an automobile, it would be irrelevant to ask a salesman if he had sold any automobiles in the past.' This was what Max had been waiting for, the first chink in the Broillie armour.

'But to use your metaphor, Mr Broillie, it *would* be a relevant question to ask the salesman in question if he had *fraudulently* sold an automobile in the past?'

Broillie knew he had taken a wrong turning, sadly for him down a one way street with reversing an impossible rectification.

'That might ... under certain circumstances ... be a reasonable question.'

'And to dispense with the metaphors and return to the issue we are dealing with, it would be irrelevant to ask if you had experience of the corpses of murder victims, but relevant to ask if you yourself had ever murdered anyone?' Broillie maintained his poker face, but Max could tell that behind this facade there was some feverish activity going on. Eventually, the Presidential aide responded, obviously having taken the decision that as he could not go backwards the only way to go was to elevate the conversation upwards to a higher gear.

'That might be a relevant question if I were a suspect for the murder of Professor Quark. Is that what I am?'

'As one of a very small number of people on this planet when the Professor was killed, then the answer is yes. Whether I, as the Space Detective investigating this incident, have any reason to suspect you of having committed this crime over and above any of the others, then the answer is no. The fact remains, though, that the behaviour of yourself and Mr Joyce immediately following the discovery of the body would strike any neutral observer as being suspicious. Firstly, the fact that you requested that Mr Portent leave the room. I accept that he may have been in a state of some anxiety, as we have already established, but surely you would acknowledge, and would have been aware, that as the manager of the hotel the primary responsibility for dealing with the incident was his, not yours. Secondly, when Miss Rose Saturn reached the Professor's room, yourself and Mr Joyce were removing the body. Surely you are aware that it is not normally considered a prudent course of action to remove a body from a potential murder scene without at least making an adequate record of the most basic details. Did you, for example, make any notes as to the position in which the body had been discovered, any signs of activity in the room such as a struggle or fight, or was the room searched for the murder weapon? Did you compile any photographic evidence?'

'No, Detective, we didn't. Our concern was to remove the body to a safe place. Our initial thought was that one of the hotel's overflow refrigerators would be ideal for the task, as this would preserve the state of the body prior to a post mortem examination. I grant that, with the benefit of hindsight, it may seem that this was not the most prudent course of action, but perhaps that was down to the situation. Perhaps Mr Joyce and I were not as cool-headed as we thought.'

'Or perhaps, Mr Broillie, you were being absolutely one hundred per cent cool-headed. You are obviously an intelligent man, and I have no reason to doubt that your associate Mr Joyce is not similarly blessed. I therefore have some difficulty in my own mind in reconciling this fact, and your self-proclaimed cool-headedness, with the seemingly illogical, thoughtless and panic-ridden idea that it was necessary to immediately remove the body to a refrigerator rather than conduct a reasonable appraisal of the scene. I simply cannot entertain the notion that you were of the firm belief that a recently deceased body would almost instantly begin to decompose. This makes me wonder whether or not these were your true intentions when you took the decision to firstly remove Mr Portent from the room, and then the body. Or, to put it another way, I cannot discount the possibility that you had other plans for the remains of Professor Quark, but that it was the appearance of Rose Saturn as you carried the body out that made you instantly have to concoct an alternative version of your intentions, hence the illogical, some would say daft, story about taking it to the refrigerator.'

'And in your great theory, Mr Quadrant, to which by the way I afford no credence whatsoever, what did Mr Joyce and I originally intend to do with the body, and for what reason?'

Max let this question hang in the air for a while. He had managed to rattle Broillie, and he had him on the defensive. He didn't, however, have any evidence against him at this point and, aside from his suspicious behaviour on the night in question had no other reason, let alone motive, to suspect that this man might be the murderer.

'Only you know the answer to that question. At this point.' said Max.

The poker face remained, but Max noticed a slight relaxation in the muscles of Edward Broillie's frame.

'Then in that case, Detective Quadrant, may I suggest that

this conversation be adjourned until such time as you have something more concrete to discuss?'

'I would be generally in agreement with that proposition,' said Max, consciously and deliberately aping the tones of the aide's earlier responses.

Broillie rose, shook hands with Max, and strode out of the room quickly, but in Quadrant's estimation not as quickly as he would have liked to. Turning back to the Visiscreen on the desk, Max noticed he had a message from Horatio Tacitus stating that he had called by, but that Max had been in conference with someone else and would it be OK to meet up first thing in the morning instead? Max sent a brief reply stating that, yes, the morning would be fine, and decided to draw to a close the first day of investigating the death of Samuel Quark. He was reluctant to circulate in the hotel until he had had a chance to speak to each person individually, so took his dinner in his room before going to sleep.

# 10

The next morning, Max took breakfast in his room, sipping on a glass of fresh orange juice and nibbling at a bread roll. His first priority was to try to meet with President Shrube after he had spoken to Professor Tacitus. Basic protocol demanded that Shrube be one of the first people he should speak to, and he felt that he had perhaps already pushed him too far down the list, albeit unintentionally. It had been a natural move to talk to Portent first, with him being the manager of the hotel in which the murder had been committed, and Rose Saturn and Edward Broillie had rather forced themselves on Quadrant, so it was only Tacitus that Max had consciously placed above the President in his running order. This had certainly been a deliberate move, for the reason that Max felt the Professor would be the man to provide perspective to the case. Context was what Max was seeking to gain from his talk with Tacitus. Context. Given the small cast of people and the location, he was convinced that this was no random, spur of the moment killing. Not a case of tempers lost over a spilled drink or a disputed bet. On the other hand, if it were a premeditated act, and someone had made the decision, that for whatever reason, Quark must die, then there were a thousand better places to commit the act than on Solauric, where the number of suspects would be small (and exalted) and the chances of escaping the scene unnoticed near impossible. Therefore the reason behind the killing must be part of something wider, something which existed before the guests arrived, but where something must have occurred, or developed, since their arrival, which had necessitated the immediate termination of Quark. Hence, context.

Max looked out of the window in his room. It was another extraordinarily beautiful and idyllic day on the planet Solauric, and he was tempted to go outside for a stroll in the fresh morning air and sunshine before commencing his day's work but, sticking to his resolution of the previous evening to try and stay out of circulation as much as possible until he had spoken at least to the main protagonists in this fatal drama, he headed directly to Portent's office to await Professor Tacitus.

Tacitus was already there waiting for him, and greeted him with a beaming smile and warm handshake. Despite his professional inclination to remain dispassionate and neutral towards all potential suspects, Max took an instant liking to Horatio Tacitus. He thanked the Professor for coming, and asked him to be patient for one moment while he composed a short message to President Shrube requesting an interview with him later on in the morning. Aware of Tacitus's loquacious reputation, he did wonder whether he should have arranged an afternoon meeting with him, but he was very aware of the time pressure he was under, both professionally in terms of closing this high profile case so that the innocent people could leave and return to the business of being important elsewhere, and the personal pressure in terms of making it back to Centrum H in time for Dan's Millennium bash at Uranium. No, much as he had warmed to Professor Tacitus, he would have to be firm with him if he started to digress. Having sent the message to Shrube via the Visiscreen, he turned his attention to Tacitus.

'Professor Tacitus.'

'Please, Detective, call me Horatio. Professor Tacitus is too formal.'

'OK, Horatio it is. Now, Horatio, you are, I understand, an adviser to President Shrube. Much as the late Professor Quark was?'

'That is correct, although of course we are, or rather were in his case, advisers in completely different capacities. Samuel advised on science, I on history. More importantly, Samuel's was the advice the President wanted, whereas mine was the advice the President felt he needed to be seen receiving. There is a very great difference between the two.'

'I appreciate that. In what way do you think the President desired Quark's advice above your own?'

'It was obvious. You see, Shrube views science as the future and history as the past and, like all politicians, views the past as an irrelevance. The future is what matters to them, because the next election is always in the future. On a simplistic level, of course, he may be right, but on a deeper level he is much in error. The past does matter to the future. The past is often what shapes the future. Virtually nothing is what it is without the past. You, for instance, Detective. Without your mother and father, you would be nothing. You would not exist. They, likewise, would not exist without their parents, and so on and so on, right back to the time which our ancestors were sharpening pieces of flint and driving them into sticks to throw at each other.

'Imagine, if you will, a small battle between two opposing groups of what, for the purposes of this debate, we will call cavemen. One throws a flint-tipped spear at another. The spear misses by a few millimetres, just brushes the hair of his opponent. This opponent then reciprocates by hurling his own spear which pierces the heart of his rival and kills him dead on the spot. The surviving caveman goes back to his social group, takes a mate, and produces a child, starting a lineage that ultimately propagates millions and millions of totally forgotten and nondescript people throughout time until the modern day, but also produces among them a small number of the most notable leaders, generals, scientists and artists in the whole of human history, the people who have shaped the development of humanity. But what if the first spear had not missed? What if the first assailant's aim had been better, or what if the man who was his target had moved his head slightly at the moment of delivery? The second man would have taken the first spear directly through his head, would possibly have been killed and would not have spawned the line that produced those great men and women of history. Instead, the man whose heart had been pierced by the second spear may well have returned a hero from the battle and gone on to produce his own offspring of completely different characters, and the whole history of mankind would have been different. Multiply this one instance by several billions, several trillions, for every event or situation where there is more than one possible outcome, and you will appreciate how much of our history, and by definition how much of our present, is down to sheer chance. Shrube cannot see this. For him, there are no votes in history. Science, on the other hand, gives him voter appeal, or so he imagines. Science is exciting, it creates wealth, it creates jobs, it creates dreams, no – it represents the fulfilment of dreams and aspirations. No one makes money out of history. Plenty make money out of science. No one ever voted for a man who understands the past. Many will vote for a man they think understands the future.'

'So you felt that the President did not value your advice, that he was only interested in the views of Samuel Quark?'

'Correct. Yes, the President was anxious to be seen in public with both of us. You know, a balanced view, past and future, all that nonsense. But has the President ever actually sought my advice on anything? No, never. I've given him plenty, mind you, although I've not always been convinced that I have, how shall we say, had his full attention?'

'But he sought the advice of Professor Quark?'

'Constantly. He was always consulting him. Too much, in the opinion of Samuel. He often tried to avoid him.'

'Avoid him? Why?'

'You must remember, Detective, that Samuel Quark had the mind of a supercomputer, whereas Mr Shrube has the mind of a rusty tin opener. Shrube interested him insofar as his role as adviser gave him power and influence, but no more than that. Besides, in recent months I got the impression from Samuel that he no longer felt he needed Presidential endorsement, that he had perhaps, how can I say, moved onwards and upwards?'

'Onwards and upwards? From being scientific adviser to the President of the Universe? As a scientist, where is there to go onwards and upwards from there?'

'You do not strike me as being a naive man, Detective Quadrant. I cannot believe, therefore, that you do not appreciate where lies the real power in this universe in which we reside.'

'D'Arqueville?'

'Of course.'

'You think Quark was also advising D'Arqueville?'

'Think is the right word. I have no evidence to substantiate my thoughts, but I believe them to be true. Why else would Quark lose interest in his role for the President, if not because he had moved on to greater things? And what greater role could there be than working for Jerrand D'Arqueville?'

# 11

Max took a few moments to absorb this potential twist in the tale. If he had thought that a case involving President Shrube and a host of celebrities was slightly daunting, the possible involvement of Jerrand D'Arqueville was something entirely different. Shrube and the others were powerful, without doubt, but D'Arqueville was power itself.

'Professor, what do you know about Jerrand D'Arqueville?'

'Probably the same as you. Practically nothing. Richest man that ever lived. Owns his own planet. Whereabouts unknown. Personality unknown. Political allegiance unknown. Intentions and ambitions, unknown.'

'Any ideas why he may have wanted the advice or knowledge of Samuel Quark?'

'Impossible to say. No one really knows where D'Arqueville's commercial interests lie these days, or if they do they keep it to themselves. I would imagine, however, that he probably has interests in pretty much everything. You simply don't get that rich by having only one string to your bow, however gilded that string may be, so I'm sure that amongst all his interests there would have been some, perhaps many, where Samuel could have been of use to him. Don't forget, Samuel Quark did not work alone. He had a large team of some of the greatest scientific brains in the universe working under his control. His group was continually working on a multitude of projects.'

'Do you know the nature of any of the projects he was working on when he was killed?'

'Of course not. He was an intensely secretive man, both personally and professionally, with good reason. There were always rival scientists trying to get hold of his team's research. Developments made by Quark in the fields of science made many people very wealthy including, incidentally, Quark himself. The only research he was conducting that was not a secret was his lifelong fascination with the size of the universe and the search for alien life.'

'Do you think he found it?'

'Perhaps. Perhaps not. Probably not, I would say. You have to bear in mind, Detective Quadrant, that the question 'are we alone?' has been one which has both intrigued and plagued mankind since the dawn of civilisation, perhaps even before that. Granted the methods we use now in this eternal search are more sophisticated than ever before, but we could have said the same thing with just the same degree of truth a hundred years ago, two hundred years ago, a thousand years ago. We will doubtless be able to say the same thing a hundred years hence. Doubtless at some point we will find the answer, but statistically speaking we have no reason to believe that this will happen in our lifetime. In fact, statistically speaking, if we take the fact that this search has been going on for a few thousand years and may well continue for several thousand more before it is resolved, then one given man's chances of making that discovery, however bright that individual may be, would seem to be slim. We may feel that it is inevitable that the discovery will be made soon, as we naturally view ourselves as being at the forefront of scientific advancement and discovery, as being immensely superior to everyone who has gone before, but of course every generation views itself in this way as it can only compare itself to what has gone before, not to what is to come after. Modern man is not innately more intelligent than his predecessors, unless you go right back to his development from the Neanderthals. He simply starts out from a stronger position, having the benefit of the knowledge of those that have preceded him. Once humans developed language and, more importantly, writing, they then had the ability to pass on knowledge not just to their contemporaries, but to their future descendants, allowing each subsequent generation to start off with the knowledge of the previous generations, and add to it as one adds bricks to a wall. The ability of the bricklayers does not need to improve over time for the wall to continue to grow. I speak, of course, as something of a layman on this subject as it is not my field of expertise. Ask me something to do with Third Millennium history and I will be able to answer with more authority, although even then I would be forced to apply my traditional caveat concerning any so-called "knowledge" of human history.'

'Which is?'

'I am sure that you are familiar with the expression which goes something like "history is written by the victors". This is largely true, and does serve to draw attention to the underlying fact that all history is a version of the past, and that one man's interpretation of events is inevitably different from another's. Whereas much of the world of learning and knowledge deals with specific facts, for example two plus two equals four, or the boiling point of water is one hundred degrees Celsius, or the population of Centrum A is approximately eight and three-quarter billion, history can be more, how can I say, subjective? Yes, there are certain known facts – a certain individual may have been King or President at a certain time, a battle or war may have taken place on or between certain known dates, but the answers to the questions of how that individual came to be King or President, whether his performance in that role was a triumph or disaster, or why a particular war or battle was fought and why a particular side won or lost, the answers to these questions will vary depending on whom you ask, and the time in which you ask the questions. It is true that history is written by the victors, but it is also re-written by subsequent victors, usurpers and anyone and everyone with a political agenda to serve. This is a fact that President Shrube has always neglected. He sees history, like science, as immutable fact, and could never understand why my answers to his questions were not as definitive as those he got from Samuel Quark.'

Much as he liked Horatio Tacitus, Max could to a certain extent sympathise with Shrube on this fact. He took Tacitus's point about history not being the exact science that, well, science was, but he also strongly suspected that had Tacitus been a professor of science rather than history, then his naturally loquacious and digressive character would have determined that his responses would still never have been either definitive or, most certainly, concise. He sensed that the Professor's propensity to monologue, which was either natural to him or had evolved during his long and distinguished career in university lecturing, had the distinct potential to both elongate the investigation and, more importantly, make it difficult to obtain any exact answers, and that the only way to counter this was to try and be as precise in his line of questioning as it was possible to be. A precise question may still be met with a rambling and somewhat vague reply, but a question with any degree of generality seemed doomed to failure from the start.

'Professor, as you know, I am here to investigate the death of Samuel Quark. I did not know Quark on a personal level, nor, as a layman in the field of science, am I fully appreciative of his work. There are no known witnesses to the killing, nor is there seemingly any forensic evidence which may conclusively serve to identify the perpetrator. My prospect of success in this case therefore lies in the establishment of a motive for the crime: if I can formulate a likely and reasonable theory as to why he was murdered, then, given the limited number of people present on this planet, the shortlist of who may have killed him should be very short indeed.'

Max paused, wondering how much at this stage he should take Tacitus into his confidence. His years of experience had taught him that, until proven otherwise, everyone was a suspect, especially in circumstances such as this where the murderer had to come from a small group of known individuals. There was no reason for him to believe that Tacitus hadn't held the laser pistol that sent the fatal beam through Quark's head. Tacitus had already shown signs of professional jealousy towards his scientific counterpart. Was that reason enough to kill? Perhaps. Max had known people killed for less. Jealousy could be a deadly passion which could lie dormant for years, festering in and corrupting a person's soul, with every subsequent perceived injustice increasing the pressure and temperature of the person's inner lava until one day, without warning, the top of the seemingly benign volcano blows off and the pent up fury erupts.

Yes, experience told him that Tacitus could well be the killer. In fact for all the suspicious activity of Broillie and Joyce on the night of the murder, he had no motive for them killing Quark, so the only person he currently had any semblance of a case against in these terms was Tacitus. However, despite this, something told him that Tacitus was not the killer. He wasn't sure why he felt this. He had no logical reason to think this way, but despite his firm belief in the powers of logic and reason, he also recognised that sometimes you just knew, even if you didn't know why or how you knew. In the case of Tacitus, Max Quadrant knew, he was sure that Tacitus had not killed Quark. He was also sure that Tacitus was not hiding anything or anyone, that he didn't know the identity of the killer or killers. He knew that Tacitus could help him. He had known Quark personally and, whilst not a scientist himself, was quite familiar with the Professor's work. He decided that, to progress, he must trust Tacitus.

'If we take the possibility that he may have been killed for personal reasons, we must consider what those reasons might be. Of course, knowing little about the man, the list of potential motives is almost endless – love, jealousy, hatred, money owed to him, money owed by him, blackmail – as I say, I have no idea. What I do know, however, is that he was murdered here on Solauric, and so I asked myself, "why here"? Why here, on an isolated planet from which it would be impossible to escape undetected, and where the small number of people present inevitably dictates that the murderer will be investigated as a suspect? Professor Quark normally resided on Centrum A, a planet with a population nearing nine billion people. Why not kill him there? Also, he regularly travelled to other planets, including ones with significant numbers of people on them. Why not kill him on one of those trips? Or somewhere in transit? In short, planet Solauric is one of the absolute worst places in the universe to murder anyone and hope to go undetected. So why? Why do it here?'

'Your field rather than mine, Detective,' said Tacitus, 'but I would imagine that the inevitable conclusion was that the person who killed him did not possess the desire to kill him before his arrival here on Solauric.'

'Precisely,' said Max. 'But more than that. Not only was the desire or need to kill Samuel Quark not present prior to his coming to Solauric, the reason why he was killed must also have determined why he could not have been killed after he had left. If we accept that there was no reason to kill him prior to his arrival, but that circumstances or events which occurred while he was here meant that the killer took the decision that he must die, then for the same reasons I stated earlier, why did the killer not simply wait until Quark had left Solauric and gone somewhere else where he or she had a much greater chance of being able to perpetrate the crime without being caught? The answer has to be that the killer took the decision to murder him here on this planet because the killer could not allow Quark to leave Solauric.'

'I have to say, Detective, that I cannot think of any logical reason to dispute your conclusions on this point.'

'To return to my original point, Professor, he was killed either for personal or professional reasons. My theory that the reason for his death arose first here on Solauric, and that this also determined that it was here that the deed must be done, to me does not rule out the possibility of a personal motive but does make it unlikely, unless you can think, from your knowledge of the man, that anyone here might possess such a motive?'

'Samuel was not a man who openly discussed his private or personal life. It may be that there were things about it which he needed to keep secret. It may be that he simply wanted to keep his private life private. If you want my personal opinion, the reason that he never discussed his private life was that he didn't really have one. He was not married, had no children, never appeared to have either a girlfriend or a boyfriend, in fact I'm not aware of him having any personal relationships outside of his work. You see, to be as brilliant as he was, of course you have to have a fantastic brain, but it takes more than that. You have to have absolute dedication to your task, and that is what Samuel Quark had. He was totally obsessed with his research. Like all great scientists, he was acutely aware both of his own mortality and of the almost infinite number of discoveries still to be made. Once you are aware of those two things, your life becomes a kind of frantic race to discover as much as you can in the time you have available. That was the way he was. He lived for science.'

'And possibly died for it too,' said Max.

# 12

The more Tacitus revealed about the personality and behaviour of Samuel Quark, the more Max became convinced of his feeling that the great scientist had not been killed for any personal reasons. Prior to leaving Centrum H, Max had conducted a good degree of research on the Solauric guests, and Quark was the only one on whom there was not the slightest scent of personal scandal. Even Tacitus had been the subject in the past of unproven allegations of sexual harassment from female students. The rest of them, being rich and famous, were continually the subject of rumours regarding their honesty and morality, especially Karl Shernman, who dismissed all such talk as jealousy, or, when facts were proven against him, as mere misunderstandings brought on by the inability of others to take a joke. Blane Levitas, being an Actor, was of course the subject of countless stories of bad behaviour and anguished liaisons, but these did not really count on the grounds that most of these rumours were actually started by Levitas himself, although no one knew whether he did such things to boost his public image or whether he was such an egomaniac that he genuinely believed that he couldn't possibly not have done such things.

Having received confirmation of his appointment with President Shrube on his Visiscreen, Max was aware that the time for that meeting was fast approaching so he would need to curtail his discourse with Tacitus. Before he did this, though, there was one more point on which he wanted to have the Professor's thoughts before he talked to anyone else.

'Horatio, before we finish here, I would be interested to hear your perspective on the historical position of Samuel Quark, where you think he fits in.'

Horatio Tacitus stood up and put his hands in the over-sized pockets of his undersized and well worn woollen cardigan. Then he began to pace around the room, composing himself and ordering his mind ready for another of his monologues.

'As I have said before,' he began, 'Samuel Quark was a great scientist. He was certainly the best scientific mind of our generation, and his achievements put him in exalted company, science-wise. It is difficult to compare great people from different periods in history, as a person may only become great because of the particular circumstances which exist at the time when he is alive. However, if you trace the greatest scientists through time, from Archimedes through Newton, Faraday, Einstein, Hawking, Allport, Vorkitowtsky, you would have to end with Quark. He was, in scientific terms, a colossus. I am sure that at some time after his death, someone will come along and challenge one or more of his theories, but no one would have dared to while he was still alive.

'However, one of the greatest dangers when viewing a great historical figure is the application of hindsight. Take Horatio Nelson, for instance. He has his place in history as one of the greatest military commanders of all time, certainly in naval terms, but if we were to look at his early career as a midshipman, should we view it in the context of what he became, or what he was at the time? And so with Quark – I do not know of his personal history prior to his starting to achieve fame as a scientist, but if, for example, there was an incident in his teenage years when he mounted a personal challenge to the accepted wisdom or authority of the time, it would of course be tempting to interpret this as being a sign of his great mind, that even in his young days he refused to accept the status quo, that he was drawn to question accepted fact and strive for reinterpretation and discovery, as was borne out in his later career with his theories on the infinite size and nature of the universe. Tempting as this may be, it would of course be much more prudent to interpret such an act as merely being representative of him being an ordinary teenager, and doing what ordinary teenagers do: rebelling against accepted practices. Perhaps the pertinent question is how many teenage boys, or girls for that matter, have vigorously challenged the accepted facts of the day but have not gone on to develop new theories on the infinite nature of the universe? However, historical perspective is what you have requested and historical perspective is what I shall endeavour to provide you with, albeit within the confines of the inexactitude of the interpretation and reinterpretation of history.

'The early part of Samuel Quark's life was, in most ways, unremarkable. He was, I believe, a very bright student in his youth, but no more than that. He graduated with a First Class Degree in Physics from Centrum A's Cambridge University and for the next twenty years held a number of research posts for various governmental and educational institutions. His reputation steadily grew within his chosen scientific field, but outside of that he was unknown. When he was in his late forties, he was appointed as Chief Research Officer on the Universal Government's Space Research Programme, and it was whilst working in that capacity that he developed and published the theories that were to make his name.

'The question of a finite or infinite universe has not only dogged scientists for all time, but has proved of equal fascination for all of mankind, although the bigger question, of course, has always been the existence of other life forms, where they are and what they are like. It is a question which both fascinates and scares us. We are all frightened of the Thorians, for instance, but there cannot be a human soul alive who is not anxious to find out what they look like. Despite the waves of destruction and slaughter they have wreaked across the outlying planets of human colonisation, we are still out there, searching, hoping to make formal contact with them. We don't know yet whether or not this is just some form of collective blind optimism, that perhaps their actions are all part of some great misunderstanding, and that once we all sit down around a table everything will be sorted out and the humans and Thorians will live together in peace and harmony in a brave new world of shared values and shared technologies, a giant leap forward of mutually beneficial co-operation and co-existence. Of course, even the most cursory examination of human history reveals this type of thinking to be blind folly. Whenever and wherever different groupings of humanity have encountered each other, one has always dominated or destroyed the other. That has always been so, particularly in the earlier stages of civilisation when mankind was compelled to co-exist with his fellow man on a single planet. We know, of course, that since man has had an infinite number of planets to populate, things have changed somewhat, so it is perhaps worth looking at that period in our history in some detail. Fortunately for us, that is my chosen specialism, and I will be delighted to enlighten you in this area. However, I do detect, Detective, that you are becoming to some degree anxious to terminate this interview. The increased movement in your chair, the frequent glances at the time display on your Visicreen ...'

'You are correct, Professor,' said Max. 'You may have made a good Space Detective yourself. Whilst I am most interested to hear what you have to say on this subject, I do have an appointment with President Shrube. Perhaps we could continue this discussion later on today?'

'Of course,' said Tacitus. 'My dear Detective Quadrant, my ego is not so great as to be offended that a man in your position feels the need to talk to the President of the Universe as a priority over my own humble ramblings. It may be preferable if we were to continue our discussions in altogether more pleasant circumstances and surroundings. I would be delighted if you would join me for dinner tonight in my suite. We can enjoy some of the excellent food and wine on offer in this hotel, and I will bore you with my favourite subject.'

'It's a deal,' grinned Max. 'Thank you for your understanding, Professor Tacitus.'

As Tacitus left the office Max followed him outside to greet the President. The President himself was not there, but instead there sat a small man in a dark suit, with thinning hair on top of a thin, almost skeletal face. When the man spoke his voice was soft, in one way soothing but in another way disquieting.

'You must be Space Detective Quadrant,' said the man. 'My name is Hal Joyce. I am aide and Security Adviser to President Shrube.'

'Nice to meet you, Mr Joyce. Is the President unavailable at present?'

'No, no, Detective. The President is very much available and ready to meet with you. I have come to escort you to the President's Suite.'

Oh dear, thought Max. The old psychological power game. Making me go to him, rather than him come to me. A pretty basic, transparent and naive attempt to assert dominance. The man on home ground has the advantage. Well, that's fine with me. If that's the level of his cunning, he shouldn't be too difficult to break down if he's got anything to hide.

Max walked with Joyce down the corridor in which Portent's office was located, across the reception area of the Hotel Solauric, past the bar, which Max noted was empty, and

69

down the most exclusive corridor of this most exclusive of hotels, where the best suites were situated. The suites here were so large that even along this huge corridor, there were only three, one on each side and one across the end. Being President of the Universe, Aldous T. Shrube occupied the most prestigious suite across the end, the two slightly less prestigious but nevertheless impressive suites on either side being occupied by the extravagantly wealthy Karl Shernman and the extravagantly egotistical Blane Levitas. Joyce and Quadrant stopped at the door to the President's Suite. Joyce knocked sharply once and they both entered.

# 13

President Aldous T. Shrube was seated behind a desk in the office area of his suite with a stack of official-looking papers in front of him and a gold fountain pen poised in his right hand. He looked up and made a sideways gesture to Joyce with his head, indicating the small seating area to the side of the desk. Joyce extended his arm to point Max in the direction of this area, and the Space Detective duly obliged by lowering himself into one of the offered armchairs. Shrube, for the moment, ignored Max completely, carrying on intently examining the papers in front of him, alternately nodding his sagely consent to the contents therein and then slowly shaking his head in disapproval. Max noted that despite the presence of the hovering fountain pen, and despite making the impression of being in disagreement with some of the various documents in front of him, Shrube was making no notes or amendments at all.

First, I have to come to him, thought Max, secondly he makes me wait in his presence whilst he finishes some task which is obviously meant to be far more important than talking to me. Oh well, if this kind of petty dominance ritual makes him happy, then so be it. What did confuse Max was the fact that Joyce had neither left the room nor sat down. Instead, he stood by the side of one of the vacant chairs, still, as if on some kind of guard duty. Quadrant thought maybe this was some kind of presidential protocol, his not being able to leave the room until the President had formally

71

begun his interview with Max. This possibility increased in likelihood when Shrube eventually put down his pen, raised himself from the chair behind the desk, and slowly stepped over and seated himself on the small sofa opposite Max, at which point Joyce pointlessly announced, 'Detective Quadrant – President Aldous T. Shrube.'

This is getting ridiculous, thought Max. Now he has to sit on a sofa while I have to sit on a chair? What next? Is he going to sit on a cushion so he appears taller than me? Am I going to have to sit on the floor? Are we going to drink coffee out of different sized cups?'

Once President Shrube was seated, Joyce suddenly sat down in a chair next to Max. There was a brief, awkward silence before Max turned to the President's aide.

'Mr Joyce. I don't want to appear rude, but it is customary in these instances for a Space Detective to question any potential witnesses alone, unless of course you are acting in some kind of legal representative capacity for the President?'

Joyce looked startled. 'Why would the President need legal representation? Are you about to make a criminal accusation against him?'

'I don't see that it is necessarily of any concern to you if I am,' said Max, 'but if it will make you more relaxed then no, I am not.'

'Not my concern?' said Joyce in his slow, quiet, almost ghostly manner. 'I am a Presidential aide and Head of Presidential Security, Detective. Everything which concerns the President is my concern. It is, accordingly, absolutely vital that I am in attendance for this interview. I could not conceive of any situation where it might not be advantageous for me to be present.'

Max paused for a second, before delivering his reply.

'What is advantageous for you, Mr Joyce, is not necessarily synonymous with what would be advantageous for myself, or indeed for the President. I shall of course, in due course, wish to speak to yourself independently, and alone, about the events that have transpired in this hotel surrounding the death of Professor Samuel Quark, but surely you of all people would recognise that basic protocol dictates that I should conduct the interview with President Shrube prior to conducting a similar exercise with one of his aides?'

Joyce stared at Max. Not a malevolent stare, more of an intense but detached gaze, before almost repeating himself.

'I am an aide to President Shrube. And the Head of Presidential Security. What concerns the President therefore concerns me.'

'Hey, Hal,' said Shrube. 'The Detective is just going to ask me a couple of questions about Samuel. No big deal. Look, I just want to get this over with as quickly as I can so that I can get back on the campaign trail. This man has a job to do, so let's let him do it. I'll be fine. Why don't you take a walk, grab a drink or something.'

'If it's all the same to you, Mr President,' said Joyce, 'I'll stay. I am your aide and Head of Security. I think I should stay.'

Shrube glanced at Max. Max's face made it quite clear that this interview was not going to start whilst Joyce was present. Shrube looked straight at his aide (and Head of Security).

'Hal. Take a walk. Please.'

If looks could kill, Aldous T. Shrube would have been dead, embalmed and buried in a fraction of a second, but Joyce gave a brief nod of assent before slowly getting up and silently pacing across to the door, opening it, stepping outside and closing it behind him without making a sound.

'Now then,' said Shrube. 'How can I help?'

'The first thing I would like to establish,' replied Max, 'is how you first became aware that Professor Quark was dead.'

'I was very shocked by the news, you understand. Profoundly shocked. It was a great personal tragedy for me,

73

personally. Samuel was a great personal friend of mine, so his death naturally affected me in a very … personal way.'

Max realised straight away that this would be a difficult and potentially inconclusive interview. The President was clearly used to having all his responses pre-drafted for him by his advisers, and in the first reply he could instantly detect the words of Edward Broillie, although Shrube was clearly not as familiar with the script as his aide would have wished him to be.

'I appreciate that, sir,' said Max, 'and I am sure that this has been, and perhaps continues to be, a difficult time for you, but what I'm really interested in here is the precise timetable of events, that is, the specific timing of when you were informed, and by whom, that the Professor was dead.'

'You will forgive me, Detective, if my memory as to exact timings is a little vague. This whole horrible business occurred some time ago now, and whilst at the time it was a traumatic experience for me, I have had to put those feelings to one side and carry on the business of governing the universe. It's the nature of the job, I'm afraid. However personally one is affected by things, and in this case I was deeply upset, personally, you have to carry on. The affairs of the Universal Government do not stop. The threat of the Thorian invasion does not go away. The problems of taxation, interplanetary trade, corruption, education, welfare. All of these continue, and do not allow a man time to wallow in personal grief, however deep and personal that grief may be.'

Shrube paused. Max was unsure whether this was because he wanted to gauge whether or not his tactic of answer-avoidance had succeeded or if he had simply forgotten something that Edward Broillie had told him to say. Max said nothing. He wasn't going to engage in another game of verbal gymnastics like he had with Broillie the previous day. That in some ways had been both challenging and intellectually entertaining, but with a leaden-brained fool like Shrube it would just be tedious. Instead, Max adopted the policy of saying nothing, just staring intently at the President, making it quite clear from his expression and body language that he was still waiting for an answer, and inferring that he was going to persevere until he got one. Without his advisers present to bail him out, Shrube seemed lost and exposed.

'Now ... let me see if I can remember. I was alone here in my suite at the time. I had had dinner here in my suite with my aide, Mr Broillie, and I had returned up here to catch up on some urgent correspondence which had been received earlier in the day. People think just because I'm on an LRP that I'm relaxing and having fun. What do they know? The business of being President never stops. The whole universe doesn't shut down just because I'm on an LRP!'

Despite his intention to force an answer out of Shrube as to how he had first learned of the murder, Max saw the chance to force a different question, one which he had originally been meaning to leave until the end of the interview on the grounds that it could possibly be viewed as being an impertinent enquiry to a man who was President of the Universe.

'So, is that why you came to Solauric then, President Shrube? For a holiday?'

'No, no. It was never intended to be a holiday. It was simply a nice place to meet. You know, beautiful surroundings, and very discreet.'

'Did your meeting require some degree of discretion?'

'Detective, when you are the President, all meetings require discretion.'

'But you don't hold all your meetings here on Solauric. Am I to infer, then, that this meeting perhaps required more discretion than usual?'

Shrube looked either side of himself. Max was convinced

he wasn't looking to see if he was being overheard, more that it was a reflex action of his that as soon as he began to panic or lose control he immediately looked to his aides to dig him out of trouble, but alas for Shrube, they were not there.

'As I said, all my meetings require discretion, and we would always choose the venue according to the level of discretion which was required ...'

He's starting to flounder, thought Max, let him keep going.

'... but in this case, the level of discretion required was not an issue which was imposed upon my office as we were not the persons arranging the meeting in question.'

Got him. If the President didn't call the meeting, then who did? How many people in the universe had the clout to summon the President on a lengthy journey through space to a remote planet like Solauric? The list of such people would not be a long one, and one name immediately sprang to the forefront.

'Mr President, if you didn't call this meeting, then may I ask who did?'

'You may ask, Detective, but it may not be possible or perhaps prudent for me to answer. I am not convinced that the identity of such a person bears any relevance whatsoever to the nature of your enquiries here.'

'It may not,' said Max, 'but then again it may. If you are not prepared to reveal it to me, at this stage,' (he could feel Shrube bristle at this comment, the inference being that he may be forced to divulge this information at a later time) 'then perhaps you could tell me what the meeting was to be about.'

'Again, I don't see that the nature of the meeting for which I came to Solauric has anything to do with your enquiries, especially given the fact that the meeting never actually even took place.'

Max leaned back in his chair. Shrube interpreted this as

evidence that he had successfully fought off Quadrant's attack and that the Space Detective had conceded this line of questioning. His interpretation could not have been further from the truth. Max was simply information processing, working out the option paths before him on what was proving to be a productive route of enquiry.

'Mr President, please correct me if I'm making assumptions here, but if a man in your position travelled all the way to Solauric for this meeting, it must have been highly important, and I'm struggling to comprehend why such a meeting would then be cancelled simply because a murder had taken place at the venue, for the purposes of which I am assuming that the Professor's death and your intended meeting were entirely unconnected. As you said yourself, the business of being President has to go on, irrespective of the unpleasantness of the circumstances, irrespective of your own personal feelings. So, no matter how distressed you may have been on a personal level at the death of your scientific adviser, you would presumably, under normal circumstances, put those feelings to one side and continue your duties as the head of the Universal Government. I may be mistaken, and please correct me if I am, but the only reason I can think of for the meeting not taking place following the death of Professor Quark would be if the Professor himself was to have attended, and to have been central to, the proposed meeting. Consequently, once the murder had been committed it was a case of no Professor, no meeting.'

Shrube sat in silence, looking at the door, unwilling to look directly at Max for fear of his eyes betraying the turmoil going on behind them. He shifted uneasily in his chair, which Max took as a revelation that he had chosen the correct path. He decided to tighten the screw another revolution.

'But as I said, President Shrube, please correct me if I'm wrong on this. There may well be some perfectly simple and obvious reason for the cancellation of the meeting which I have overlooked.'

Again, silence from Shrube. Another slight movement of the head from side to side, just to check if his advisers had miraculously materialised beside him. Then came the reply, altogether softer, bordering on confessional.

'No, you are not wrong, Detective. Samuel Quark was also due to be at the meeting. And yes, you are right, once he was dead the meeting could not take place.'

'Who else was supposed to be attending the meeting?' asked Max. 'I have checked the hotel records and it appears that most of the guests currently here arrived around the same time and all were due to depart around the same time as well. Were they all summoned here to attend the same gathering?'

'Goodness, no! What could I possibly have to discuss with some of them? No, they were not invited. Just myself, plus my aides naturally, Professor Quark and Professor Tacitus.'

Tacitus? thought Max. Interesting.

'What about from outside?'

'Detective, there are no other buildings of residence on this planet. There are no other people here, apart from the hotel staff, and I am sure you will believe me when I tell you I had no intention of conducting a meeting with any of them.'

'I accept that, sir, but it does lead me to make certain other conclusions.' Max could feel Shrube's body make a kind of physical groan at this statement. 'If we have established the fact that all the guests had arrived on Solauric around the same time, some three days before the murder, and that this highly important meeting was scheduled to take place between yourself and the two professors, plus Mr Broillie and Mr Joyce, then my question would have to be why the meeting had not already taken place by the time of the murder? Granted this is a uniquely beautiful planet, perfect for rest and relaxation, but surely any such activity would have taken place after your business here had been concluded? It makes no sense to me for the most important man in the universe to undertake a space journey of that magnitude, for a meeting of such importance, and then spend the best part of three days doing nothing before its commencement. Unless, of course, you were waiting for someone else.'

Shrube looked as if he had just been struck by a bowling ball, his carefully laid out pins normally so well protected by Broillie and Joyce scattered by Quadrant's last statement. Why had he agreed to talk to this Space Detective alone, he thought to himself? Did he have to? Well, he did now. To curtail the interview now would look like an admission of guilt. But he had already revealed too much. He couldn't let this man know any more. Calm down, don't say anything else. Broillie and Joyce will sort it out. Backtrack where necessary. Nothing concrete has been established. It's all assumptions at the moment. Keep calm.

'Detective Quadrant, I'm afraid I can reveal no more on this matter unless you can establish that my answers to these questions are necessary to the enquiry into the death of Samuel Quark. The confidentiality which is required by my position requires it to be so. If the investigation cannot be resolved without my providing details of that meeting, then in the interests of justice I will be forced to reveal what I know, but until you have established that that is where we are, I must keep this knowledge to myself for the protection of all concerned.'

'I am slightly concerned here, Mr Shrube, that you feel that by withholding information from this enquiry you are protecting some person. Protecting them from what? Not, I hope, from being exposed as a murderer?'

The look of panic returned to Shrube's face.

'No, no, Detective. Believe me, I have no idea whatsoever of who could possibly have committed this terrible crime. I have been deeply affected by it, personally, and I can assure you that if I had any information at all which I thought could in any way help you to apprehend the killer I would be only too happy to divulge it to you, but I must also consider the duties of my office and that includes the duty of confidentiality to others. Forgive me, Detective Quadrant, but I must insist on finishing this interview now. I will certainly be available to talk to you again, but there are certain matters which I feel I must take advice on before I comment further.'

'Certainly, Mr President. I will respect your desire to discuss these issues further with whoever you desire, and until then I will not press you further on the identity of the other person or persons who were due to meet with you here. I would, however, before we finish, just press you to answer my original question.'

'Which was?'

'The circumstances by which you became aware that Professor Quark was dead.'

This was the question which, at the start of the interview, Shrube had done his best to avoid, and in fact had been determined to avoid, but now Quadrant was dangling it in front of him like a carrot. Just answer this and it would be over. He could then talk to Broillie and Joyce and get them to sort this mess out. Pull Presidential rank for the rest of the enquiry, get Broillie to deal with it. That's what he should have done at the start. Why did he agree to talk to this man? Why did Joyce let him agree? He should have known. Hal Joyce should have known. It was his job to know. Being President was tough enough without having to do other people's jobs. Broillie would have known, he would have kept this Detective away. Hal had really let him down. Just tell him. There's nothing to hide. Just tell him and be done.

'As I stated earlier, Detective, I dined in my room that night with Mr Broillie, then remained alone dealing with some urgent correspondence.' Shrube paused before delivering his final statement on the matter. 'My duties took me some time, until the early hours of the morning, I think. When I had finished, I decided I needed a change of scenery before going to bed, so I strolled down to the bar for a drink. The barman informed me that Professor Quark was dead.'

# 14

After his interview with President Shrube had concluded, Max's next scheduled appointment was not until dinner with Horatio Tacitus. Although he was reasonably sure in his own mind that it would serve no useful purpose in his investigation, he felt it would be prudent at this point to at least conduct a cursory examination of the body of the late Professor Quark. Rather than endure another conversation with the explanatorily-challenged hotel manager, Max decided to execute this task alone. He knew that the body was being stored in one of the overflow freezers, and simple logic told him that this would probably be in close proximity to the kitchen. When he reached the kitchen, he found the place spotless but deserted. He looked behind various doors, which all opened onto storage areas for food and cooking utensils, but at last he opened one that seemed a bit more promising, revealing as it did a lengthy and brightly-lit corridor which led to a large open-plan area at the end.

Having walked the length of the corridor, he found himself standing on the white-tiled floor of a large room about twenty metres square, which was divided into two distinct halves. Down one side was a series of disposal units for various categories of waste material, and down the other side was a succession of what Max assumed were the hotel's overflow refrigerators and freezers. He open the first. Empty. He opened the second. Empty. Also the third and fourth. He tried each one with the same result until he reached the last one standing by the back wall. Locked. Max grinned to himself. Whatever else you thought about Portent, he did things by the book. Broillie and Joyce may have dumped a body in his freezer, but at least he had made sure it was locked and every scrap of food removed from the room. Oh well, nothing else for it. He would have to go and get the key from him.

As he was approaching the manager's office, he could hear Portent's voice in deep and meaningless conversation, and as he looked round the open door of the office he saw him sitting at his desk with Rose Saturn opposite.

'Sorry to disturb you, Mr Portent,' said Max, 'but could I just talk to you briefly? Sorry for the interruption, Miss Saturn.'

Rose looked up and smiled warmly at him. 'No problem,' she said.

Portent got up from his desk and hurried out into the corridor.

'I need to see Quark's body,' said Max. 'I need the key.'

'Yes, yes, of course,' said Portent.

On another day he might have launched into a lengthy discourse over the issue, but even Barrington Portent was not immune to the attractions of Rose Saturn and so today he saw the request for the key as simply an inconvenience when he had her sitting at his desk. He reached into the inside pocket of his jacket, handed the key to Max, and without another word, went back into his office, this time closing the door behind him.

Back in the storage area, Max unlocked the last freezer, a top-opening chest cabinet which had now taken on the role of an arctic coffin. He lifted the lid and gazed upon the lifeless corpse of the universe's foremost scientist. Ignoring motives for a second, the actions of the President's aides had done a remarkable job of preserving the body as, some three months after the murder, there were as yet no major signs of deterioration. There were, of course, large entry and exit wounds on either side of the professor's head, and these were, in Max's view, entirely consistent with the use of a laser pistol at short range. He looked over the rest of the body, still adorned in the clothes the professor had been wearing on the night of his death. He checked the body for other wounds. Nothing. He checked the pockets. Nothing. He lowered the body back into the chest, then stood a while simply staring at the face of the dead man. Why? he said to himself. Why did they kill you? What did you do? What did you know? What were you about to do? He shut the chest and turned the key in the lock. As he had anticipated, the examination of the physical body had provided him with nothing. He had to work out why. Why Quark had been murdered. Then he would know who.

When Max reached Portent's office, Rose Saturn had gone. He quietly returned the key and made an exit before the manager could engage him in conversation, and began to walk back to his room. As he passed through the reception area, he paused briefly to admire the late afternoon sunshine reflecting gently off the lake outside. It was then that a thought came into his head. Although he hadn't yet formally interviewed all the hotel guests, it was a relatively small building and he had seen them all at various moments around the place. Except one. The athlete Sun Gord was supposed to be on Solauric, but the runner had so far been conspicuous by his absence. Strange. Perhaps it's just chance that we've never been in the same part of the hotel at the same time, Max thought. Perhaps it's nothing stranger than that.

Max returned to his room and took a hot shower. His mind drifted back to his conversation with Shrube. This man was the President, the holder of the most powerful political office in the universe. One of his advisers, the most famous and respected scientist of his time, had been found murdered in the same hotel as the President, and Shrube had heard the news from the barman? Were his aides really disturbing the murder scene and removing the body without informing their boss of what was going on? There were two possibilities. Either Shrube was lying, in which case he was trying to conceal something or someone, or he was telling the truth and Broillie and Joyce were trying to hide something from the President.

Max used the Hotel Solauric's secure communications service to send two messages - one to his boss Lars Jettessen, and one to his son Dan. Possible solutions were now beginning to germinate in the head of Max Quadrant, and there was only certain information which he was going to be able to discover from the Solauric guests. He was hoping that the answers he got from Lars and Dan would, by the time they arrived, help to prove which solution was the truth.

With thirty minutes to go before dinner, he decided to leave his room and call in for a drink at the bar on his way, hopefully getting a chance to talk to the barman who had supposedly been the bearer of bad news to the President some three months earlier.

# 15

Jerrand D'Arqueville stood in front of his Visiscreen. As befitted the richest man that had ever lived, his Visiscreen was the largest and best ever built, taking up the whole of one wall in the central room of his living quarters. The definition on the screen was so fine that even across the immensity of space from his planet to the planet Solauric, the form of his interlocutor was so crystal clear that they might have been standing in front of him. In his quiet, authoritative voice, he began.

'I gather the Space Detective arrived yesterday. What is your first impression?'

'He doesn't seem overawed by the situation. The opposite, in fact, he is as cool as a penguin in a fridge. He's either totally inept or very, very good. I suspect the latter.'

'He has the reputation of being the best. That was what I demanded.'

'How do you want me to play this?'

'I trust you to play this the right way. You are one of the few people in this universe who I trust absolutely. Use your instincts. They have never let you down in the past. What has he been doing today, this Detective?'

'He's spent most of the afternoon talking to Shrube.'

'Does he think Shrube is the murderer?'

'Who knows? Like I said, he's quite cool this one, doesn't give a lot away.'

'How are my other guests bearing up under these circumstances?'

'Nervous. Most of them are keeping themselves to themselves. Difficult to socialise comfortably with people when you know that one of them is a murderer.'

'True. Still, if this Quadrant is as bright as they say he is, this will all be resolved in a few days. I'll leave it to you – involve yourself as much or as little as you want in this. Just make sure you know what is going on.'

'Will do.'

# 16

Max walked into the bar of the Hotel Solauric. As had seemed to be the case since he had arrived on the planet, the place was empty, save for a tall young man busy polishing the large stack of crystal glasses behind the bar. Max walked over and sat himself down on a stool at the leather-padded bar. The barman put down his glass and polishing cloth and turned to face Max.

'Good evening, Detective Quadrant, and welcome to the Solauric bar. What can I get you to drink?'

'Orange juice, please. You seem well informed.'

'Part of the job, sir. We don't have that many guests here on Solauric, and all of the staff are told in advance of new guests arriving. As you can appreciate, you are the first new guest we have had for three months, so I didn't need to be Sherlock Holmes to figure out who you are, if you know what I mean.'

'Sherlock Holmes. I haven't heard that name in a while. Are you a fan?'

'Sure. I read Ancient Literature for my University Degree. Conan Doyle was my favourite. You read that kind of stuff, or would that be a bit like taking your work home with you?'

'I love Sherlock Holmes. And Hercule Poirot. It's from the same era. By Agatha Christie.'

'Can't say I've heard of him, or her, but I'm sure it's cool. I'm Caleb, by the way.'

'Yes, I know,' said Max, 'Caleb Khorklory. Part of the Khorklory banking family.'

The barman placed Quadrant's drink on a small mat in front of him.

'You, too, seem well informed.'

'Like you said, it's my job.'

Caleb smiled at him. A genuine smile, thought Max. This is one of the few people he'd met on this planet who didn't seem to be acting as if he might be hiding something. Max took a sip of his drink.

'So, Caleb, how do you go from rich banking family to studying ancient literature to working in a bar on a remote planet like this?'

'Don't know, really. Just sort of happened. But it's cool. I like it here. Bit quiet at the moment, what with everyone having gone to ground a bit since the murder. But normally, we get people in here every night, and they're usually some interesting guys.'

'Like Blane Levitas?'

'Yeah. He's a cool guy. He was in here every night until the murder. Good business for me. He drinks like a suction pump. A bit loud when he's had a few, but no trouble or anything. And the bonus is, if he's here then Rose Saturn is here as well. Maybe that answers your question. What would you rather do, work in banking or serve cocktails to Rose Saturn?'

Max raised his glass. 'Point taken.'

He took another sip of his orange juice and sat silent as Caleb Khorklory finished polishing the last of his glasses before quickly and expertly stacking them in a pyramid shape next to the various bottles on the counter behind him.

'Have you seen much of President Shrube in here?' asked Max.

'He was in here a bit on the first couple of nights he was on Solauric. Not much since the Professor was killed.'

'What about on the actual night he was killed?'

'Yeah. He was here. Came down very late, I seem to remember. Everyone else had left, and I was just thinking about closing up for the night. You see, any of the guests can get any drinks they want taken to their room. Whoever is on night duty does it. I don't actually have a set time to close. If people are in here drinking, I stay open all night if need be. If there's no one here, I close up. As I said, I think I was about to close that night when President Shrube came in. I remember because on the previous nights he hadn't been a big drinker. You know, a couple of glasses of wine, a gin and tonic, that sort of thing. But on that night, he drank Russian vodka, neat. Large ones too.'

'Did he mention the murder?'

'We talked about it, yeah. There was no one else in here.'

'Can you remember who spoke about it first?'

'Caleb thought for a second before replying. 'Definitely me. I remember he was very quiet, and I wasn't sure whether it was because he didn't know what to talk to me about or whether he just didn't think me worth talking to, you know, with him being President and me just being a hotel barman. I'd heard the news earlier in the evening from Mr Portent, so I assumed that if I knew it couldn't be much of a secret, and that if I knew something had happened then the President of the Universe must have known for ages. So I think I just sort of said it, you know, sort of "a bit of a shock about Professor Quark being killed tonight," that kind of thing.'

'And what was Shrube's reaction when you said this?'

'He seemed cool. Just asked me what I meant, which I thought was a bit strange. I mean, if you say it's a bit of a shock that someone has been killed, it can only mean one thing, right? That someone has been killed and that it's a bit of a shock. But then it turned out that he didn't know about it. I mean, what are the chances of that? Of me knowing a piece of news like that before the President? I felt quite bad for bringing it up then, with the Professor being a friend of the President and me being the first to tell him rather than one of his other friends, but he was cool about it.'

'Tell me, Caleb, can you remember, you said Shrube drank large Russian vodkas that night. Was he drinking that before you told him about Quark or did he order it after you told him?'

'Definitely before. He came in and ordered the drink, sat at the bar with it. In fact, he drank it and ordered a second, then a third I think, and it was then that I brought up the subject of the Professor being murdered. I only brought it up to kind of move the conversation along, because you know some customers when they are on their own don't want to talk, but some do but just don't really know how to get things going with some barman they've never met before. I got the feeling that the President wanted to talk, so I kept trying to think of things he might want to talk about. I thought I'd made the wrong choice there because after I brought it up and he had asked me about it he went away from the bar and sat on his own in the easy chairs over there. He had another one, maybe two drinks, big ones mind you, but sitting on his own. I got a bit worried, you know, thought I might have upset him, but he was cool when he left, you know, said thank you and goodnight and all that.'

Max glanced at the clock behind the bar. It was almost time for his dinner with Horatio Tacitus. He thanked Caleb for his company and began to walk out of the bar area, just as Blane Levitas, Rose Saturn, and Darren and Karen Farren were walking in. Levitas made an extravagant gesture to allow Max to pass, and Rose Saturn smiled at him.

'All hail the Great Detective!' roared Levitas. 'The man that is too grand to question a humble thespian such as myself, unless perchance my reputation dictates that I am above suspicion.'

'Certainly not, Mr Levitas' replied Max, deliberately vague as to which part of the question he was answering. 'I would very much like to talk to you when you are available. Tomorrow morning if that would be convenient.'

'Sir, that would be most convenient' said Levitas, accompanied by a bow so deep he nearly fell over. 'I look forward to affording you the pleasure of my company. Until tomorrow, then.'

With that, he strode across to the bar, with the Farrens in tow. Rose Saturn stayed where she was, looking up to Max in a way he found somewhat disconcerting.

'You must excuse Blane.' she said, 'I think he's gone a bit crazy, well ... crazier, being cooped up here for three months. Now that you are here, he is convinced that this matter will be cleared up and we'll be allowed to leave. To celebrate, he has declared the self-imposed moratorium on public drinking by the Solauric guests to be over, hence his reappearance in the bar tonight. Would you care to join us, Max? I think we could be in for quite a night.'

Max wavered for a brief moment. He knew that what Tacitus had to tell him could be vital to solving this murder, and besides that, he enjoyed the old Professor's company enormously. Likewise, the thought of spending an evening in the presence of a pompous, posturing egomaniac like Blane Levitas was enough to make him seriously consider re-enacting the last moments of Samuel Quark. However, the thought of spending the evening with Rose Saturn had the potential to override any other considerations. He felt like he was made up entirely of iron-filings and she was the most powerful of electro-magnets. He knew that if he stopped to consider, he would be doomed to snub Horatio Tacitus and remain in the bar, so he quickly began to propel his reluctant body away from the bar area, saying as he went, 'Sorry, but I have a previous engagement. I may call in later, depending on what time I finish.'

As he walked off down the corridor towards Tacitus's suite, he heard the quiet voice of Rose Saturn, almost whispering.

'I'll see you later then, Max.'

# 17

Max was shaking slightly when he reached Tacitus's room, due mainly to the extreme concentration required to override the desire of both his body and mind to be drawn back to the presence of Rose Saturn. He composed himself, knocked lightly on the door, and entered.

'Ah, my dear Detective Quadrant!' rang out the voice of Horatio Tacitus. 'Come and sit yourself down.' The Professor himself was already seated at the table in his room, and a small trolley next to it contained their dinner in heat-retaining compartments. A bottle stood in the centre of the table, with a cork lying beside it. Max took off his jacket, hung it over the back of his chair, and sat down.

'Will you join me in a glass of wine, Max?' said Tacitus. 'It's a very good one, I'm told. I'm not an expert on wine, you understand, but it was recommended to me by the young man who works in the bar here.'

'Then I'm sure it's good,' said Max. 'I'm no expert either, but I'll gladly join you.'

Tacitus poured them each a glass of wine, then served the food from the trolley. Both were, as you would expect on Solauric, of the absolute highest quality.

'From my understanding, Max, what you are looking for is some idea of where Samuel Quark fits in, and what it means now that he is dead. As we all know, mankind has always had a fascination with space. From the early civilisations' belief that it was the home of the gods, and in some cases that the stars which they could see were the gods themselves, through to the realisation that the objects they could see in the sky were other planets very much like the one they were standing on. Once we reached that point we started to get the development of theories as to the nature of these planets, and to the nature of space itself, with one theory replacing another and so on. This was the case until the last years of the Second Millennium, when we had advanced sufficiently to build rockets capable of breaking away from the force of gravity on Centrum A, or "Earth" as it was then called. There followed various manned space missions, and some landings on Centrum A's moon, as well as various probe craft sent out to explore the nearest other planets. This takes us, without, I hope, being too dismissive of ten thousand years of human evolution, to the beginning of the Third Millennium.'

Professor Horatio Tacitus took a small mouthful of food and began to chew rapidly. Before he had finished it, he began speaking again. 'One very important thing you have to be aware of, Detective, is that man's ability to invent and create, to push back the boundaries of science, is directly and inextricably linked to his desire or need to kill and maim his fellow man. In short, the greatest advances in mechanical engineering and scientific development have always come in times of war, either actual or threatened. The first landings on the moon of Centrum A were only a mask, an illusion of peaceful scientific exploration. Anyone with any sense knew that governments did not spend such huge amounts of money to find out what moon rock was made of, or how far a golf ball would travel in reduced gravity. It was all about developing weapons that could be fired from space. When a war was not being fought, they seemed to engage most of their time in preparing for the next one. The more you have war, or the threat of war, the more money governments provide for scientific research, the bigger and better ways we devise to kill each other. The main problem with this sequence of events is that, while the physical existence of the planet Centrum A was finite, man's capacity for destruction was infinite, and so, with a certain inevitability, the early stages of the Third Millennium saw one pass the other. Bombs were developed of such magnitude that they had not only the power to destroy completely your opponents, but also yourself and everyone else on the planet.

'Once we reached the point where weapons were made which could destroy the whole planet, it became pointless to develop any bigger and better ones. Having a larger bomb, or more of them, is no use at all. Therefore, everyone who gained possession of this weapon became exactly equal with everyone else who had one. It was the first great military equaliser in history.

'This was, of course, of great concern to those governments who had previously been the most powerful and therefore able to dominate the rest. Suddenly, their military power was, to all intents and purposes, gone. Their economic power, too, was under threat, for economic power has always had to be backed up by the ultimate threat of military superiority in order to be sustained and effective.'

'And so ... space was the answer,' said Max.

'Precisely, my dear Detective. They came to the conclusion that while everyone was living on the same planet, no one could possibly gain a military advantage. The only solution was to colonise other planets. If this could be achieved, then Hey Presto! The equilibrium is dashed and imbalance is restored. So, you see, even what is arguably mankind's greatest achievement, the ability to escape from the planetary environment on which he crawled from the sea and evolved, is not down to any lofty philosophical aspirations, but purely down to his aggressive desire to dominate, and ultimately kill, his fellow man. Forgive me, Detective, if this seems to be an overly cynical viewpoint, but I'm afraid it is the truth. I am not, by nature, a cynic. I am an eternal optimist, but such optimism is eternally tinged by my knowledge of the enduring nature of humanity.'

The Professor took advantage of the natural break in his speech to take another mouthful of food. 'This really is most excellent,' he said with his mouth full. 'It's the one thing I will miss about this place.'

'OK, Horatio,' said Max, 'I get it so far. The end of the arms race, even though it was temporary.'

'Stalled, if you like,' said Tacitus, 'put on hold. It could not develop further until the restriction of being bound to the same physical environment had been overcome. Once the settlement of other planets could begin, it was intended that the race would be back on again.'

'But,' said Max, 'between the point of the development of these weapons and the settlement of other planets, there must have existed the very real danger that someone would use one of these weapons and destroy everything.'

'Quite,' said Tacitus. 'That was a very real possibility, and one which troubled many people at the time. Such weaponry is arguably fine while confined to the hands of sane and rational men where controls exist such that it will never be used. But as ownership expands it inevitably becomes the prized possession of men who are neither sane nor rational, and with such people it becomes not only a possibility that they might be used, but a distinct probability.'

'So how did we survive?'

'It's a long story, but I shall endeavour to deliver to you as short a version as I can.'

Max tried hard not to laugh, and managed to contain himself as Tacitus continued.

'By the end of the third century of the Third Millennium, we had a single World Government, English had been adopted as the common World Language, and the dollar adopted as a single currency unit. This unification was not confined purely to economics and politics. Prior to this point, Centrum A had been home to many and varied schools of religious belief, which had caused mankind no end of trouble. People were regularly discriminated against, and actively persecuted for, their particular brand of religion. Wars had been fought, individuals assassinated, and billions of hours had been expended in ultimately fruitless unresolved debate. Then, around the year 2222, there emerged a young man called Videon Kranke, who argued that this was all pointless, that ultimately they all shared the common belief in a superior being, and what was more they were all wasting their time disputing what this superior being had or hadn't said or done, or the way in which he or she wanted them to lead their lives, when of course such questions could only ever be conclusively resolved if the superior being in question chose to actively and definitively communicate with mankind. Kranke went on to argue that since this superior being had chosen not to reveal himself at any previous point in the whole history and evolution of humanity, then the chances of him doing so in their lifetime seemed in all honesty to be pretty remote, so it might be a bit better for all concerned if they stopped worrying about it and just got on with their lives. Besides that, he also argued, they had enough trouble with all the cynics and doubters who continually poured scorn on their beliefs without constantly fighting and bickering with people who ultimately believed the same thing as themselves.

'Videon Kranke became known as "Vid the Analogiser" for his constant use of analogies to explain his thoughts on religious unification. "If God is a fruit," he would say, "does it matter if he is an apple or a banana?" and, "If worship is a method of transport, does it matter if it is a racing car or a bicycle, as long as you finally get to where you want to be?" and so on. His over-use of analogies rather than just saying what he meant did actually cause more argument and debate than solving any great theological questions, but gradually

97

the religious believers of the world began to see the logic in Kranke's teachings, and eventually all the major religions of the world joined behind him in the Universal Church of Belief. This Church allowed you, fundamentally, to believe in whatever you liked without fear of persecution, as long as you believed in the existence of some kind of supreme being or beings, or other things which were not beings but were nevertheless supreme. The only strict rule of Vid the Analogiser was that you had at all times to wear something purple to denote your belief. With the establishment of the Universal Church of Belief, many of the problems of Centrum A disappeared in an instant, and Videon Kranke was lauded as the greatest spiritual leader in the whole history of man. Some years later, Vid the Analogiser was hounded from office as Head of the Universal Church of Belief following his exposure as the owner of Centrum A's largest purple dye manufacturing company, but his church survived.'

'I can see why the elimination of religious differences would drastically reduce the potential for war,' said Max, 'but surely not eliminate it? Wars have been fought over many things apart from religious differences.'

'True,' replied Tacitus, 'very true. The primary causes of war are usually religion, politics or economics. As we have seen, the establishment of the Universal Church of Belief put paid to any future religious conflicts. This left politics and economics. Let's take economics first. Historically, the principal point of wars fought on economic grounds was to destroy the economy of an opponent and/or to create new economic market potential for the aggressor nation. With the establishment of the Global Economy, these aims became almost redundant. The biggest corporate entities were operating on a global basis and already had access to every marketplace. War could not therefore serve to open up or create new markets for them, and as their competitor companies also operated on a global basis it was not possible to have a war which would destroy your competitor's business but not your own. War would only serve to disrupt business, not to augment or expand it, and so became frowned upon in corporate circles.

'So we have dealt with religion and we have dealt with economics, two of the three traditional causes of armed conflict. That leaves politics.

'In the early stages of the Third Millennium, if you were a resident of Centrum A you would have been forgiven for thinking that everyone else apart from yourself was a lawyer, unless of course you were a lawyer yourself in which case you probably thought that everyone else on the planet was a worse lawyer than you. Of course, not everyone on the planet was a lawyer, just most of them. The reason for this was that the population had collectively managed to convince itself that every single problem which existed or occurred could be solved by litigation, that everything that happened which was not to your liking could be blamed on the actions or inactions of somebody else. People began to litigate against companies and against each other for all sorts of bizarre events. Parents sued their children for causing them emotional distress through their behaviour, children sued their parents for conceiving them without their approval or consultation. Surgeons who had performed life-saving operations were sued by their patients for the increased costs that they would now incur through being alive rather than dead. It seemed that the proliferation of litigation was going to strangle the whole of human society, that the whole system of social order was going to break down when to simply be alive was to expose yourself to immense liabilities to all around you. Just as it seemed that lawyers would prove to be the downfall of mankind, their actions unexpectedly turned out to play a major part in its possible saving from total destruction. We come here to the case of Benjamin Zoot.

'Benjamin Zoot was an unremarkable private soldier in a government army, but when instructed one day to carry out the task for which he was employed, that is to go to war, he sued the government. In what became known as the "Zoot Suit", he alleged that the action of his government in ordering him to go and fight was negligent, in that as a consequence of such actions he would be exposed to potential bodily and mental injury. The court found in his favour, granted an injunction against the government preventing them from knowingly sending him into a dangerous situation, and awarded substantial punitive damages in his favour. The Zoot Suit had two momentous consequences. Firstly, it established the legal principle of pre-emptive negligence, that is you could sue someone if you suspected that they were about to commit an act of negligence, rather than waiting for them to actually do it. Secondly, Zoot's fellow members of the armed forces, when they saw the amount of punitive damages awarded in the Zoot Suit, all began launching suits of their own, leading to colossal expenditure which almost bankrupted the government and made it impossible for them ever to contemplate going to war again.

'Actions arising from, and similar to, the Zoot Suit began to be brought in any country of the world wherever and whenever there was the slightest whiff of armed conflict in the air, and the whole military infrastructure of the planet began to slowly grind to a halt. With the establishment of the principle of pre-emptive negligence claims, the entire legal system of the planet also very quickly ground to a halt, as there were simply not enough courtrooms, judges and juries to hear even a fraction of the mass litigation which arose. There were, of course, more than enough lawyers to bring these actions on behalf of all those people who suddenly believed themselves to be in mortal danger through some impending act of negligence by one or more parties.

'And so, my friend, we come to the middle of the Third Millennium. Two hundred years of breathtaking scientific advancement, resulting in the beginnings of the colonisation of new worlds. The biggest problem they faced was the immense distances between inhabitable planets, and they spent much of the first hundred years of this period trying to build faster and faster spacecraft in order to make interplanetary travel feasible, but the problem was eventually solved by the great scientist Allport, who invented the process which we now know as Spacesleep. With the subsequent invention of the Element Bomb (interestingly, like most great inventions, the accidental by-product of weapons development) a large number of planets could be made habitable worlds, and colonisation began. There was no shortage of volunteers ready to explore the brave new world of outer space. The expanding population of Centrum A had been outpaced only by the expansion in the number of lawyers, and the small percentage who had resisted the temptation to study law were only too glad to escape to a new life of more room and less litigation.

'By 2500, everything seemed fine for humanity except, of course, that there was no one to fight against. This was troublesome for mankind as a whole, for fighting others was something in which he had been almost continuously engaged for thousands of years, and without it life appeared on some levels to be rather pointless, but it was even more troublesome for the numbers of people who had made, or more importantly were making or intending to make, their fortunes from arms manufacture and dealing. What would be the point in making weapons if there was no one to use them against? More importantly, who would buy them? It could be said that at this point mankind missed the opportunity to pass into a new era of peace and enlightenment, giving up thoughts of aggression and dominance to share the wondrous bounties of their new inter-planetary environment. As you can imagine, this opportunity was not given a second thought, perhaps not even a first thought. We immediately became obsessed with the threat from non-humans, from the devilish alien species which were living unseen in the greater cosmos. As we expanded into the infinity of space, it was surely only a matter of time before we encountered these other beings, and, while admittedly they may be friendly and well disposed towards us, we could not afford to take the chance that they might not be. Furthermore, whilst inter-human conflict had always taken place on a relatively level playing field militarily speaking, we had no idea what kind of martial technology these aliens possessed. They could be centuries or millennia ahead of us. Therefore, it seemed the only path ahead was to embark on weapons development of a scale and at a pace never known before. Massive amounts of money and resources were channelled into arms development in the hope that when we encountered the aliens we would be ready to fight and beat them.

'And so, over the next four hundred years, the expansion of the human race across the wilderness of space continued. More and more planets were colonised, always under the control of the single Universal Government. Likewise, the development of weaponry continued at a frantic pace, and with the other potential protagonists in any future war still an unknown quantity, there could be no limitation on the required scale of these weapons. In the field of science, opinion was still divided. Some believed in the infinite nature of the universe, some in a finite universe. Theories and counter-theories abounded, although this was all they were – theories. Still, as to this day, no one could offer any kind of conclusive proof one way or the other. Certainly the further mankind explored the depths of space, the more it appeared to be endless, and outside of laboratory and lecture-room theorising there was no concrete evidence to prove that there was an end to space. As many pointed out at the time, proof of infinity was impossible. If you could travel through space for a billion billion light years and not reach the end, it did not prove that there was no end, just that if there was one it was a long way away. If you could find the end of space, you could prove the case for a finite universe without a doubt, but proof of infinity would always be an unattainable goal. Similarly the existence of alien life. Possible to prove, if you find it. Impossible to prove that it doesn't exist.

'Let us fast forward now to the middle of the last century of the Third Millennium, and to the work of a young professor by the name of Samuel Quark. Now, as I have already explained, since the beginning of civilisation the scientific world had continually argued within itself over the question of the infinite nature of the universe. Then, Samuel Quark announced to the world his radical new theory on the nature of matter and the universe. As you know, Detective, I am by profession a historian, not a scientist, so please do not ask me to explain Samuel's theories to you, for they are of such complexity that even some of our most brilliant scientists today will readily confess to maintaining only the briefest and most superficial understanding. That's how good Quark was. By common consent, there have been few individuals in history who could have honestly stated to truly comprehend the Quark theories. Nevertheless, such was Quark's reputation, coupled with people's understanding of the basic "headline points" of his theories, that it became universally accepted he was correct and that space was of an infinite nature. When it came to it, Quark said the universe was infinite, so it was, but even Samuel himself tried to give credence to his new theories by quoting the now long dead Vid the Analogiser, who had famously espoused, "The universe is like the edge of a circle, it has no beginning and no end, but if it has no beginning it cannot really be said to exist, although of course it does, and if you travel round the edge of a circle you eventually end up back where you started, which is not the case with the universe, and also you have to consider what lies within the circle itself, and outside it as well, so really it is very complicated indeed and so best left to those who truly understand it." Well, Quark did understand it, and such was the awe in which he was held by his contemporaries that most research in this field ceased almost immediately. That was that, they said. Quark has solved it.

'This acceptance led, of course, to two distinct emotions within the collective mass of humanity. Firstly, there was a kind of universal agoraphobia. If space was indeed infinite, as had now been proved, then whatever was the largest distance you could possibly imagine, and in these days of interplanetary travel on a vast scale that could be pretty huge, then that distance amounted to virtually nothing, and in mathematical terms so close to nothing as indeed to be considered as nil, in comparison to the infinity of space. Secondly, it served to reinforce the belief that there absolutely must be other life forms out there. If space was infinite, they must be there somewhere. This led to calls in various quarters for more and more wealth to be poured into arms development, so as to give mankind the greatest chance of victory and survival in the seemingly inevitable conflict. This call was answered, but as this unilateral arms race began to drain more and more resources across the universe, there emerged a school of thought that perhaps this expenditure was unnecessary, not on the grounds of any other life forms being likely to constitute a peaceable bunch who would only want to swap jokes and technology, but on the grounds that in an infinite amount of space the chances of two life forms encountering each other would surely be so slim as to be negligible? This alternative theory gradually began to attract a significant number of backers, to the extent that there emerged a serious political will to cease weapons research and production altogether and possibly to decommission existing arms. This movement, however, was quickly quashed on discovery of the Thorians.'

'Forgive me for interrupting,' said Max, 'but my understanding was that the Thorians have never actually been "discovered" as such.'

'That depends on your viewpoint,' replied Tacitus. 'True, no one has returned from an encounter with the Thorians with any kind of physical evidence. In fact, to date, no one has returned from an encounter with the Thorians at all. However, the inhabitants of many of the remoter planets have been slain, and many a space liner destroyed. As you know, Detective, armed conflict between humans on any kind of scale has been virtually non-existent for centuries and the kinds of weapons used in some of these planetary attacks are not possessed by humans outside of the control of the central Universal Government, with the exception of course of Jerrand D'Arqueville, who I believe protects his own planet with a fearsome array of military hardware. Purely for his own defence, of course. No, these attacks had to come from somewhere and someone, or something, outside of humanity, and when stories began to trickle back from space merchants about encounters with a race called the Thorians, that was that. Of course we may be doing the Thorians a great injustice. They may in fact be an entirely peaceable and friendly race, and these attacks may be being carried out by an alien race of which we currently have no knowledge at all. Only time will tell, but if in fact the Thorians are not responsible, it really changes nothing. The danger is still there. It doesn't matter that much if we are being attacked by the Thorians or by someone else, we are still being attacked and logic dictates that we should prepare to defend ourselves in the best and most effective manner possible.

'So, that's it. A somewhat brief and potted history of a thousand years of human evolution, but I hope I've covered the main points as far as you wanted to know, how Samuel fits in and the effect his theories had on how we live today.'

'Professor Tacitus, that was perfect,' said Max, 'exactly what I needed to know. Context was what I was looking for, and context is what you have provided. In addition, you have provided excellent food, excellent wine and above all, pleasant company. I cannot thank you enough. I am in your debt.'

'Max, that debt will be fully repaid when you discover who killed Samuel Quark. Samuel and I were not especially close, but he was a great man and the murderers of great men should not go unpunished.'

'Don't worry, Horatio. I will find out who killed him. And why. In the meantime, I must thank you once again and allow you to get some rest.' With those words, Max put on his jacket and left Professor Tacitus's room. It was now late, and he really should be returning to his own room to rest himself. He was well aware, though, that he had no intention of doing so just yet.

# 18

Max walked briskly down the corridor of the Hotel Solauric, desperately trying to stop himself breaking out into a full-scale run. In the near distance, he could hear voices coming from the bar. One voice in particular, the thespianic roar of Blane Levitas. As he turned the corner, he could see Darren and Karen Farren sitting either side of a small low-level table, seemingly convulsed with a mixture of awe and laughter at Levitas, who was standing on the table re-enacting some outrageous theatrical tale with accompanying expansive gestures.

'... and then I accidentally bumped the elbow of this rather large lady,' exclaimed the great Actor, '... and before I could apologise, which naturally in the gallant tradition of my craft I was about to do, before I could apologise, she turned around and gave me a veritable broadside of the most foul abuse I had heard in many a year. Now, many a man would have replied in kind, matching obscenity with obscenity, but not I, not Blane Levitas.' He paused to take another drink, downing the measure of colourless liquid in his glass in a single gulp. The Farrens simply sat there silent, mouths gaping, waiting for the punch-line.

'So ... I simply turned to her, waited for a natural break in her invective, and announced with a bow, "I'm sorry madam, but I seem to have misjudged your width".' At this, the Farrens could barely contain themselves, roaring with drunken laughter as tears ran down their cheeks. Max viewed all this with some distaste, but it was not Blane Levitas or the Farrens he had come to see. Looking to his right, he saw Rose Saturn sitting at the bar, drink in hand, talking to Caleb. In contrast to her three companions, she appeared to be relatively sober and in control of herself. Max strolled over as casually as he could manage, and took up a position standing at the bar. Rose looked round and smiled warmly at him.

'Good evening, Max, or should I say good morning?'

'Depends whether you are an optimist or a pessimist,' came the reply. 'If you are an optimist, it is still evening. If you are of the gloomier persuasion then I guess it's morning.'

'And which are you, Detective Quadrant, an optimist or a … or the "gloomier persuasion"?'

'In my profession you have to be a bit of both. Dealing with murder on a daily basis does lend itself to cynicism and a tendency to look on the dark side of things, but you also have to retain a sense of optimism that you will eventually apprehend the perpetrator and take him or her out of society and by doing so make whichever world you happen to be in at the time a marginally better place.' Max ordered an orange juice and sat down on the bar stool next to Rose, who looked at him with a mischievous grin.

'Really, Max, I have to say I'm disappointed. That was the sort of equivocal answer I would have expected from Edward Broillie. I had you down as much more decisive than that.'

'I'm sorry to disappoint you. But believe me, I can be decisive when I need to be. I don't think I would solve many cases if I couldn't. When the time comes, you will see.'

'Apologies. I consider myself chastised. Anyway, how was your important appointment? The one that stopped you joining in our little celebration? Has it got you any further in identifying the killer of dear old Professor Quark?'

'Possibly. I had dinner with Professor Tacitus. He has been filling me in on the history of everything and where Quark fits in to the grand scheme of things.'

'Is that relevant? I thought you detectives looked for clues and stuff, you know, threads of people's clothing that had been left behind, hairs, fingerprints, DNA, that sort of thing.'

'Sometimes, yes, but that's not really my style. I try to work out the reason why someone has been killed. Once you have established that, the identification of the perpetrator is usually straightforward. Besides, in this place, mere physical evidence may not be of much help. There are only a few people on this planet and none could be viewed as not having had good reason to be in any particular place at any particular time. Quark's room, for example. All of the hotel staff had reason to go in there, and it's perfectly feasible that Quark himself could have invited any of the other hotel guests in there at any time. Therefore, if I found someone's DNA there, for instance, what would that prove other than that they had been somewhere they had no reason not to be? No, to solve this puzzle I need to know why. Why he was killed.'

'And do you know why he was killed?'

'No … but I will. But what about you, sitting here all on your own. Do you not share the same celebratory mood as your associates? You don't seem to have indulged in their drinking activities to the same extent?'

'On the contrary, my good friend Caleb here will testify that I have in fact drunk considerably more than my "associates", as you call them, it just happens that I am a better drinker. Despite his reputation, Blane has never been able to drink, so he doesn't. He once played a magician, you know, and to prepare for the part spent almost a year training to be one and got quite good at the basic tricks. Concealed beneath his jacket is a small plastic bottle which every now and then he uses to substitute the vodka in his glass for water.'

'What does he do with the vodka?'

'Watch him. He either puts it in someone else's glass or

simply pours it on to the floor. He's very good. If he'd drunk even half what they think he's drunk tonight he would have passed out hours ago.'

'He seems drunk enough.'

'He's an actor. That's what we do. Pretend to be something we're not. Of course he's one big fraud, but at least he's an honest fraud.'

'Pretending to be a great drinker when he isn't is honest?'

'Max, I'm surprised at your naivety. All of us act a part every day of our lives. When we're at work, at home, or out with friends. We all take on different personalities depending on the situation. A man may appear ruthless and businesslike at work, loving and caring at home, and humorous and a little outrageous and devil-may-care when out with his friends. Three different scenarios, three different personalities, but they are still the same man. And is any of those three different personalities the real man? The answer is no. A man's real personality exhibits itself only when he is alone. His real personality is known only to himself, and every man wishes he was something different. As soon as a man comes into contact with others he will immediately change, or at least adapt, his character to what he thinks the situation demands. In one way, you could say that acting is the most honest of professions. At least we make no pretence about what it is we do. We openly state that we are pretending to be someone we are not.'

'I see your point,' said Max, 'but I'm not sure I agree with it. I'll admit that people change the way they behave in different circumstances and situations, but couldn't it just be that they are simply all just variant aspects of the complex nature of personality?'

'No. It's acting. No one is truly happy with who they are, so they spend most of their time trying to convince others that they are who they would like to be. You see, Max, man is essentially an aspirational being, he always wants to be something better than he actually is. This is fine for humanity as a whole, as it is this force which constantly drives us forward, the urge to improve our situation, and it has worked. Look how far we have come in a few thousand years. But for the individual it is a disastrous trait, for the reality of living can never equate to the aspiration.'

'Are you saying that no one is ever happy?'

'Don't confuse happiness with mild contented forbearance, Max. It works on two levels, you see. On the surface, a man may be content with his position in life. He may have a good job, nice family, nice friends. But underneath he will still yearn for something else, something better, always something which is out of his reach. A poor man may dream of wealth, but a man who has that wealth may dream of even more wealth.'

'Not everyone equates happiness with wealth.'

'That was just an example. OK, take yourself as another example; let's look at Max Quadrant, Space Detective. Now, I've only known you a short while, Max, but here's my guess. You make a good living, because you are very very good at your job, but I think that you don't much care for money. I don't think you care whether or not you are as rich as Karl Shernman. Money would only worry you if you were poor.'

Max gave a mildly assenting nod of his head. Rose smiled at him and continued.

'Now – friends.' She paused for a moment, placing her index finger on the end of her chin in a stagey show of contemplation. 'Now, Max, don't take this the wrong way, but my guess is that the nature of your work means that you don't have a great number of close friends. You have spent most of your adult life either on various different planets all over the universe or in Spacesleep travelling between them. That kind of life must lead to some degree of isolation, and make truly close friendships a logistic impossibility.' Max couldn't argue with this, it was true he had no real close friends. He

111

couldn't. Not when you might go away on cases to a series of remote planets, spend time in Spacesleep and return to find everyone had aged ten years to your one. He knew it was true, but it made him uncomfortable to hear it from Rose Saturn. She wasn't finished there, though. Gradually, the smile began to fade from her face and be replaced with a look of great intensity. Was she acting a part here, thought Max? Or was she being genuine? He couldn't tell.

'Home life,' she said. 'I think you are happy in your home life, when you are there. I think you love your wife and son, but feel guilty about the amount of your life you have spent away from them. I think you love your wife, but you are also troubled by the fact that while you are still a young man your wife is fast approaching the age of retirement. You see, you love her, but you still yearn for something else, for someone else.'

Suddenly, Max's mind was in a state of panic. How did she know all this? Had he made it that obvious? She was right, he did love Chloe. He loved her very much, but he would be lying to himself if he didn't admit that in his dreams he was wandering the universe with a younger, brighter, vivacious woman, and in those dreams he could almost inhale the sparks of energy and vitality, of wit and emotion, that emanated from her. This had been the case ever since the age gap between himself and Chloe had become generational, but before, this other woman had simply been an idea. Now she had a face.

Rose Saturn's face began to change again. It was almost a mirror image of the previous transformation, but this time in reverse, from intensity back to smiling, carefree and mischievous.

'I'm sorry, Max.' she said, 'I didn't mean to upset you.' If Max had thought what she had said to be unfair, the return of the smile to her face quickly banished any thoughts he may have had of offence or admonishment. He simply smiled back, a weak smile, but one that conveyed the sentiment that whatever transgression had occurred was forgotten.

There was a lull in their conversation. Max's initial inner panic at Rose Saturn's comments about his personal life had quickly crystallised into the logical analysis of a Space Detective. Having certain psychological insights into his personality was explainable given that she was obviously a highly perceptive and intelligent woman. To a certain extent, such insights could in the cold light of day be dismissed as a mere party trick. But she knew he had a wife and son. What's more, she knew how old Chloe was. He hadn't mentioned Chloe or Dan to anyone since he had been on Solauric. He had sent messages to Dan via the Visiscreen but these had been sent via the hotel's most secure encryption and transmission system. So how did she know these things? They were not the things you could guess at with any great degree of accuracy, or rationally deduce from any superficial assessment of his personality. The only conclusion to come to was that she had received this information from someone else. The questions were, from whom and for what purpose?

During this brief silence, the voice of Blane Levitas hurtled across the bar room once more.

'… so I simply fixed the man with a stare and, after a suitable dramatic pause, exclaimed the retort, "Sir, your life may be as a drama critic, but my drama is a critic of life".'

Right on cue, the Farrens burst out into uncontrollable shrieks of laughter, which this time appeared to slightly offend Levitas, believing as he did that his latest quotation was of earth-shattering profundity rather than a cheap late night gag. But, ultimately he was an Actor and so would take acclaim whenever, wherever and in whatever form he could get it, so he smiled an indulgent smile and, Max noticed this time, used the temporary disablement of the Farrens to perform once more his trick of vodka to water substitution.

113

As Max turned his head back to the bar, he noticed Rose receiving another drink from Caleb Khorklory.

'So, are you drinking for real, or are you doing the same magic trick?'

'No, rest assured Max, whatever gets put in front of me, I drink.'

'But you don't get drunk?'

'Eventually I do, but it takes a long time. You must remember, I come from a theatrical family. My family have been in theatre for so long that the ability to drink has become genetic.'

'I must make a mental note never to take you on in any kind of drinking competition, then.'

'Are you not a drinker then, Max?'

'Not much. I had a few glasses of wine earlier tonight with Horatio Tacitus, but I can take it or leave it. I only drink excessively under very particular circumstances.'

'And what might they be?'

'Now that, Miss Saturn, is my secret, and one which you will have to strengthen your otherwise remarkable powers of psychoanalysis to find out.'

'Is that a challenge?'

'Only if you take it as such.' Again, a brief pause, but this time they stared at each other. Max could read nothing at all in her face, nothing at all, although that didn't make looking at her an unpleasant experience. He could have looked at her for years without tiring of it, but her earlier comments still disturbed him, and he knew he had to get some rest before the coming day so resolved to return to his room, check to see if there were any messages from Lars or Dan, and finally get some sleep.

'Well, Miss Saturn,' he said. 'I have enjoyed your company, but I regret I must retire to my room and leave you to resume your celebrations with your friends. I fear I have already detained you too long from their company.'

'Not at all, Max. The Farrens are a couple of bores, and I've heard all of Blane's stories a hundred times before. None of them are true, by the way.'

'An honest liar, perhaps?'

'Maybe not honest, but harmless.'

'Goodnight, Miss Saturn.'

'Goodnight, Max. See you soon.' With that, she leant over and kissed him gently on the cheek.

As Max walked out of the bar, he caught the end of another Blane Levitas tale.

'… and some of the dialogue was so awful I took the liberty of changing it on the opening night, and then this dreadful little man who had written the stuff accosted me backstage and said, "Mr Levitas, it took me three years to write that play. How dare you forget your lines!" To which I replied, "My dear man, I did not forget my lines, I simply chose not to say those lines which were forgettable!"' For one of the few times in his life, Max genuinely did not know whether to laugh or cry.

It was very late when Max got back to his room. He checked his messages, two from Lars and one from Dan, both over the secure channel. He sent one back to each with further requests for information, then went to bed.

# 19

The next morning, Max Quadrant awoke feeling slightly jaded from lack of sleep. He had drifted off quickly enough the previous night, or in reality early morning, but it was the relatively short gap between that point and his awakening that was the problem. He showered, took breakfast in his room, and got dressed. His first appointment of the day was to interview Blane Levitas, but considering that when he had eventually left the bar a few short hours ago Levitas had still been in full drunken flow, he did not hold out much hope of the Actor putting in a punctual appearance. As a result, he was in no great hurry and somewhat idled over his preparations, followed by a rather casual stroll through the hotel building, stopping to admire the sheer magnificence of the new day on Solauric via one of the picture windows in the reception area. By the time Max reached Barrington Portent's office, he was about fifteen minutes late, but was already mentally prepared for a long wait for, and a potential 'no show' by, Blane Levitas. To his surprise, when he opened the door of Portent's office, Levitas was already there, seated resplendent in his oversized white shirt and undersized red trousers. Max suddenly remembered the magician's trick with the bottle of water. Levitas hadn't been drinking at all, it was all an act. He was less hungover than anyone else who had been in the bar last night.

'I'm sorry, Mr Levitas,' said Max, 'I appear to have kept you waiting.'

116

The Actor rose from his seat and proceeded to offer Max another of his absurdly extravagant bows.

'I am at your service, my dear Detective,' said Levitas. 'Please do not fret yourself. You are certainly not the first person to observe my bar room performance and make the natural assumption that no ordinary man could possibly surface until late the next day, if at all. As you are about to discover, sir, I am no ordinary man, but alas often find myself being judged by the standards of ordinary men. No apology is necessary, as I have long ago resigned myself to the fact that to be so judged is a cross I have to bear.' With that, he resumed his seat, although even this was done with an exaggerated flourish. Max sat down behind Portent's desk and momentarily composed himself before beginning the process of questioning the overblown ego sitting in front of him.

'Yes, I would imagine that you are used to being subjected to other people's judgement, being an actor.'

'An actor? An actor? I, sir, am the greatest living Actor in the universe.'

'Mr Levitas, if that is how you choose to style yourself, that is no concern of mine, nor is it a claim I am in any qualified position to either contradict or endorse, but the fact remains, does it not, that you are an actor?'

'Sir, you misunderstand me. Please do not think that my ego is so monstrous as to proclaim myself the greatest living Actor in the universe. It is others who make such proclamations, not myself, who, as you so rightly point out, am merely a humble actor. Here, I will demonstrate, hopefully to your satisfaction, that I am not a self-obsessed egomaniac making exorbitant claims above my station.' With these words, Levitas proceeded to reach into the inside pocket of the jacket which lay over the back of his chair, and produced a small collection of rather tatty old press clippings which he almost ceremonially laid out on the desk in front of Max.

117

'If you read these carefully, you will note that my status as the greatest living Actor has been bestowed upon me by the words of others and is entirely outside of my control.' Max merely glanced at the material presented before him, being indifferent as to whether they indeed heralded Blane Levitas as the greatest living Actor or whether they dismissed him as the greatest living example of an ego over-inflated to the point of bursting. Rather than prolong this pointless discussion any further, Max simply replied, 'I see what you mean, Mr Levitas. Others do seem to possess some strong and heartfelt opinions regarding your abilities.'

Levitas seemed satisfied with this response and carefully retrieved the objects of his self-affection from the table before returning them to the security of his jacket pocket. Max was wondering how any man could carry plaudits of his own talents around with him, presumably permanently, and then claim to exhibit them as evidence of his own modesty. He had encountered a number of self-deluded egos in his time, but even against these Blane Levitas stood out in a class of his own. Determined not to get distracted by the actor's eccentric behaviour, Max commenced his interrogation.

'Mr Levitas, when looking at the various people here on Solauric, one of the first questions I asked myself was why are they here? I have now got the answer to this question from many of the guests, but your reason for being here remains something of a mystery to me.'

'Are you familiar with the term "resting", Detective?' said Levitas. 'Not in the ordinary sense of the word, you understand, but in the theatrical sense?'

'Yes, I think so. It's a euphemism for a period of unemployment, isn't it?'

'Absolutely not! Nothing could be further from the truth. You are obviously not at all familiar with the concept, and so as an aid to your understanding I shall seek to enlighten you. When one takes on a role, it is more than just taking on a job.

If, for instance, I were a banker and took on a banking job, I would turn up in the morning, do banking things, then return home each night to carry on my life as normal. The job would occupy part of my day, but otherwise my time would be my own to do with as I please. But, when I take on a role, it transforms my entire life, twenty-four hours a day, every day. Everything I do from the moment I take on a role to the moment the role ceases is done in the character into which I have chosen to transform myself. I talk in character, walk in character, and think in character. I eat, drink, see, smell, hear and taste in character. I even sleep and dream in character. That, as I am sure you cannot imagine, is a massive undertaking and includes a commitment stratospheres above that which is required for conventional employment. When the role is completed, and the applause and accolades finally begin to fade, I have to begin the process of resuming my own identity, which becomes harder and harder the more roles you have played. You see, when you achieve a certain level of greatness, your portrayal of your character becomes so good and all-consuming as to almost transplant your real personality, and part of the recovery process, or "resting", involves the rediscovery of yourself, of your own emotions, your own thoughts and opinions, your own speech patterns and physical mannerisms. That is why I rest, Detective. To go straight from one role to another would be tantamount to personality suicide, as within a short time I would be unable to recreate my true self, which would be a travesty. And so, I rest. And it was for this purpose that Rose and I decided to take this ill-fated break on the planet Solauric.'

'So Miss Saturn is "resting" too?'

'Not as such. She is a very talented actress and, as I am sure you have observed, both stunningly beautiful and deeply charismatic. She is not, however, a great Actress, and her character portrayal does not involve the same emotional and physical commitment as my own. She therefore finds it acceptable to sometimes take on consecutive roles without the danger of being exposed to catastrophic loss of self-identity.'

Max was already beginning to tire of this pompous self-aggrandisement.

'What you mean,' he said, 'is that she learns her lines, turns up and tries not to fall over the furniture.'

'To put it very crudely, yes,' said Levitas. 'Anyway, Rose chose to take a break to coincide with my resting period and accompany me here, so that answers your question, I believe, as to why I am here. I am resting.'

'Thank you. That gets that one out of the way. Forgive me though, for a brief moment, if I step down from my role as Space Detective and temporarily don the mantle of a fan of the dramatic arts. If you had recently finished one role and had come to Solauric to "rest" before the next one, may I enquire as to what the next role will be? I know you usually take on the most challenging roles, and I would be intrigued to find out which one is the next to be installed in your pantheon of great theatrical creations. Although, of course, your detainment on Solauric for the past three months may have had implications for the commencement of this next project?'

For the first time in this interview, the self-confidence of Blane Levitas seemed to take a momentary dip.

'No, Detective ... it has had no ill effect. As yet, my next creation is undecided. Not for want of offers, you understand. I am constantly in demand, and have the pick of all the available roles. I turn down ten times the roles that I take. It's just that in this case, I had decided to make my resting period open-ended, so my extended stay here has not really inconvenienced me at all as far as my work is concerned. On the contrary, my elongated period of resting has enabled me to fully restore my own natural personality, which can only be good for myself, for those around me, and for the public at large.'

'Yes. I am sure that is the case. Tell me, Mr Levitas, did you know the late Professor Quark prior to your stay here on Solauric?'

'No. I am an Actor, Detective, I tend not to mix in the same social circles as scientists. I had vaguely heard of the Professor before, and knew he was something of a renowned expert in his field, but I had no idea what his field was. I did meet him briefly when I first arrived here on Solauric, and to my surprise he turned out to be a huge devotee of my work. He was familiar with all of my greatest roles, almost slavish in his intimate knowledge of my distinguished career. He was, I believe, quite overcome with emotion at finally coming face to face with me, and almost begged to meet with me later during my stay in order to relive some of those moments straight from the mouth of Blane Levitas. Alas, sadly for the great Professor, it was a dream which was cruelly snatched away from him, something which I know would have made his last moments alive even more agonising.'

'How did he seem when you met him? From a professional point of view, you must be a keen observer of the characters of others. Did he seem like a man who knew his life was in danger?'

'I don't believe so. He did seem a little nervous, perhaps distracted, and certainly overawed. But I am accustomed to that reaction from people when they meet me for the first time. I am sure you felt the same when we met in the bar room last night.'

'I was distracted, yes,' said Max. He began to wonder if there was any question he could ask of this man which would not elicit a reply concerning his own greatness, and he strongly suspected that the answer was no. He continued, 'Where were you on the night the Professor met his death?'

'I was drinking in the bar area with Rose, the Farrens and Karl Shernman. All night, well at least up until the time that

121

we heard the news about the murder. That did serve to put something of a dampener on our proceedings.'

'You were all there all night?'

'Yes. Well, apart from Rose. I believe she was involved to some degree in the discovery of the murder.'

'Did she hear about the murder while she was in the bar with you?'

'No, she left the bar at various points in the evening. I don't know where she went. For a walk, I presume. You see, most people find being in the presence of Blane Levitas an intense and somewhat overwhelming experience. Even short-term exposure has been known to lessen the self-esteem of otherwise great men. For Rose to spend as much time with me as she does, it must be difficult for her to say the least.'

'Yes. I can imagine it would be,' said Max.

'So even as charismatic and enigmatic a person as Rose Saturn must repeatedly distance herself from Blane Levitas on a temporary basis in order to reinstate her own personal self-worth. Like a planet orbiting around its sun, she has to constantly force herself away to avoid being pulled in by the strength of my gravitational field and being consumed in the fire of my personality. As I once said to a then-famous theatre critic, "Sir, however much you value your own opinion of my work, you are still only the moon to my sun, in that any light you may cast upon the public is simply a reflection of my incandescent and blindingly flaming talent".'

# 20

That last comment almost sent Max Quadrant over the edge, and he quickly concluded his interview with the great Blane Levitas. He was under the impression that Levitas could and would talk about himself all day and all night if given the chance, but Max felt he had little more to gain from this posturing peacock of a man. Having left Portent's office rather rapidly before Levitas could start another one of his stories, Max had decided that he needed some kind of stimulant to kick his brain back into the real universe, so headed towards the bar area with the intention of consuming a large vat of the Hotel Solauric's finest coffee.

He ordered coffee and had a chat with Caleb as the banker's son prepared his drink. Out of the corner of his eye, Max noticed Hal Joyce sitting in the darkest corner of the seating area and, once his coffee was ready, Max decided to go and attempt to ascertain the current mental state of the man who had, with his partner, been attempting to dispose of Professor Quark's body on the night of the murder.

'Mr Joyce. May I join you?' Hal Joyce looked up sharply. He had obviously been deep in thought and was previously unaware that Max Quadrant was in the room.

'Yes. Yes, of course, Detective Quadrant. Please sit down. How is your investigation going?' Max seated himself and took a sip of his coffee before replying.

'Not bad. How about yours?'

'Mine? My what?'

'Your investigation.'

'I'm sorry, Detective, I'm not sure what you mean.'

'I apologise, Mr Joyce. A bit of a habit of mine, I'm afraid. Jumping to conclusions. The very thing I shouldn't do in my profession. I had merely assumed that as you were the Head of Security for President Shrube, and as one of the President's closest advisers had been murdered, a man who was, to use the President's own words "a great and close personal friend" of his, that you would perhaps be conducting some kind of investigation yourself.'

'No. Not as such. Of course, I will, in my position as Head of Security, be taking a keen interest in the case as it develops, but I do not want this to become a jurisdictional issue. The investigation into the murder has been clearly assigned to the Space Police, with yourself as the designated investigating officer. Whatever my personal feelings may be, whatever my professional feelings might be, I am bound to defer to this allocation of duties and decline to involve myself in any activities which could be viewed as impeding your duties.'

'That's very kind,' said Max, taking another sip of coffee.

'As a fellow professional in the area of criminal activity,' said Joyce, 'as a fellow "good guy", I would obviously be more than willing to assist you in any way possible should you so wish. I just thought that, under the circumstances, it would be better to wait until asked rather than impose myself.'

'Again, very kind, Mr Joyce. I am assuming, however, that in the three months since the murder you have not been entirely idle. With the killer still at large, you have surely had serious concerns over the safety of the President?'

'My duty is, as you rightly point out, the protection of the President. For that reason, I must be close to him at all times and cannot go off in some wild pursuit of those responsible for the death of the Professor. I assume, Detective, that your continued presence here on Solauric suggests that you are confining your investigations to those persons who are present here. That is not something which I should have done.'

'No? Interesting. You would look outside Solauric? But surely, if the Professor was murdered here on this planet, and no one has left here since the murder, wouldn't you come to the inevitable conclusion that the murderer is one of the people here on Solauric?'

'I grant you that the person who shot Quark may be one of those still here, but that is perhaps a too simplistic route to take when it comes to solving the crime, in my opinion. To truly solve the crime, it is often required to look beyond the actual perpetrator of the physical act, for such person may simply be a tool of the true murderer, the person who actually planned and ordered the killing, the person who would derive the material benefit from the Professor's death. In the greater scheme of things, the identification and apprehension of the person who pulled the trigger may be almost insignificant if the person behind the crime escapes justice.'

'So you think the murderer was acting on the orders of a third party?'

'Certainly. Have you established any concrete motive for anyone on Solauric killing Quark? No. Of course you haven't. None of the guests here have anything to gain by his death, so you may find yourself having to look at the staff. As I said, none of the guests would have any personal motive to murder Quark, and they are all independently wealthy in their own right so murder for money would seem to be out of the question. The staff of the hotel, on the other hand, are presumably not independently wealthy, and would be open to suspicion of having committed murder in return for personal financial gain.'

'So you think one of the staff pulled the trigger in return for payment from someone on the outside?'

'That would seem the most likely scenario in my opinion, yes.'

'Any ideas as to who this mysterious outside person might be?'

'Well, it could be anyone,' said Joyce. 'There's a whole universe to choose from. But my money would be on one of two sources. Firstly, Professor Quark was a major figure in our society. He was both an icon in terms of his past work and a colossus in terms of his current and potential future work. Eliminating him seems just the sort of terrorist activity which the Thorians seem to specialise in. Apart from that, Quark's scientific consortium was the prime developer of new weaponry. With him gone, the arms business is bound to go through a period of instability while they reorganise, which will slow down the research and production of new weapons. That could provide the Thorians with a window of opportunity to catch up, or even overtake us.'

'You mentioned two possible sources ...'

'Yes. The Thorians would be the prime suspects, but if I were looking somewhere else it would definitely not be on Solauric. No, I would be looking at a different planet altogether. A specific planet. A planet which has only one resident.'

'D'Arqueville?'

'Certainly.'

'Why D'Arqueville? What would he have to gain from Quark being killed?'

'Who knows? No one knows much about Jerrand D'Arqueville. One thing we do know, though, is that a large portion of his wealth was generated from the arms business, a business in which Quark was a major figure.'

'But you just said that Quark's death would potentially throw the arms business into chaos, and at the very least stall new development. How would that benefit D'Arqueville when he makes money out of that business?'

126

'As I said, I don't know. That's something you have to find out, I guess. D'Arqueville makes his money in all kinds of places, has a financial interest in just about everything, but I know he is especially prevalent in the arms trade. He has a significant stake in all the companies that produce weapons, and the main producer of new weaponry, Novae Systems, he owns one hundred per cent and keeps it very much a secretive organisation. Quark was involved with Novae Systems too, heading its research team. What we do know is that Quark came to Solauric for a meeting with President Shrube, but was killed before that meeting could take place. That might be significant. Maybe Quark was going to tell the President something D'Arqueville didn't want him to hear.'

'Does D'Arqueville have a history of eliminating problems in this way?'

'Detective, your guess is as good as mine. Jerrand D'Arqueville is the most secretive man in the universe, as well as the richest. Most of the general public don't even know he exists. There are no pictures of him anywhere, no first-hand accounts from people who have actually met him, and there is no access to his personal planet except by direct invitation from the man himself, and then only under strict terms of secrecy followed by an absolute confidentiality agreement, so even people who have met him can't say so.'

'Perhaps he doesn't exist. Every society needs a bogeyman figure, always have done, always will do. A figure upon whom we can all project our collective fear and anxiety. Maybe that's what he is, an invention.'

Joyce slowly shook his head. 'Believe me, he's real. He's very real. Between you and me, Detective, I think that the President has had a number of meetings with him in the last few years, both before he became President and after. He always goes alone, and there are never any minutes of these meetings, in fact he never even makes direct reference to those meetings, or to D'Arqueville. It's almost like we all have to pretend that they don't take place. You see, even the President has to conform to the confidentiality agreement. That's how powerful D'Arqueville is.'

'What would happen if he broke that confidentiality agreement?'

'Couldn't say. One thing's for certain if he did, and that's that he wouldn't get re-elected. D'Arqueville has enough money in pocket change to buy any election he wants, even for President.'

Max noticed Karl Shernman enter the bar area, get served a drink by Caleb, hesitate for a moment, then disappear through the doors to the seating area outside.

'Mr Joyce,' said Max, 'thank you for your time and most valuable insights into this investigation. Your comments have certainly provided me with some fresh avenues to explore.'

'No problem,' said Joyce. 'Any time. Glad to be of help.'

# 21

Karl Shernman sat at a table on the paved area overlooking the magnificently sculptured gardens of the Hotel Solauric. He had a drink of cola on the table in front of him, and was smoking a large cigar. This struck Max as something of a surprise, for a number of reasons. The planet Solauric was something of a jurisdictional anomaly, being as it was a privately owned planet. It was illegal even to land there without a prior confirmed reservation at the hotel, and the prices at the hotel meant that it was effectively closed to the general populace. While the Space Police had jurisdiction to apply universal law anywhere and everywhere, Solauric had (due to its private ownership) never been formally recognised as being part of the Universal Federation of Planets and was consequently not subject to any planetary laws. Whilst the smoking of tobacco was illegal on all publicly owned planets except when alone in a private house which had a smoking licence, it was, theoretically at least, perfectly legal to smoke anywhere on Solauric, including within the hotel buildings. However, to preserve its public image, and to avoid gaining a reputation as a place where otherwise unlawful practices could be freely engaged in by people purely because they were rich and famous, the Hotel Solauric did not permit smoking within the confines of its buildings, but did allow it in the outside areas. What struck Max as curious was not the fact that smoking was allowed, but the fact that the smoking in question was being practised by

Karl Shernman, the business tycoon who was famous for his clean living lifestyle and was a noted fitness fanatic. Max was enough of a realist to recognise that a man's public image and his private behaviour were often of such diversity as to be unrecognisable from each other, but having observed Shernman for a few minutes he noticed that the man was simply going through the motions of smoking the cigar, rather than actually smoking it. Surely, thought Max, if you were a man who enjoyed smoking cigars, but this particular pleasure, irrespective of your fame and fortune, was routinely either denied or severely restricted by the law, then being on Solauric would be a release of the highest order. To be able to sit with a drink and a cigar in the open air, you would celebrate it, luxuriate in it, enjoy the moment of supreme satisfaction. Instead, Shernman merely took the odd tentative puff, just enough to keep the thing alight, and immediately exhaled the smoke from his mouth. It seemed to Max that he was smoking a cigar because he needed to smoke a cigar, not because he wanted to. Curious.

Maybe he was just doing it because he could, as if it was some kind of demonstration to himself of his own achievement, as if he was saying to himself, 'Look Karl, look how far you have come. You have enough money to be able to stay on Solauric, where the rules that apply to ordinary people will not be applied to you. You are so great and successful that you are above the law.' Possible. Given the ego of Karl Shernman, very possible, but Max didn't think so. There must be some other explanation.

Max got himself another coffee from the bar then passed through the doors into the glorious sunshine outside. He stood for a moment taking in the view, and then glanced round hoping to catch the eye of Karl Shernman, which he did. Shernman nodded his head to Max in recognition, and gave him a broad, gleaming-toothed smile, before gesturing over that he should join him at his table. Max smiled back, walked over and placed his coffee on the table before engaging the over-firm handshake of the famous entrepreneur.

'A pleasure to meet you, Mr Shernman,' said Max.

'Likewise, Detective Quadrant,' replied Shernman, 'or may I call you Max?'

'Certainly.'

'And please, enough of the Mr Shernman. Call me Karl. Everyone does, my staff included. Just because a man has a bit of money, it doesn't make him any different to other men. Or women. Well, different maybe, but not better. I can't abide all this bowing and scraping to people just because they are wealthy or famous, or both in my case. No, Max, I'm an ordinary man. Just one who has been fortunate to succeed in everything he does.'

'Well, Karl, that's a very refreshing attitude for a man in your position. There aren't too many of your peers who would adopt such an enlightened approach.'

Shernman suddenly remembered his cigar, grabbed it hastily from the ashtray in front of him and tried to inhale, but it had gone out. He threw it back into the ashtray. 'Damn things,' he said, 'I'm trying to give them up anyway.'

Max pretended not to attach any significance to the cigar, going along with the apparent pretence that Shernman was a habitual, although now reluctant, smoker. The easy smile quickly returned to the face of Karl Shernman.

'So, Max, how are you enjoying life on Solauric? It's a fantastic place, isn't it? Certainly when you have the kind of background and upbringing I had.'

From his research, Max was aware that Shernman liked to peddle the image of the working-class hero, the boy from the backstreets who had risen to the top through sheer brilliance and hard work, without the aid of family wealth or connections. In fact, it was well known after various media

131

exposures that he had come from a very comfortable, although admittedly not wealthy, background. His father had been a middle management office worker, and although the young Karl Shernman had attended state school, his father had been wealthy enough to provide some private tuition outside school hours. Max felt sure that it would not constitute the greatest start to their relationship if he were to remind him of this fact, so instead contented himself with the reply, 'I agree, it's lovely here. I'm working of course, but if you're going to be working there's nowhere better to work. How about yourself, are you treating your enforced stay here as an extended holiday or are you managing to keep in touch with your business?'

'It's the nature of what I do, I'm afraid, Max, I'm always in touch, always doing business, no matter where I am and whatever the circumstances. Obviously, nothing would give me greater pleasure than to take a complete break from it all, to just relax, but you see when you're in my position your life is not your own. I have too many people relying on me. The businesses I run employ thousands upon thousands of people, and they are all relying on me to keep their jobs going. Sure, I'm wealthy enough to stop working tomorrow, just cash it all in and walk away. If I lived to be a thousand I still couldn't hope to spend all the money I have. But, as I said, it's not about me. It's about looking after others. I don't know, I suppose most people in my position would do just that, walk away and go and enjoy themselves, but I have this great sense of moral obligation to my employees. What would my businesses be without me at the helm? Who knows, but general sentiment seems to be that they would deteriorate quite rapidly. You see, I have what the media refers to as the Midas Touch. I make things successful which would otherwise not be successful, and as a result I create wealth and success for others. It's quite an awesome responsibility to bear, but it's one I've learned to live with in my own way.'

'It must be tough to have that kind of responsibility,' said Max. 'So, you've managed to keep in touch with the outside worlds then, while you've been here?'

'Yes, you could say that. A man in my position is never alone, Max. Never. I have some of the best communications systems money can buy, so I've been in contact with my companies and with the markets. That's why you've not seen me around much since you've been here. I spend most of my day, and most of my night, sometimes, in front of the VisiScreen in my room, running my family.'

'Your family?'

'Forgive me. I mean what the media would call my "vast business empire". To me, it's my family. I feel very paternal towards all my companies and my staff. So I keep in constant touch. All very secure, naturally, even here on Solauric. Fantastic encryption they have these days, you know, Max, unbelievable what they can do to make it all safe. Costs a fortune, mind you.'

'I'm sure it's all worth it, Karl. A man like you must have many secrets. Secrets which would be of great value to others.'

'You're right there, Max. In my business, information is your primary asset, so you have to keep it safe. If there's even a sniff of a rumour that I'm about to buy into a company the price rockets up in an instant. It's that Midas Touch thing, you see. Whatever state a company is in, people think that if Karl Shernman is going to be involved then it's going to be a licence to print money. To be fair, my past record would lend some credence to that assumption, but it does mean that I have to be very careful about what I say and to whom, so a lot of the time I just have to keep myself to myself. That's another reason you haven't seen me about too much around here.'

'So is that where you were when Professor Quark was killed? In your room doing business via the VisiScreen?'

133

Karl Shernman's face broke out into a grin so broad that Max felt the entrepreneur's ears were going to be enveloped by his mouth.

'My dear Max,' he laughed. 'And there was I thinking we were just having a pleasant conversation in the morning sunshine, and all the while you were doing your "detecting", all leading up to the old "and what were you doing on the night of the murder?" question.'

'Sorry to disappoint you,' said Max, 'but like you, I always seem to be working.'

'Now,' said Shernman, 'I think I've read enough detective stories to know that this is the part where I say, "That's correct, I was alone in my room all evening on the night of the murder," and then you say, "but Mr Shernman, other guests in the hotel have given statements that you were in fact, on the night in question, drinking in the hotel bar with Blane Levitas, Rose Saturn and the Farren couple".'

Max smiled back at Karl Shernman. 'OK, you've got me there,' he said, 'I did know from other people that you were in the bar that night. The next slightly lame question, as I'm sure you've already anticipated, is did you notice anything suspicious going on that night?'

'What, you mean people walking around with laser pistols asking the whereabouts of elderly professors? Only joking, Max, I know you're just trying to do your job. As you know, I spent all night in the bar, so you can cross me off the list straight away. As for suspicious activity, well there was one thing that struck me as strange at the time, but I'm sure it had nothing to do with the actual murder.'

'Really? What was that?'

'Well … no, I'm sure it had nothing to do with it. It would be unfair of me to put doubt in your mind where there really shouldn't be any. Sorry, forget I said anything.'

'Karl, with all due respect here, I appreciate that you are a great businessman, one of the greatest, if not *the* greatest, but you do not solve murders for a living. I do. So please, let me be the judge of what is significant and what is unimportant.'

Karl Shernman sat silent for a moment, staring past Max to the hills beyond, adopting a slightly pained expression that suggested he was engaged in the process of trying to resolve some great personal moral dilemma. Then, the standard smiling countenance returned in an instant and he looked Max straight in the eyes.

'I agree,' he said. 'I am an expert in many things, but murder is not one of them. You obviously are, and I believe that I can rely on you to treat the information objectively and quite quickly dismiss it from your investigation without placing any lingering and undue suspicion on the individual concerned.' He paused, and once more stared out to the hills, as if having second thoughts about his impending revelation, but almost immediately turned back to Max.

'On the night Quark was killed, I was, as you know, in the bar area with Levitas and Rose and we were joined by those two that won the lottery money, the Farrens. We were there all night, at least until it was announced that there had been a murder, at which point we all retired to our rooms, not necessarily through any fear for our own safety, but more because it didn't seem right to carry on drinking when someone had just been killed in the same building. Anyway, thinking about it when I got back to my room, what I had thought rather strange was that throughout the evening, well at least up until the point we became aware of Quark's murder, was that Rose Saturn had been continually disappearing from the bar. Three or four times, in fact, she left the bar area, completely unannounced, and then would return later and carry on as if she hadn't been anywhere. I'm sorry, it's embarrassing really, I shouldn't have said anything. I'm sure there's a perfectly logical explanation, and I've probably really put my foot in it by telling you. It'll probably turn out to be some really sensitive personal issue. Usually is where women are concerned, in my experience. Not that there's anything wrong with women having personal problems, please don't think I'm some kind of sexist dinosaur. Women are very valuable contributors to my business, and they are just as valuable as men, notwithstanding their personal issues and sensitivities.'

'Karl, when Rose, as you say, disappeared, how long was it for, each time, roughly?'

'Difficult to say really. You see, as I said, she went unannounced. No "won't be a moment, I'm just off to do such and such or talk to so and so". I just remembered turning round and her not being there. And then I would look back later and there she was, sitting next to me again.'

'Just roughly. How long on average? Five minutes? An hour?'

'I'd say perhaps twenty minutes to half an hour each time. You see, if it had just been five minutes, I wouldn't have thought anything of it, you know I would have just assumed she had gone to the lavatory, or gone to touch up her make-up, or just doing the sorts of things that women do, and I think that if it had been an hour I would probably have asked Levitas if everything was all right, you know, should we go and look for her, that sort of thing.'

'How about the others? Did they seem to think it strange that Miss Saturn was absenting herself for these periods of time?'

'To be honest, Max, I think I was the only one who noticed. You've got to remember we had all had rather a lot to drink. Levitas was being ... well he was being Blane Levitas. He was telling story after story about his life and profession and his encounters with famous people, and to be quite honest he appeared to be so obsessed with talking about himself that it wouldn't have surprised me if we'd all left and he didn't notice. I think he would have carried on regardless even if the sole audience was the bar room furniture. As for the Farrens, they were so obviously in complete awe of Levitas that I am convinced that they were, at that point, completely oblivious to everything else in the universe. Jerrand D'Arqueville himself could have walked in and sat beside them doing conjuring tricks and they wouldn't have noticed he was there.'

'Why D'Arqueville?'

'I'm sorry? What do you mean?'

'I just wondered why you used D'Arqueville as an example.'

'No reason really. Just that he is famously reclusive, so it would be a surprise to see him.'

'Although of course they wouldn't recognise him if they saw him.'

'True, but it was just a comment. I appreciate it doesn't stand up to scrutiny and analysis, but it wasn't intended to be significant.'

'How about you, Karl? Would you have recognised Jerrand D'Arqueville if he had come into the bar and sat beside you?'

'Max, it was just a comment to illustrate how infatuated they were with Levitas, it wouldn't have mattered if it had been D'Arqueville or anyone else, they wouldn't have noticed any one or any thing. You know, I could have said "if a Pterodactyl in a pinstripe suit wearing a bowler hat and smoking a pipe had sat down", that was my point.'

Shernman sat back in his chair, adopting another of his expansive grins in reaction to his self-perceived amusing quip. Max remained serious, and now it was his turn to look straight into the other man's eyes.

'The question remains. If Jerrand D'Arqueville had walked in and sat down, would you have recognised him?' The smile slowly disappeared from the face of Karl Shernman. He was clearly a man who was used to having things his own way, and did not seem to take kindly to being asked the same question twice, especially when he felt he had effectively dismissed it as an irrelevance at the first time of asking. His eyes narrowed and he stared back at Max, making the detective think for a moment that he might be about to walk out on him. However, as before, the intense look was quickly replaced by an affable smile, and Karl Shernman simply shrugged his shoulders and extended his arms sideways in a gesture of helplessness.

'No … the truth is, I wouldn't. I told you before, Max, I'm just an ordinary guy. I'm just like everyone else. They've never met Jerrand D'Arqueville or even seen an image of him, and neither have I. For all I know, you could be D'Arqueville. So could anyone else on this planet. In fact, the guy is so secretive about his identity, maybe I am Jerrand D'Arqueville, I just don't know it because I'm too touchy about it to even tell myself.'

'Do you seriously think D'Arqueville may be here on Solauric?'

'Well, it's possible I suppose. I mean, hardly anyone knows what he looks like, so he could be here masquerading as someone else. It's possible, but I don't think it's probable. Certainly, popular belief is that he never leaves his own planet these days, hasn't for years. Still, if he's going off on jaunts here, there and everywhere passing himself off as other people then I guess we would all think that. When it comes down to it, and forgive me here, Max, if it seems like I'm trying to do your job for you, when it comes down to it, if D'Arqueville wanted to get rid of Quark, why would he travel all the way to Solauric in person and risk being exposed as who he was, or worse, get caught as the murderer, when the guy has so much money he could hire any and every hit man in the universe to knock off the old professor and remain in the security of his own planet? D'Arqueville is effectively above the law, Max. Even if a crime could be traced back to him, there's no way he would ever be held accountable for it.

Firstly, he has so many lawyers in his pay that the case would struggle to ever get to court, and secondly, even if it did, how are they going to arrest him? My people tell me that D'Arqueville's arms companies manufacture the most advanced weapons purely for the defence of his planet. If anyone, and I mean anyone, goes there and he doesn't want them to be there he has the power to blast them into space dust. His planet is impregnable. As long as he stays there, he's untouchable, so why would he leave? No, my money would be on him paying someone else to do it, no doubts, one hundred per cent. You might catch the assassin, but you'll never pin it on D'Arqueville.'

'I'm sorry, Karl, but we seem to have made something of a quantum leap in this conversation. I don't recall the part where we actually established beyond reasonable doubt that Samuel Quark was killed by Jerrand D'Arqueville, either in person or by proxy.'

'No, no, of course not, I was just theorising out loud. Maybe that's why you're the detective and I'm not. You manage to stick to the point, and to the law. No, I fully accept that nothing at this point has been proven, as you say, beyond reasonable doubt. I agree there is a chance that D'Arqueville may not be behind all this, although I have to say I can't think of any reason anyone else would have to want him dead.'

'And you can think of a reason why D'Arqueville would have wanted the Professor dead?'

'Well, surely he's the prime candidate, isn't he? I mean, everyone knows that Quark was well and truly in bed with D'Arqueville. Most of his big commercial research projects were funded by D'Arqueville, and I think D'Arqueville took most of the profits.'

'So why would he want him dead? If Quark's research was making him money, why would he want to stop him?'

'Who knows? Maybe he had found out something about D'Arqueville, what he looked like, some great secret or other.

Maybe D'Arqueville was scared having Quark out there knowing as much as he did about his weapons systems. Maybe he simply outlived his usefulness to him.'

'Perhaps,' said Max, 'you could be right. But there's no evidence. No evidence at all.'

'Well, evidence, that's your department, Max, although I may be able to help you a little there.'

'Really? In what way?'

Shernman looked either side of himself and behind in a deeply conspiratorial way, totally unnecessary given that they were quite clearly alone. Nevertheless, Shernman lowered his voice.

'Max, as I said to you earlier, in my business information is king. Not only do I have to protect my own information, it also serves my business well if I can learn as much information as possible about my competitors. I agree it is possibly not altogether ethical, and may be a bit underhand arguably, but I do from time to time make use of certain outside agencies that gather certain information that may be of commercial use to me. Nothing illegal, you understand. No real industrial espionage, information theft, hacking, that sort of thing. While I have to be constantly on my guard against that kind of behaviour from others, I absolutely forbid my people from engaging in that kind of practice, and anyone who did would be instantly dismissed from the company. I want to make that absolutely clear, Max. I do not indulge in any illegal activity of that type, and everyone who works for me is made fully aware of the standards of behaviour I expect and the penalties for failing to totally adhere to those standards. However, there is certain information which can be of some assistance to me and which it is perfectly legitimate to obtain, and which I sometimes employ people to obtain for me. Examples might include which people are rumoured to be about to join or leave certain companies, whether certain people working for my competitors whose services I might be interested in securing are contented in their jobs, that kind of thing. I might also want to keep an eye on the whereabouts of my peers, as their physical presence in a particular place may be mildly indicative of their present or future plans.'

'So you keep tabs on Jerrand D'Arqueville?'

'Not as such. As we know, or rather as we all believe, D'Arqueville doesn't leave his planet, and if he does, of course we don't know what he looks like. For the purposes of this discussion we assume the former, that he stays put on his planet safe behind his huge array of high-tech weaponry. We can't therefore monitor his physical movements, as for all intents and purposes he doesn't have any. We can't monitor his communications, primarily for the reason that that would be both unethical and illegal, and as I stated just now, I will not stand for that kind of behaviour within my organisation. The fact remains that even if I didn't have such high ethical standards it would in any event be impossible to break the encryption in D'Arqueville's communications. It's the best there is. Totally impenetrable, even to the best hackers there are. Well, the best hackers that don't already work for D'Arqueville, anyway. So what does that leave? If I can't, as you say, "keep tabs" on him if he doesn't go anywhere, and I can't monitor his communications, the only way I can get any idea of what he's up to is to watch those who are known to be close associates of his.'

'Including Samuel Quark.'

'Precisely. I've had Quark under observation for some years, ever since he began to work for D'Arqueville. Nothing illegal, you understand. Just where he goes, who he meets with, that sort of thing. Well, shortly before I came here to Solauric, I received an urgent message from the agency whom I had charged with keeping track of the dear old professor. Normally, theirs was a fairly routine job. Quark stayed mostly at the University of Cambridge on Centrum A, occasionally going on a trip to speak at some scientific conference or other. Mostly, he just met other scientists. Then, one day he suddenly boards a privately owned space cruiser and departs Centrum A for destination unknown. Now, my people managed to track this space cruiser while it was in Centrum A's solar system and were able to get one of their own small ships to follow it through space. Presumably Quark was in spacesleep, but my men kept on the case for several months travelling through space, determined not to lose their target, which they didn't. Our ship was sending regular reports back, simply providing their current co-ordinates and repeating the same message that they were still tracking and following the space cruiser containing Professor Quark. Then we received a message stating that the ship in front was beginning the process of deceleration, which as I am sure you know normally indicates that it is nearing its destination. The co-ordinates in this transmission were in an area of space where D'Arqueville's planet has been rumoured to be situated. After that, nothing. We have been trying ever since to contact our ship, but we receive nothing back. It has, as far as we can make out, vanished.'

'So you think Quark went to see D'Arqueville before he came to Solauric, and that D'Arqueville knew his ship was being followed and so destroyed it.'

'It would seem the most likely explanation, Max. After that, who knows? The next thing we know is that Quark turns up here on Solauric and is promptly murdered. Either they had some kind of dispute or showdown on D'Arqueville's planet, or D'Arqueville realised after Quark had gone that he knew too much.'

'Interesting. Obviously, we have no real evidence here. We have no proof that Quark was on that space cruiser, and even if we did, we have no evidence that wherever it was that he went was the personal planet of Jerrand D'Arqueville. Further, we have no evidence that the ship containing your surveillance team has been destroyed. If it was destroyed, we have no evidence that it was by anything other than natual phenomena or mechanical failure. If it was destroyed by weapons, we would have no evidence that such weapons were under the control of Jerrand D'Arqueville. Still, it is an interesting story, and I thank you for sharing it with me, Karl. It has been very helpful.'

'Max, I'll do anything to help. I have no personal grudge against D'Arqueville. We're both businessmen. I don't know him personally, but I respect him as a rival. Speaking of being a businessman, I'm really sorry but I do have to get back to my room. As you know now, I'm never truly on holiday. I have a business to run, decisions to make. There's a lot of people out there relying on Karl Shernman to keep them in a job.'

Shernman stood up and they shook hands, Max's hand being almost annihilated in the entrepreneur's iron grip.

'Thanks for listening, Max, and for the pleasure of your company.'

'Likewise,' said Max. 'Thanks for the information.'

# 22

Having still failed to encounter Sun Gord, the elusive athlete, the final appointment Max Quadrant had scheduled in his round of interviews was with Darren and Karen Farren, the wealthy lottery winners. He had left them until last as he had been convinced from the start that they of all people must be innocent bystanders in the whole affair of the murder of Samuel Quark. He was good enough at his job to know that he could never rule anyone out completely until he had firmly identified the murderer, and so it was a necessary part of his due diligence that he question them, but he could not see any possible connection between them and Quark, nor could he imagine any way in which they would stand to gain by the Professor's death. If he were absolutely honest with himself, Max would also have admitted that one of the reasons why he had put off the Farrens to last was that, from what he had seen of them so far, they seemed such awful, shallow people. Max was certainly not a snob in the material sense, and generally treated everyone the same be they millionaire or nillionaire, but he was, albeit subconsciously, something of an intellectual snob. Some of this was out of a slight sense of frustration when other people's minds did not function at the same speed as his own, but although he would have denied it vigorously had he been questioned on the subject, he did have a tendency to look down upon those whose minds resembled the bottled water shelf of a shop shortly before a predicted hurricane.

He had arranged to meet the Farrens for lunch in the hotel restaurant, and they were already seated there when he arrived. They were the only diners in the room, but Max still felt embarrassed when Karen Farren saw him and leapt to her feet, waving and screeching, 'Over here, Detective, we're over here!' Thanks for pointing that out, thought Max as he walked over and took his seat at the table. The Farrens were both dressed in ridiculously expensive clothing, although unfortunately for them not only did each item they wore seem to clash with every other item they wore, it also clashed with everything their partner wore. They were, he thought, sartorially speaking, the conjugal incongruants.

Following a requisite bit of small talk about the weather and the planet Solauric, and ordering their food, Max got down to the business in hand.

'The Professor's murder must have come as something of a shock to you.'

'Oh yes, it certainly did,' said Karen, 'a real shock. We didn't know him of course. We didn't actually know who he was until he had been killed. We had seen him around the hotel a couple of times before that night, but we didn't know he was anyone important. To be honest, we thought he was maybe someone who worked here, odd-job man or something. A funny looking man. Quite odd.'

'Yes,' said Darren, 'it was only when he had been killed that we found out he was a professor of space or something like that. Apparently he was the man that discovered the Thorians.'

'Something like that,' said Max. 'Now I gather that when the murder took place you two were in the bar area of the hotel, and had been for some time.'

Darren opened his mouth to speak but years of being married to Karen had still not taught him that he needed to be quicker than that to get the first word in.

'We certainly were,' said Karen, 'we had been there all

evening with our friend Mr Shernman and that lovely Mr Levitas. Ooh he's ever so handsome that Mr Levitas. I never in all my days ever dreamed that I would ever be sitting in a hotel like this with Blane Levitas. He's ever so clever as well, you know. And so talented. He's the greatest living actor in the universe, you know. Of course he'd never say that about himself, he's much too modest, but that's what other people say about him.'

'That's right,' said Darren. 'He showed us some papers with it on.'

It struck Max as strange that Karen Farren had referred to Karl Shernman as 'our friend Mr Shernman' even though they had quite clearly been consumed by their fascination with Blane Levitas. Was this simply their way of showing their respect for the great entrepreneur, or was it something more significant than that?

'Yes, he did,' interrupted Karen, 'he had some papers in his pocket. It was very kind of him to let us read them. He's such a gentleman. So very charming. He was so kind to us. We don't normally get treated like that by people like him, you see. It's hard, you know, in a way, having all this money. Well, not having the money, I don't think that's the problem, I think it's how we got it that upsets people. You know, a lot of people seem to hate us for it. Especially other rich people, and especially if we've got more money than them. They seem to think that we don't deserve to have it, you know, that we haven't earned it, even when they only got their money because their parents had it before them. I hate that. You know, before we won the money, me and Darren had never had anything. We both came from poor families and we'd both worked for more than twenty years, Darren on building sites and me as a cleaner. Twenty years of hard work just to keep our little house going and put some food on the table. We never had holidays, never had new clothes, never had anything new, and then one day, bam! Suddenly we are two of the richest people in the universe, we can have new everything, as many holidays as we want. It's brilliant, really lucky, but don't say we've never worked for anything. I'd like to see those snooty lot who look down on us do what we used to have to do, to live the lives we used to live.'

'Yes,' said Darren, 'I'd like to see them do that. It'd kill them.'

'Twenty years without a holiday,' said Max, shaking his head. 'That must have been tough. I hope you've made up for it since your win.'

'Oh we certainly have,' sighed Karen Farren, 'we've been everywhere. First to all the parts of our own planet that we'd always wanted to go to, then to all the other planets that we'd dreamed about going to.'

'Including Solauric?' asked Max.

'No, we never knew it existed, Detective. Not until Mr Shernman kindly invited us here.'

So, thought Max, 'our friend Mr Shernman' invited them to stay here. This was interesting.

'Was this the first contact you had with Mr Shernman, or did you already know him?'

'Oh, we've known him for quite a while,' said Karen. 'Well, obviously not before we won the money. We didn't know him before that, what with him being who he was and us being who we were. But after we won the money, like I said before, most rich people were really horrible to us and looked down on us or ignored us, but Mr Shernman, he sent us a personal message congratulating us on our good luck, and then a few weeks later he turned up at the hotel we were staying in and took us out to a really posh restaurant for dinner. He was so kind to us. You know they say a lot of these famous people who are known to be really nice are actually really horrible when you meet them in person, but not Mr Shernman, he's just like they say he is, a real gentleman. He's been really helpful to us, he's acted like a kind of financial adviser to us.

147

We'd never had any spare money in our whole lives before, and suddenly we had so much of the stuff we didn't know what to do with it, but Mr Shernman was so kind, he really helped us, you know, he advised us what to do with it, you know, to keep some handy to live on but to invest the rest to make even more money.'

'That's right,' said Darren. 'Mr Shernman said that once you have money, it is easy to make money.'

'You wanted to make more money?' asked Max. 'My understanding was that you had won more than you could ever hope to spend. What's the point of making even more?'

Again, Darren Farren opened his mouth to speak but failed miserably to beat his wife to the conversational draw.

'I know what you mean, Detective,' she said, 'and that's what we thought at first, and we said that to Mr Shernman, but he got very serious and told us that with great wealth comes great responsibility, and that we had been very very lucky in winning what we had and that if we didn't use it to do good then that would be an abuse of our good fortune. He said that if we were to invest the money in companies then that would be good as it would help other people by giving them good jobs and stuff. And we would make more money as well, so everyone would win out of it. So that's what we decided to do, and we've now invested some of our money into companies and we're helping to give people jobs. It's very satisfying.'

'We like to think we're doing our bit,' chipped in Darren, 'you know, giving something back.'

'Very admirable,' said Max, 'that's very nice to hear. I like to think I'd do the same if I were to suddenly become wealthy like that, but I don't think I'd have the first idea where to start. I wouldn't know which companies to invest in and which ones to steer clear of.'

'Well of course neither do we,' replied Karen, 'that's where Mr Shernman has helped us. He's been advising us which companies to put our money into. What with him being who he is, and with what he has done for himself and all that, then it's practically the best advice you can get. And you know what? He doesn't charge us anything for it at all!'

'That's right,' said Darren, 'nothing at all. All that advice. From Karl Shernman himself. For free!'

In the midst of this Karl Shernman love-in, their food had arrived and they had all begun to eat. The standard of the cuisine was such that there followed a period of relative silence as all three of them devoured the various dishes in front of them, save for a few noises of culinary appreciation from the Farrens between, or sometimes during, each mouthful. Max ate somewhat faster than his usual pace and was the first to finish, although whether this was due to a conscious desire to resume his investigative questioning or through a sub-conscious desire to finish this meeting as soon as possible he really could not say. As he was wiping his lips after the final mouthful, he posed one more question.

'On that night, the night when Professor Quark was killed, you said that you were in the bar all night with Karl Shernman and Blane Levitas. Did you notice who else was in the bar?'

Karen Farren looked briefly downwards, seemingly a little embarrassed.

'Well, to tell the truth, Detective, it was a long time ago now, and we did all have rather too much to drink. You know what these actors are like. They're famous for it, and I think that Mr Levitas must be one of the worst. He drinks like a fish, although a very charming and amusing sort of fish. What I'm trying to say is, I don't really remember that well, so I couldn't really say, but I don't remember anyone else being there. Of course some people may have come and gone during the evening, but I probably wouldn't have noticed, what with all the drink and Mr Levitas telling us all his wonderful stories and that. Sorry, but the more I think about it the more I think that the answer is no, there wasn't anyone else there. I am sure it was just the four of us.'

Darren Farren's face suddenly changed, as if he had just experienced a Eureka moment.

'What about Rose Saturn!' he said. 'I am sure she was there. Yes, I am sure she was. Don't you remember, Karen?'

Karen Farren screwed up her face and closed her eyes in a slightly over the top show of trying to remember. 'No, I don't think so, I don't remember talking to her.'

'No, Karen, I don't think we spoke to her, but I am sure she was there.'

Karen quickly gave up trying to look like she was scanning her hard drive to retrieve lost memory files.

'Listen dear,' she said, 'if you say she was there, then I'm sure she was. All I'm saying is that I don't remember seeing her. I've tried, but I just don't remember.'

'It's not a big deal,' said Max, 'I don't need to know about Rose specifically. All I wanted to know was if you recalled seeing anyone else who was definitely in the bar all evening. You see, anyone who was in there all evening couldn't possibly have killed the Professor, so I can eliminate them as suspects.'

Karen Farren's jaw dropped so far that Max thought it had dislocated itself from the rest of her skull.

'Ooh, Mr Quadrant!' she almost shrieked. 'You are clever. That's really clever. I'm sure you'll catch this murderer, you know. I don't think he stands a chance what with you being so clever.'

'Mmmmm,' said Darren. 'That's clever all right.'

'Any particular reason why you think the murderer is a "he", Mrs Farren?'

'Sorry?'

'You said "I don't think *he* stands a chance" when you referred to the murderer.'

'Did I? Oh, I didn't mean anything by that. Just force of

habit, I suppose. I mean, if you don't know who did something, I think you just use he or she depending on who you think would have been most likely. I mean, if we were talking about someone doing some cleaning, I probably would have said "she", even though I didn't know that it was a she and it could possibly have been a man. So for a murderer, I just said "he".'

'So you think most murderers are men?'

'Well aren't they?'

'Slight majority, but only slight.'

'But what about here, then? There's a lot more men than women. I mean, there's only three women here – myself, the hotel maid and Rose Saturn. You know I didn't do it, because you said yourself just now that anyone who was in the bar all night couldn't have done it, and I was in the bar all night so I couldn't have done it. I can't believe the maid would've done it, I mean what would a nice young girl like that be doing going around shooting old professors for? That only leaves Rose Saturn and I'm sure you don't for one minute suspect her.'

'No, no,' added Darren Farren, 'not Rose Saturn.'

Max stood up from the table.

'No, I'm sure you're right, Mrs Farren. Unfortunately, I must proceed elsewhere with my investigation, but I would like to thank you both for your charming company throughout this delightful lunch. I hope to see you again before we leave this planet.'

# 23

Back in his room, Max sat at his table and spread in front of himself all the papers he had brought with him to Solauric. These detailed the information he had been able to gain on each of the hotel guests prior to his arrival. He now began the process of going through each of them in turn and adding notes of the information he had gained and thoughts he had had on each of them during his questioning.

Late in the afternoon, having just completed his notes on President Aldous T. Shrube, Max reached out and grabbed another sheet of paper at random from the pile in front of him. As soon as he glanced at it, he stopped dead. The name on the paper leapt out at him. Sun Gord. The runner. Was this a mistake? He hadn't seen Sun Gord in all the time he had been on Solauric. Not a glimpse of him. Not a mention of him by any of the other guests or by the staff. It must be an error. Maybe he was supposed to have been here but he wasn't, he had cancelled at the last minute. He needed to check. He moved his chair over to the VisiScreen and tried to contact Barrington Portent. Fortunately, Portent was working in his office and responded immediately, his face appearing on the screen before Max.

'Detective Quadrant. What can I do for you?'

'Sorry to disturb you, Mr Portent, but a small discrepancy has just arisen in the course of my investigation. On the list of guests that was sent to me prior to coming to the planet Solauric, there appeared the name of Mr Sun Gord.'

'Yes. That is correct. Mr Gord is a guest here at the Hotel Solauric.'

'Are you sure he's here?'

'Well, according to my records, Mr Gord arrived here and he hasn't yet checked out. I'm no detective, Detective, but that would lead me to the inevitable conclusion that he is still here.'

'Could your records be mistaken? Be in error?'

'My dear Detective! This is the Hotel Solauric!'

'It's just that I haven't seen him at all since I've been here. Not once. Of all the people I've talked to since I've been here, no one has mentioned him at all.'

'Well,' said Portent, 'that does seem to be a trifle curious. Come to think of it, I haven't seen him myself for some time. I remember greeting him when he arrived. Very quiet sort of man. Not much to say for himself at all. But no, you're right, it is strange. He's been here over three months now and I don't think I've seen him since the day he arrived. You see, we take our guests' privacy very seriously here on Solauric. Some people don't like a lot of fussing and attention, like to keep themselves to themselves, and if that's what they want that's what we give them. On the other hand, three months without being seen does seem a bit excessive. You don't think something dreadful has happened to him, do you?'

'It's possible. I don't know.'

'I tell you what, Detective, leave it with me for a few minutes, and I'll check with my staff. I'm sure one of them will have been in some sort of contact with Mr Gord. I mean he can't have gone for three months without eating or drinking anything, can he? Well, assuming he's still alive, of course. What am I saying? That's the last thing we want, a second dead body. Our reputation would take years to recover. Let me check and I'll get back to you.'

'Thanks for your help, Mr Portent. I'm sure there's a perfectly innocent explanation behind all this.' As the words

153

came out of his mouth, Max grimaced at his own error and awaited the inevitable reply, which Barrington Portent summarily delivered.

'Well, Detective, I am sure there are many ways to explain it, but perhaps we'd better wait until I have concluded my own mini-investigation.'

# 24

Having just despatched an urgent message to Lars Jettessen requesting some final pieces of information, Max sat silently awaiting the results of Barrington Portent's questioning of his staff concerning the whereabouts of Sun Gord, the fastest man in the universe. A light began to flash on his VisiScreen, and his hand instantly shot out to touch the connection square in front of him. The familiar face of the hotel manager appeared in front of him.

'Mr Portent. What's the news on Sun Gord?'

'Quite odd, really. I've spoken to the staff, and I can confirm that Mr Gord is still a guest of the Hotel Solauric, and that he has been so for the past three months. The odd thing is that, much like myself, none of the staff have seen him since he arrived here either.'

'But as you said yourself, he must eat and drink.'

'Well, it seems he does. He just doesn't do it in the company of others. It seems that he has initiated some kind of routine here which ensures that he doesn't come into contact with any other human beings. When the maid goes into his room every morning to tidy and clean, he has always left. He has clearly been there, as the bed has always been slept in, but he has always gone by the time she arrives. On the instructions of Mr Gord, a light meal and four bottles of water are left in his room every afternoon. Mr Gord is never present when they are delivered, but when the maid enters the room the next morning the food appears to have been

155

eaten and the water bottles are empty. It's been like this for three months. I don't know what else to say. It is most unusual.'

'I agree,' said Max. 'It's unusual. He's either just an eccentric or he's avoiding something or someone. Still, it's good to know at least that we don't have a second death on our hands. I'm sure we're both relieved about that. Thanks for your help again, Mr Portent. I'll contact you again if I need anything further.' Max pressed the disconnect square on the VisiScreen and sat back in his chair and thought. Sun Gord could not be concealing himself in the hotel anywhere. It was totally impractical to do that all day every day for three months without being observed. He must be getting up before dawn, leaving the hotel, staying out all day and sneaking back after dark to consume his waiting food and water and catching a brief sleep in his room before heading off again. But why?

Max Quadrant's thought process was broken by the sound of a knock on the door. Annoyed, he strode over and opened it sharply.

'I'm sorry, Max. Have I disturbed you?' It was Rose Saturn.

'No, no. Not at all,' said Max. 'Come on in.' He stood back from the door to allow her to pass, and she walked slowly past him and across the floor of his room before sitting down in one of the chairs. As always, Max tried valiantly to act as the consummate professional and not stare at the body of Rose Saturn as she passed. As always, he failed. When she was seated, he closed the door and sat opposite her.

'What can I do for you, Rose?' he said.

'Nothing specific. I happened to be passing, and hadn't seen you today. Thought I'd just pop in for a chat. See how it's all going. Your investigation.'

'Oh, fine. It's going fine.' There was a pause.

'Is that it?' asked Rose. 'It's going fine? Sorry, Max, but I don't do this kind of thing for a living. What does doing "fine" mean? Does that mean you've solved it, or that you're nearly there, or that you don't have a clue but are nevertheless having a great time?'

'The middle one is probably the closest. I've spoken to everyone here, well almost everyone, and I've received some information from outside that's given me some ideas. Nearly everything is there now in my head, I just have to go through the process of sorting it all out, putting it all in order so that it fits together and all makes sense.'

'And how do you do that?'

'Well that's the secret of my success. And that's what it is. Secret.'

'Fair enough, Mr Mystery.' She smiled at him, momentarily make him lose his concentration and drop his guard. She continued, 'So you say you've talked to most of the people here. Who have you got left?'

'Just one. The runner. Sun Gord.'

'Oh him, yes, he must be a bit of a difficult man to track down.'

'A bit difficult? No one has seen him since the day he arrived here over three months ago.'

'I wouldn't go as far as to say that.'

'What do you mean?'

'I mean I wouldn't go as far as saying that no one has seen him since he arrived here over three months ago.'

'Meaning someone has?'

'Max, you know, for a man with a reputation as a great detective you are very slow on the uptake. Of course someone has seen him. I have seen him. A number of times, as it happens. I've even spoken to him once.'

'But where?'

'Out in the hills beyond the lake. He's a runner. He runs. Where would you expect to find him? In the bar?'

'When was the last time you saw him?'

'Probably about ten days ago. It was then that I had a chat

with him. He wanted to know what was going on. I told him you would be here shortly to investigate Quark's murder.'

'And how did he react to that news?'

'Difficult to say. He seems to be very nervous about it all. Bordering on paranoid I would say, but it's difficult to judge really. I've never met him before, you see, so I've nothing to measure it against. He might be like that all the time for all I know.'

'Did he say why he is living such a secretive life here?'

'I don't think that what he is doing here is really any different to how he lives his life the rest of the time. He's famous for being reclusive. Even when he runs in an event he turns up just before the race starts and leaves as soon as he has picked up his medal, and in between races no one ever sees him. So what he is doing here is hardly out of character. He obviously prefers his own company. Maybe he just doesn't like other people. That's not a crime.'

Max thought for a moment. 'What strikes me as odd, though,' he said, 'is that a man of such a misanthropic disposition should choose to come here, to Solauric. Why put yourself to the trouble of going into spacesleep, of travelling millions of miles through space, to come to a planet where you are not going to have any contact whatsoever with anyone else? It doesn't make sense. What he's doing here, he could have done at home, or on any of the planets that are nearer to his home. Why come here?'

Now it was Rose Saturn's turn to sit back in contemplation, before replying, 'Well, it can only be one of two things. If he didn't come here just to run, which as you say makes no sense given the alternatives, then either he came here to kill Quark and now having done it he's happy to stay out of the way, or else he came here to do something else and hasn't done it yet.'

'Or maybe,' said Max, 'what he came here to do cannot now be done as it involved the Professor? You've spoken to him, Rose. Do you think he could have killed Quark?'

'He could have, I suppose. I think that under the right, or should I say the wrong, circumstances, any one person is capable of killing any other person. He could have killed him, but the question is why would he have killed him? People usually kill for reasons of anger or advancement, occasionally for fun. He didn't strike me as a man who would kill for fun, certainly not a man who would travel all this way to kill for fun. Anger might be a better bet. As I said, he did seem a bit paranoid, so I guess that if he felt threatened he could possibly react in a violent way, but the circumstances of Quark's murder do not suggest that. You would suppose that if Sun Gord had murdered Quark in a snap paranoid reaction he would have killed him with his bare hands in some kind of violent rage attack, which he could easily have done – Gord is an athlete of almost physical perfection, whereas the Professor was a frail old man. But Quark was killed in what appeared to be a cold-blooded act of elimination, shot straight through the brain with a laser pistol, so that seems to take out killing in anger. As for advantage, who knows? Nothing obvious, as far as Gord is concerned; that he would stand to gain by Quark's death.'

'Well,' said Max smiling, 'if you ever get fed up with being an actress you can come and work with me as a Space Detective. You obviously have something of a feel for it.'

'You never know, Max, one day I might just do that.' Max felt slightly uncomfortable. Was she always this flirtatious with everyone, or was it simply with him? If it was just for him, then why? Was she trying to distract him from something? Was there something out there which he couldn't see because she was masking it? Or did she genuinely like him? Oh come on, Max, he thought, she's an interplanetary superstar, beautiful beyond comprehension, wealthy, successful, charming and highly intelligent. Besides, she was with Blane Levitas, the greatest living Actor, even if Max doubted that this was necessarily the universally held opinion as proclaimed by the

159

man himself. Personally, Max thought he was nothing but a big fraud. But perhaps he was just jealous? Perhaps Levitas was a great man, perhaps he was ultimately a good man, and Max was just envious of the fact that Levitas was with Rose and he wasn't. What was he thinking? He was married, he had a wife back on Centrum H. How could he possibly be jealous of Levitas? What was going on in his head?

'Are you solving it, Max?'

'I'm sorry?'

'Is this your secret? Putting yourself into some kind of trance to solve the crime. You looked like your mind had deserted your body.'

'I'm sorry, Rose. Very rude of me. Yes, I was just doing some thinking.'

'And your conclusions are?'

'Oh, none really. I didn't get very far that time.'

'OK, so where were we?' said Rose. 'We think that Sun Gord didn't kill Quark, but we can't be sure, he may have done. One thing we do know is that he must have had a reason to come to Solauric, although we have no idea what that reason is, or whether or not his reason for coming here has any connection with Quark's death. So what's the next step, Max?'

'I need to try and find him. To talk to him.'

'Do you want me to come with you? He knows me now, might be more willing to talk to you if I'm with you. What do you think?'

'It's possible. But then again if he's a recluse he might feel more comfortable talking to one person rather than two. Two might seem like a crowd to him at the moment. No, I think I'd better go alone, but I could do with some help in tracking him down. Any suggestions?'

'I can do better than make suggestions. I can tell you where to find him. You see, like most recluses, he is a creature of habit, of routine. It's easy to achieve this if you have no contact with other people, because generally it's other people who interrupt your life and make you change your plans. Not that that's always a bad thing. I mean you might be feeling lonely and would love to go out but have no plans to do so, so you decide to stay at home, but then someone arrives unexpectedly at your door and offers to take you out for dinner, and you want to because you feel lonely. So you change your plans in a good way. But if you live in isolation then you probably never change your plans. You just make them and stick to them. That's why I know where to find Sun Gord. Once I'd seen him the first time, which was purely by accident when I was out walking in the hills, I suspected that if I went to the same place at the same time on another day, I would see him again, and so it proved. I would imagine that he gets up the same time each day, runs the same route, and because of what he does, goes at roughly the same speed all the way round, arriving back at the same time. Have you got a map?'

'Of Solauric?'

'No, of the fourth moon of Centrum R! Max, you really are an idiot sometimes.'

'Sorry. No, I don't have one. Portent's probably got one in his office.'

'Don't worry, I'll draw one for you.'

Rose took a pencil and a sheet of paper from the notepad on the desk and proceeded to sketch out a rough map of the local area, showing the hotel and its gardens, the lake, and the small hills beyond. She drew a path from the hotel to the place where he could intercept Sun Gord on his daily exercise routine at the specified time.

'Are you sure you don't want me to come with you?' she said.

'I'm sure,' said Max, even though he wasn't.

# 25

The next morning, Max Quadrant took an early breakfast and then left the Hotel Solauric. Clutching Rose Saturn's hand-drawn map he walked through the gardens before taking the path which gradually ascended into the small hills surrounding the lake. He did not doubt Rose's word on the timings involved, but was slightly sceptical that Sun Gord's athletic abilities were such that he could be relied on to pass a particular place at an exact time. Consequently, he allowed himself plenty of time to be sure of seeing him, and when he found the place indicated on the map he sat down to wait and began scanning the horizon. After sitting there for about half an hour, Max glanced at his wristwatch. About five minutes to go until Rose's predicted time. He looked up, and again began to scan the horizon in the direction of where he had been told Gord would be approaching from. Sure enough, a small figure began to appear running over the brow of the next hill. He watched the figure run down the hill, momentarily lost him as he passed through the small wooded valley below, and then caught sight of him again as he began running up the hill the other side. He was on schedule, almost to the minute.

As Gord drew nearer, Max moved slowly out into the middle of the path and raised his arm. Having had no previous experience in this field, he was unsure of the best way to stop a paranoid athletic recluse in full flow, and had taken the view that the best way would be to put himself in plain view so as not to startle him, but not to wave about too much to avoid any panic-stricken reaction. Whatever the merits of this approach, it seemed to work as Sun Gord slowed down and then stopped in front of Max. To Max's amazement, despite the fact that Sun Gord had presumably already been running for several hours, he was not in the least bit out of breath or fatigued when he stopped. In fact, his breathing was more like a man who had just got out of bed after a good night's sleep.

'Mr Sun Gord?' said Max. 'Good to meet you. My name is Max Quadrant. I am a Space Detective investigating the murder of Professor Samuel Quark.' Sun Gord looked straight at Max. What was that in his eyes? Was it panic or guilt? Or perhaps both? Gord held out a tentative hand.

'Pleased to meet you Detective. I'm Sun Gord.'

Max shook his hand, and was struck by the athlete's surprisingly limp handshake for such a physically perfect man. If he could have given him one piece of advice there and then, it would have been never to shake hands with Karl Shernman, as he felt sure the entrepreneur's vice-like clasp would probably put the runner in hospital.

'I'm sorry to interrupt your training schedule, Mr Gord,' said Max, 'but I just need to ask you a few questions. I've spoken to all the other hotel guests, and you're the last on my list. It probably won't surprise you to learn that you were the most difficult one to track down.'

'I'm sorry, Detective, I had no idea that you would be wanting to talk to me. If I'd known, I would have stayed behind in the hotel one day.' Gord's voice was shaking, and Max knew already that this was not from his recent physical exertions as they had not appeared to trouble him in the slightest. No, despite his claims that he would have made himself available had he known it was necessary, this man was an extremely reluctant interviewee.

'That's not a problem,' replied Max, 'we're here now. Shall

we sit down?' Max gestured to the grass bank behind them and, following a brief nod of assent from Sun Gord, both men sat down. For a few moments, Max said nothing, simply stared straight ahead, seeming to take in the beautiful view before them. Out of the corner of his eye, he could see Sun Gord already restless, fidgeting about, unable to relax and keep himself still. This man was showing textbook signs of guilt, but Max kept telling himself not to read too much into it, bearing in mind that he was an established recluse, and from conversations with Rose Saturn there was a definite suspicion that he had a tendency towards paranoia. These traits were just as likely to be the cause of his current behaviour as feelings of guilt.

'Mr Gord, as I have already told you, my job here is to talk to all those people who were guests of the Hotel Solauric on the night that Professor Quark was killed. When I have finished this interview, that process will be complete. The questions I shall be asking you will be the same as, or substantially similar to, those which I have asked the other guests.

'What I am trying to say,' he went on, 'is that you have not been singled out here in any way. At this stage, you are no more guilty in my eyes than anyone else on this planet. Obviously you are, at this stage, no more innocent than anyone else either, although the answers you are about to give me may change that of course.'

'You mean I may incriminate myself?' said Gord.

'That's not what I meant at all, Mr Gord. I meant that this is a chance to tell me the truth, and to establish your innocence in this matter, if that is the case.'

Gord suddenly became agitated and rose to his feet. 'If that is the case? You obviously think that I killed him then? I had always understood that a man was innocent until proven guilty, but you seem to be requiring me to prove my innocence. I don't like this at all. I feel I have been condemned in my absence, condemned without a trial, without a chance to defend myself, it's just not right, I will appeal against this, I will –'

'Mr Gord, please calm down.'

'I will sue you. You and your Police Force. I will bankrupt you both, I will –'

'Mr Gord! I don't want to appear rude but you are totally overreacting to the situation. No one has accused you of anything. Look, let's just forget all this. I will ask you a couple of quick questions and then you can be on your way and resume your training. How does that sound?'

Gord stood silent for a moment, staring down at the ground, his breathing starting to return to normal. Max noticed patches of sweat appearing on the athlete's shirt, and small beads of perspiration were also forming on his hair line. These had definitely not been there when Gord had first stopped running.

'OK,' said Gord, 'just two questions. And then I go. Agreed?'

'Agreed. OK, easy one to start with. Can you tell me where you were and what you were doing on the night that Professor Quark was killed?'

Gord answered, but continued to stare at the ground as he did so.

'I was out running. All day. I went out before dawn, ran, then had some rest on a hillside, then ran again. I arrived back at the hotel in the evening. I noticed there was a lot of activity going on, but I didn't think it was anything to do with me, so I went to my room and slept. I left the hotel early the next morning, and I still didn't know what had happened. It was only when I returned that evening that I saw the message from Mr Portent informing the guests that Samuel had been killed and that we all had to stay here on Solauric until a Space Detective had arrived. Of course, all that time I was alone, I've got no witnesses at all to prove that I was where I said I was, so you will probably discard my whole statement.'

'Not necessarily, Mr Gord. Granted if someone had seen you go or seen you come back, or even better seen you out here around the time the Professor was killed, then that could have gone some way to proving your innocence, but as you so rightly pointed out it is not a case of you having to prove your innocence, rather a case of others having to prove your guilt, and nothing you have said thus far could be taken as any kind of proof of guilt.'

'OK,' said the still-sweating Gord, 'next question. Final question.'

'Why did you come to Solauric?'

'To train, of course. I have money. Why shouldn't I come to a nice place to do my training?'

'No reason at all why you shouldn't. The only thing is, I'm really struggling to see why you should. You see, there are a number of planets in your own solar system which provide excellent training facilities for top athletes such as yourself, as do some of the planets in solar systems which are adjacent to yours. I'm not at all familiar with top class athletics, so there may be some finer point that I'm missing here, but I really can't understand why a man such as yourself would put himself into spacesleep, which I understand in itself causes detriment to an athlete's performance, and travel millions of miles through space to a planet which has no real training facilities at all, when there are many far more suitable planets on his doorstep. If you had said you had come here for a holiday, I could have understood. There is nowhere better in the whole universe to take a holiday than Solauric. But as a place to train? No, I don't think so. I really don't think so at all, Mr Gord.'

'Are you accusing me of lying, Detective Quadrant?' Gord was now sweating like a bear in a sauna. 'You asked me the question, I told you the answer. I came here to train. There

are certain reasons why Solauric was deemed to be the
perfect training environment, but I will not go into these for
two reasons. Firstly they are confidential to myself and my
coaches, and secondly you would not understand them
unless you had intimate knowledge of the world of top
performance athletics, which you do not. You have now
asked your two questions and I believe that under our
agreement I am now entitled to go. Is that correct?'

'Yes, Mr Gord. That will be all for now, although of course I
may need to ask you some further questions as things
develop. I would be obliged if you could check your messages
as soon as you arrive back into the hotel tonight.'

'I will. Goodbye, Detective Quadrant.'

Max began to return the farewell, but before the words
could come out of his mouth, Sun Gord was already several
yards away, running at what seemed to be a much more
intense pace than that which he had been doing on his
approach. Perhaps this was due to the fact that he had had a
few minutes rest whilst talking to Max. It could be that he was
desperate to distance himself from this Space Detective as
soon as possible.

# 26

In his softly spoken voice, Jerrand D'Arqueville murmured the word 'connect' and the VisiScreen in his living quarters immediately sprang into life, revealing the familiar face to him on the wall in front.

'Hello, Jerrand,' said the face on the screen.

'Hello,' said D'Arqueville, 'and good morning to you, or good afternoon, depending on what time it is there.'

'It's evening, actually, not that that's important.'

'So, how is my great Mr Max Quadrant, Space Detective, doing? Do you think he is close?'

'I think so, yes. He's spoken to everyone here now, so I guess it's just a case of whether or not he's learnt enough from those people to work out who killed Quark.'

'Don't be fooled. Quadrant is a highly intelligent man. He is not relying solely on what he can glean from those present on Solauric. He's been a busy man, firing off questions to his office and even some to his son, who works for the Universal Savings Bank. Some very interesting questions he has asked, and some of the answers have been even more interesting.'

'You can read his communications? But he has been using Solauric's Secure Message System – they say the encryption on that is unbreakable.'

'To an outsider, yes it is. But you forget, it was my people who designed the system. I had certain programmes built into it, just in case I ever needed to know what was going on there. A wise move as it turned out. Almost prescient, some would say. So do you think he knows yet who the killer is?'

'I don't know. I think that he thinks he has enough now to work it out, he just has to think it through, and he's just sent a message to everyone in the hotel telling them to present themselves in the bar tomorrow night, so it's either that he wants to ask some further questions to everyone assembled together, or he is confident that he will have solved it by then.'

'Ah, he's calling everyone together, is he? Excellent news! That means that by tomorrow night he will know who the killer is.'

'How can you be so sure?'

'Because I have studied Mr Max Quadrant. I know that he is something of a devotee of the literary works of Arthur Conan Doyle and Agatha Christie. It was the established form in these types of stories that at the end of the case the great sleuth would assemble all the protagonists together and slowly, dramatically, piece by piece, reveal the method by which the crime was committed, who the perpetrator was, and their motive. I believe that our Mr Quadrant is going to do the same thing tomorrow night. A trifle vain and exhibitionist, I might say, but nevertheless should provide first-class entertainment. I would be sorely tempted to put in a personal appearance myself, but I imagine I will have to content myself with being present "in kind", as it were.'

'Anything further you need me to do between now and tomorrow night?'

'No, I think not. The good Detective will, we hope, enlighten the universe regarding this crime without any further help from us. We will speak again tomorrow when this matter has been concluded. Goodbye, and thank you.'

'Goodbye Jerrand.'

# 27

Max Quadrant sat in his room, with all his notes and printed messages assembled in a random pile on the table in front of him. This was it. This was the time when he would have to decide on the circumstances surrounding the death of Professor Samuel Quark. It was possible that there were more questions he could ask, more information he could request from the outside, but he was not convinced that there was anything further he could find out that would help in solving this crime. He had put pressure on himself by calling all the guests together in less than twenty-four hours time. He had to know the answer by then or else it would be a very short, and very embarrassing meeting. His hero, Sherlock Holmes, used to say that once you have eliminated the impossible, then whatever remains, however improbable, must be the truth, and it was with this in mind that Max always approached the final solving of his cases. Any one of the guests might have had a motive for killing the Professor, and all of them would have had the opportunity to do so. Granted, the whereabouts of some of the guests on the night of the murder did serve to either expand or contract the possibility of them having carried out the killing, but Max also knew from experience that the clever murderer always took pains to attempt to establish a seemingly cast iron alibi rather than leave his or her whereabouts unexplained, or at least unproven. He had felt sure, right from the start, that the real key to this mystery was not going to be who was where at any given time, but why the Professor was killed, and why he was killed here on Solauric.

There was a knock at the door. Max stood up, walked over to the door and opened it to find Caleb the barman standing there holding a tray on which stood two large bottles and one glass tumbler.

'You ordered these, Detective Quadrant?'

'Yes, thank you, Caleb. If you could just put them on the table over there.'

The barman did as he was requested, and then made his way back to the door.

'Are you feeling OK, Detective Quadrant?' said Caleb. 'It's just that I know you're not normally much of a drinker, if you know what I mean.'

'Yes. I don't normally, no. Only on special occasions.'

'That's cool, no problem. Please let me know if you need anything else. Bar's empty tonight, so I can bring it straight up.'

'Thanks. I'll let you know.'

'Cool,' said Caleb, as he departed, closing the door behind him. Max returned to his chair in front of the table. In front of him now were his notes and messages, a litre bottle of vodka, a litre bottle of orange juice, and the glass tumbler. He unscrewed the top of the vodka bottle and half filled the tumbler, then filled it to the top with orange juice before placing the glass in the centre of the table. He picked up the pile of papers and began reading through each in turn, refreshing his memory in no particular order with the information they contained. As he finished reading each sheet, he tossed it on to the table, and after slightly less than two hours there was an unruly pile of paper on the table and none left in his hands. He sat back for a few minutes, allowing the information to sift and file itself in his brain. Then he sat a few minutes more, consciously thinking about nothing, clearing his cerebral pathways for the task ahead.

When he was ready, he leant forward, picked up the glass off the table and drank the entire contents in one series of gulps. He paused briefly, then half filled the glass with vodka, filled it to the top with orange juice, then again downed the contents in one go. He repeated this process until both bottles were empty, before sitting back in his chair feeling the sudden surge of excessive alcohol rushing through his body. The clock was running now. There would be a point at which this sudden intake would cause him to pass out, but he was confident that shortly before that occurred he would experience a moment of blinding insight, of ultimate elucidation, when all would become transparent and the reason would become clear.

He sat still, but his brain was in overdrive, working like a computer, sorting and re-sorting the possibilities, the permutations of motives, the personal agendas, the characters, the history. Why? Why? Why Quark? Why now? Why on Solauric? Why? One after another, solutions flashed into his brain, almost instantly dismissed. No, they just didn't fit. Then, suddenly, a possibility stayed a little longer. Could this be it? Yes, that would be a reason. A very good reason. But no, discard, they could have done it anywhere, any time. Move on. No, no, no. Doesn't work. Doesn't fit. He could feel that the moment was nearing when he would lose consciousness. One last effort. Come on, he told himself, it's there somewhere, the reason is there. Then, the moment of supreme clarity. That's the only reason. It has to be. The only reason there can be. But can it be true? What are the consequences if it is true? Enormous. Far greater than the death of one man, of any number of men. The greatest single event in the whole of human history. Absolutely the greatest, bar none. Now he knew, Max Quadrant knew. He knew why Samuel Quark had been killed. He didn't yet know who the murderer was, but he had most of the following day to work that out, and now that he knew the reason why, it should not be difficult to establish the identity of the killer. However, the implications of this whole event now made a murder almost insignificant in comparison. Max Quadrant's eyelids began to close, his head slumped forwards, and then he was unconscious.

# 28

The following evening, when Max Quadrant entered the bar of the Hotel Solauric, all of the guests were already assembled there. As he walked across the floor towards the bar, he noticed that there appeared to be three distinct groupings in the seating area. Nearest the window sat President Aldous T. Shrube flanked by his advisers Edward Broillie and Hal Joyce. Nearest the entrance sat Karl Shernman, Blane Levitas, Rose Saturn and Darren and Karen Farren, the drinking party from the night of the murder. In the middle of these two natural groupings sat a collection of individuals who appeared to have no obvious affiliations to any of the others, namely Sun Gord, Professor Horatio Tacitus and the hotel manager, Barrington Portent.

Max nodded to each group as he passed, and approached the bar where, as usual, Caleb stood waiting to serve.

'Good evening, Detective Quadrant. What can I get you?'

'Good evening, Caleb. Orange juice, please.'

'On its own tonight or would you like something in it?' Caleb could not suppress a small grin and, despite the seriousness of the occasion, neither could Max.

'Just straight orange juice please, Caleb. Last night was for a special purpose. Tonight my purpose is altogether different.'

Caleb placed the drink on the bar in front of Max. Unusually for him, Caleb looked a little nervous.

'Something troubling you, Caleb?' asked Max.

'No, no … well, it's just, I wasn't sure whether you wanted me to be here. You know, you've obviously got some pretty heavy business to transact here. I can go if you like … I mean, it's cool if you want me to stay, but if you want to keep this stuff between yourselves, then that's cool too.'

'No,' said Max, 'you stay. You never know, some of us might need a drink before all this is finished. Besides, you might be the murderer.' With that, Max took a sip of his drink and then turned to address his invited and assembled audience.

'Ladies and gentlemen. First of all, thank you for giving me your time and for turning up punctually to this little gathering. This shouldn't take an inordinate amount of time, and of course when this is over then most of you will finally be free to leave the planet Solauric, if you so please, and resume your normal lives.

'Now, as you all know, on the night of the 15$^{th}$ of April, Professor Samuel Quark was discovered dead in his room, killed by a single blast through the head from a laser pistol. I was subsequently assigned as Space Detective to investigate the Professor's murder, and after some three months in spacesleep I arrived here on Solauric to find you all patiently waiting. In the time that I have been here, I have managed to speak with you all at least once individually. These interviews have led to me asking myself certain questions, some of which I have answered myself through the facts that I know or through simple logic, whereas for some of those questions I have had to get help from other sources.

'The first thing that struck me about the case was "why here?" If I were planning to murder Professor Quark, why would I choose to do so here, on Solauric? The answer, of course, is that I wouldn't. It is an illogical place to murder anyone. The small number of people on the planet means that, at any given time, everyone present pretty much knows who everyone else is. Anonymity, so often the prime asset of a successful murderer, is impossible. The exclusivity and remoteness of the planet make escape virtually impossible. No craft is allowed anywhere near Solauric without express prior permission, and all space traffic is closely monitored. It is impossible to leave here without anyone knowing, and very difficult to do so without anyone knowing when and where you went. The fact that the people here exist in such a relatively small social and physical environment means that a murder could not go undetected for too long. In summary, if I were going to kill someone, then the planet Solauric as a venue would be very near the bottom of my list.

'So I return to my original question, why here? And for me there can only be one possible explanation. The person who killed Samuel Quark did not know, prior to their arrival on Solauric, that they would be required to do so. Having realised that they need the Professor dead, the next question is why not wait until he has left Solauric and gone to another planet, in all probability back to his home on Centrum A, follow him and kill him there, where the chances of doing so without detection and apprehension are far greater? Again, only one logical explanation. The reason why that person had decided that the Professor must die was to stop him doing something which he would do either on Solauric or when he had left. Certainly, it appears that the murderer could not allow Samuel Quark to leave Solauric alive.

'Next, I pondered a slightly more complex and difficult question. I looked at all of you and thought, "Why are they here?" Holidays? Well, perhaps. It is a Luxury Resort Planet after all, and after spending a few days here myself I couldn't blame anyone for simply coming here for no other reason than just to be here. But was this the case with all of you? I don't think so. So why are you all here? This was a question I put to each of you, and to which each of you gave me answers which contained varying degrees of truth.

'Some people's motives for being here are fairly straightforward and easy to establish and verify. Mr Broillie and Mr Joyce, for instance, being aides to President Shrube, are simply here because the President is here, and Miss Saturn is here because I believe she is, how shall I say, romantically involved with Mr Levitas. Professor Tacitus is an adviser to President Shrube and, as is the case with Mr Broillie and Mr Joyce, it is natural to assume that he is here because the President is here. Mr Portent, of course, works here so he of all people can be said to be a man whose presence here does not in itself raise suspicion. That leaves President Shrube, Mr Shernman, Mr Levitas, Mr Gord, and Mr and Mrs Farren as being persons whose motives for being here perhaps warrant a little closer attention.

'Let us start at the top, politically speaking, and look at the case of our President, Mr Aldous T. Shrube. When I asked the President to explain the reasons behind his visit to Solauric, he was somewhat vague in his reply. Now I'm sure that his political adversaries would claim that this is a standard response from the President, that he is accustomed to never answering a direct question directly, instead relying on the incantation of meaningless platitudes and referring any issues of substance to his aides and advisers. However, I am not here in the role of political opponent to the President, but am investigating the death of a prominent man by unlawful means, so it is not my job to judge what is or is not the usual response of a President, or whether the manner in which the President conducts himself is proper for a man holding such a position. My job is simply to ascertain whether or not the facts that the President relayed to me are the truth and, possibly more importantly, whether or not there are other facts which are relevant to the case in hand, which the President is aware of but has not divulged to me. After much thought, I have concluded that everything that President Shrube told me in the course of my interview with him was true. I have also concluded that the President has deliberately withheld certain facts from me, facts that have a direct bearing on the murder of Samuel Quark and which should have been disclosed.' President Shrube was beginning to look agitated and increasingly angry. He stood up.

'Now look here, Quadrant. What are you saying? Are you accusing me of being involved in the murder of a man who was a close personal friend of mine? I'll have you out of a job for this!'

'President Shrube, please sit down and calm down. No one is accusing you of anything. Not at this point. Please just sit down and let me do this my way. If Samuel Quark was a close personal friend of yours, then I am sure that you will be determined to see those responsible for his murder brought to justice for their crime.' Max waited until Shrube sat down again before continuing.

'I knew from my discussions with the President that the purpose of his visit to Solauric was for business, not pleasure. In fact, he was here to attend a meeting. The very fact that a man as important as President Aldous T. Shrube would, when just beginning to embark on his hectic re-election campaign, spend several weeks in spacesleep in order to come to such a remote planet for a meeting, leads me to assume that this was to be a meeting of some importance. More important to a politician than a re-election campaign? It seems so. So what was this meeting about? Well, we may get nearer to the truth of that at a later stage, but for the time being let us first consider the intended participants in that meeting. Firstly, of course, there was President Shrube himself, presumably to be accompanied by Mr Broillie and Mr Joyce. The late Professor Quark was to be there, as was Professor Tacitus, that much we know. We also know that, following the murder of Professor Quark, the meeting never took place. Was this simply out of respect for the deceased, or, as I would contend, because without Professor Quark the meeting could not take place? Therefore, whatever this meeting was to be about, Samuel Quark was central to it. In short, no Quark, no meeting.

'Then there is another problem. President Shrube and his aides, plus Professors Quark and Tacitus, all arrive on Solauric for this monumental meeting, conference, debate, whatever we want to call it. As I have said, this meeting is of such vital importance that these busy and important people have given up large amounts of their time and travelled millions of miles to attend, so you would have assumed that the moment that they were all here they would have got down to business straight away. A natural assumption under the circumstances, I think. But did this happen? No, absolutely not. They were all here, ready and waiting, for some days. No meeting took place. But why? Perhaps I have already answered my own question. They were ready, and *waiting*. Ready, in that they were all assembled in the appointed place. But waiting? Waiting for what? Or for whom? I think the answer is that they were waiting for another person. A person who was, like Professor Quark, to be a vital participant in the meeting. But who was this person? Well, there are two facts which led me to the idea of who this person might be. The first came to light when I was trying to discover why Solauric was chosen as the meeting venue. It is in many ways an illogical place for busy people to meet, being so inaccessible. Obviously it has its plus points too, such as the natural beauty of the planet, the undeniable luxury of the hotel, and the privacy guaranteed by its very exclusivity. However, there are many similar planets which run Solauric close in terms of beauty, luxury and privacy but which are much easier and far less time-consuming to get to, so on the whole Solauric struck me as an odd choice. The next fact to establish in determining why Solauric was chosen was whose planet is it? It is no secret that Solauric is one of the few privately owned planets, but its ownership was something of a mystery. It is easy to find out that the planet

Solauric is owned by Solauric Holdings. Which is in turn owned by a property company called Red Magodan, but after that the corporate structure becomes something of a labyrinth. Fortunately for me, I have a close contact in the world of corporate banking who was able to find his way through this deliberately complex maze of companies, holding companies and subsidiaries and establish to a reasonable degree of certainty who did ultimately and actually own the planet Solauric.

'The second point I discovered courtesy of Mr Shernman, who confessed to me for his own reasons that he had had Samuel Quark under surveillance for some time, and that he had a reasonable idea of the last port of call of the Professor prior to his arrival on Solauric. If that destination is true, then the Professor could only have been going to see one man, because the planet in question has only one resident, being the same man who owns this planet, Jerrand D'Arqueville. My belief is that Jerrand D'Arqueville was due to attend the meeting here. As we all know, D'Arqueville is famous for many things, one of which is that he reputedly never leaves the planet which is his home and upon which he is the sole resident. For D'Arqueville to leave his home planet to attend a meeting, that meeting would have to be very important indeed, but if it were so important that he felt the need to attend in person, then Solauric, a planet which he owns himself, would seem the most likely and logical venue. The fact that D'Arqueville owns Solauric has been established and verified as near as possible. Samuel Quark's visit to D'Arqueville's home planet is more speculative at this point, relying solely on the veracity of Karl Shernman's statement to me, but I believe it to be the truth. Therefore the reason why the meeting on Solauric had not taken place was that the participants already here were awaiting the arrival of Jerrand D'Arqueville. It would be my guess that when Quark was murdered, D'Arqueville pulled out, either through fears for his own personal safety or because without Quark the meeting could not happen.

'These facts and assumptions prove nothing against President Shrube other than that he did not divulge to me certain facts of which I believe he was aware. They merely serve to elucidate the reasons for his presence here and his initial behaviour. We will return to the President later, but for now we will turn our attention elsewhere and look at others whose reasons for being here might benefit from some further clarification.

'Let's examine next the case of our famous entrepreneur, businessman, philanthropist and all- round publicity-seeking good guy, Mr Karl Shernman. Now, when Mr Shernman made a statement to me that he had been tracking the movements of Professor Quark, I am reasonably sure that his motivation was not of an unburdening, confessional nature. Instead, I believe that his purpose was simply to attempt to incriminate Jerrand D'Arqueville. Put yourselves, for a moment, in the position of Karl Shernman. He is very successful. He is very wealthy. In fact, by his own admission, he has more money than he could ever hope to spend in his lifetime. But is wealth and success enough in itself? Well, that can depend largely on two things. One, of course, is that wealth is comparative. I, for example, am a poor man compared to Karl Shernman, but would be considered prosperous by a crop farmer on Centrum F. The other factor is mentality, how you perceive yourself in the universe, against what scale you rate yourself. Karl Shernman has never been shy of being in the public eye – on the contrary, he seems to have made it almost his life's work to court publicity, and so there is a huge volume of media articles and reports on the man, from his business activities to his pastimes and personal relationships. One thing that comes over quite clearly from this is that he is a man who likes to win. He likes to win at business, he likes to win at sport, and he likes to win in his pursuit of female companions.

'I asked you just now to put yourself in his position. How would you regard yourself and your achievements? I think that most of you would probably say, "pretty good, I've done very well". As one of the richest people in the universe, you would look around you at the billions upon billions of people making up the human population and think to yourself that you were very fortunate to be in such a position. I don't think that Mr Shernman looks at himself in this way at all. I think he wants to be what he portrays himself as. A winner. When Karl Shernman looks, he looks upwards, not downwards. For him, there is simply a winner and there is everyone else, and with Jerrand D'Arqueville around he will always see himself in the "everyone else" category. You see, for him, being second amongst billions is still being second. I think that it was for this reason that he tried to implicate D'Arqueville in the murder of Professor Quark. Despite the enormity of his wealth, he still perceives himself in terms of his relative worth compared to D'Arqueville. So, the confession of covert surveillance was, possibly, nothing more than a crude attempt to point the finger of suspicion at his bitterest rival.'

'Or,' said Shernman, accompanied by his best attempt at an angelic expression, 'a simple and honest attempt to point you in the right direction.'

'However,' said Max, completely ignoring the entrepreneur's interjection into his monologue, 'in doing so he perhaps revealed more about himself than he intended to, and set me off on a train of thought which lead me to a credible theory of why Karl Shernman was here on Solauric.

'Making the decision to have a person watched involves, I would argue, stepping over a moral line, a kind of crossing of an ethical Rubicon. I cannot believe that a man of Karl Shernman's wealth and power, having once crossed that line, would limit his spying activities to one elderly professor. No, it is my contention that Mr Shernman was in the habit of placing under surveillance most of his business rivals and those prominent figures whose actions he thought could influence the success or failure of his business empire. I have no evidence to back this up, but my guess would be that not only was Quark being watched, but also President Shrube and Professor Tacitus, perhaps even Mr Broillie and Mr Joyce. Karl Shernman also spoke to me about the large numbers of cryptographers he employed to ensure that his messaging systems were secure. Once again, I have no evidence to support this, but it would not surprise me if a certain number of these cryptographers were employed not just in securing his own systems, but in the interception and deciphering of messages sent by others. It is therefore my belief that Karl Shernman was not here by chance, rather that he had discovered that the meeting between D'Arqueville, the President and the two Professors was to take place, and guessed that something of an immense magnitude was about to happen, something so significant that he had to be on hand personally to be the first to be able to react. For all I know, he could have been intending to try and get himself invited to this famous meeting, but that is not important. What is important is that I believe I know why Karl Shernman was here – unless, Mr Shernman, anything I have said was untrue?'

All eyes turned to Karl Shernman, who simply shrugged his shoulders and gave a small grin. 'I don't know, Detective,' he said, 'you seem very sure of yourself. Who am I to contradict you?'

'Thank you,' said Max. 'I will take that for now as confirmation that my assumptions are correct. I will now move on to our esteemed thespian, Mr Blane Levitas.' Levitas, who had previously been looking bored and overtly inattentive, suddenly perked up. Whether this was because he felt he was about to be accused of playing some part in the murder, or was simply because it appeared that the conversation had moved round to a subject dear to his heart, Max could not tell, although he had a fair idea.

'Mr Levitas told me that the purpose of his stay here on Solauric was to "rest", by which he meant that he was in a period of recovery from his previous job.'

'Role, Detective,' said Levitas. 'I do not have jobs, I have roles.'

'My apologies. Mr Levitas was resting following his previous role. During the course of our discussions, I asked Mr Levitas what his next jo— ... role was going to be, to which he replied that he was engaged in a kind of open ended rest period, as he currently did not have another role to perform in the near future, a statement which I have good reason to believe may have been truthful in itself, but neglected to mention one important detail. Unfortunately for Mr Levitas, he, like Karl Shernman, lives much of his life in the public eye and thus has to live with the fact that details of his personal and professional life are freely available. I accept that much of that information may be completely untrue, or at least inaccurate, but there are nevertheless certain sources which can be viewed as being reputable and accurate. I was therefore intrigued to discover that within the acting world it was rumoured that Blane Levitas did have another role for which he was preparing. In fact, Mr Levitas, is it not true that your next role was to be that of Professor Samuel Quark in the story of that man's remarkable life? Is it not also true that the reason you came to Solauric was to meet with Quark himself in order to fully prepare yourself to play him?'

All eyes in the room now moved to stare at Blane Levitas, a development which he did not object strongly to. Milking the drama of the moment he very slowly rose to his feet, stood perfectly still and silent for a short while before launching himself into one of his trademark extravagant bows.

'Detective, I am undone. I stand here before you, exposed, a victim of my own moral equivocation. I fully accept that, while nothing I told you was untruthful, there may have been certain areas upon which I should have been more forthcoming. When I told you I had no role to prepare for, it was the truth, for when they heard of the Professor's violent death the producers shelved the project pending the outcome of the investigation and the subsequent necessary rewriting of the script to include the murder and its aftermath. They have also informed me that now that the Professor is dead they will be re-casting the role as, such is my famed dedication to my art, they cannot get insurance for me to play a character who dies at the end. However, I do accept that this information would have been useful to you, and it would have been courteous of me to provide it. That I was remiss in the free and punctual provision of this information will be forever upon my conscience, and I apologise fully and unreservedly for my actions.'

With that, Levitas resumed his seat, although when Darren and Karen Farren seemed so overwhelmed by the sincerity of his apology that they broke out into a brief round of applause, he quickly stood up again and bowed. Max gave a quick shake of his head in an attempt to bring himself back into the real universe, before moving on to his next point.

'Next, Mr Sun Gord. Universally famous athlete, often styled as the fastest man who ever lived.'

At the mere mention of his name, Sun Gord began to twitch and jerked his head around both ways, appearing to look for the fastest exit. There was little doubt that if Sun Gord wanted to make a break for it, no one was going to catch him, but on the other hand it was clear that to simply run from the hotel would be futile, as there was really nowhere to run to.

'When I questioned Mr Gord, eventually, about his reasons for being on Solauric he informed me that he had come here to train. There can be no doubt that during his stay here, he has been training. In fact, he has done little else but train, leaving the hotel before dawn and not returning until after dark. However, just because he has been training whilst he is here, it does not necessarily mean that he came here to train. Again, my question was why here, why Solauric? Mr Gord is a honed and finely tuned athlete. Several weeks or months in spacesleep must severely impair his body's performance for some time, and I presume that any benefits he may have gained by his uninterrupted stint of exercise on Solauric will in all likelihood be negated by the journey back. There are numerous worlds close to Mr Gord's home planet which provide first-class training facilities for athletes and which would have represented an infinitely better choice of location for this purpose, so my conclusion has to be that the reason for his presence here was something other than that which he had relayed to me.

'I am aware, as I am sure everyone in this room is, of the perennial problem which has plagued top-class athletics for longer than anyone can remember, namely the taking of illegal substances to enhance sporting performance. For centuries there has been an enduring war between dishonest athletes and the authorities which regulate and administer the sport. It is the equivalent of an arms race. As the administrators search for better and more accurate ways to detect drugs, so the athletes themselves search for more undetectable drugs. However, since the emergence of Sun Gord, popular mythology tells us that, in the field of sprint racing at least, we have entered a new era, a kind of golden age. Since Mr Gord came from nowhere to win the Universal Championship title seven years ago, not one sprinter has failed a drug test at a major event. Once again, popular mythology tells us that the reason for this is that Sun Gord is so supreme, so far ahead of his rivals, that they have dispensed with using illegal drugs as they know that there is no such drug that will ever get them anywhere near him on the track. It seems that people will bear the risks to win, but not when the prize will only ever be second place.

'Let us return for a brief moment to the reason why we are all here in this room. The murder of Professor Samuel Quark. A great man, a true legend. Famous for his theories on the infinity of the universe and on the existence of alien life. That was what he was famous for, but of course that was not all he did. Those theories were developed fairly early on in his academic career, but since their publication catapulted him to universal fame, he has been engaged in many different scientific projects, and whilst continuing to work on theoretical science has also, with the help of his consortium of scientists, made developments and significant advancements in a wide range of areas, most notable perhaps in weapons development, but also, and this is less well known, in the field of pharmaceutical research.' Gord could not keep still by this point, and was starting to sweat quite dramatically.

'Detective Quadrant,' said Gord, 'I think you should stop there. I can see where you are going with this and to make such an accusation in front of this audience would almost certainly be slanderous. My lawyers will bankrupt both you and your employer, even if it is the government.'

'Mr Gord, I appreciate your concern here, but I would respectfully point out that, while I am sure you have access to large numbers of top lawyers, you are not one yourself. If you were a lawyer, you would of course be aware that something can only be slanderous if it is in fact not true. The very fact that you are showing such concern does lead me to suspect that the path I am taking here is the correct one, and that my admittedly unsubstantiated thoughts on this subject are largely true. Mr Gord, I put it to you that the reason why you came to Solauric was not exclusively to train, but to meet with Professor Samuel Quark. I do not know how long Quark had been supplying you with undetectable performance enhancing drugs, but my guess would be just in excess of seven years, since shortly before the time you emerged as the exceptional performer you are. Equally, I have no idea whether you came here to discuss or receive some new wonder drug Quark had developed, or whether it was just to pick up a regular consignment. For the purposes of what I am doing here, it is irrelevant. The point is, I believe I have solved the riddle as to why you are here. For now, I shall content myself with that.'

Gord was now sweating even more and seemed to be on the verge of hyper-ventilating.

'I'll sue you, Quadrant,' he said. 'You're history.'

'You won't sue me, Mr Gord,' said Max, 'because you know you'd lose. As for history, well that's more Professor Tacitus's field than mine. Now, to conclude this section of our little discussion, we shall turn to the last of our previously unexplained guests, Mr and Mrs Farren. Here, I'm afraid, for my own purposes, I shall have to be brief. Mr and Mrs Farren are a slightly different case from those of you whom I have just mentioned. President Shrube, Mr Shernman, Mr Levitas and Mr Gord all provided me with answers which they all knew were not entirely full and truthful. Mr and Mrs Farren on the other hand gave me an answer which was untrue, but which was given to me in good faith – they believed it to be true. They told me that they were here on Solauric on holiday as the guests of Karl Shernman. All I can say at this point is that that is not the reason why they are here.' Max Quadrant turned and walked back to the bar. As he took another sip of his orange juice, there was complete silence. No one moved, no one looked at anything other than the Space Detective standing before them. There was an intense air of expectancy in the room, as they all waited for Max to continue.

'So, where have we got to so far?' he said. 'I have, I believe, now established credible reasons for each of you to be here on Solauric. The next question, the big question if you like, is one of motive. Why would any of you have had reason to kill Samuel Quark? In this part of my investigation, I had to consider each of you individually. It could have been the case that more than one of you was responsible for the Professor's death. Ultimately, of course, I had to recognise the possibility of a mass conspiracy, that all of you had made a collective decision to kill him, but for the moment I will consider each of you as individuals and to show that there is no bias in my presentation I will examine the case against each of you via the random order of your physical location within this room.'

Max took a small object out of his pocket, tossed it in the air and caught it with his hand. He looked at it, then replaced it in the pocket from which it came.

'There,' he said, 'completely random. We will start with those nearest the door and move across the room towards the window. That means that you, Mr Levitas, will be first.' Immediately his name was mentioned, Blane Levitas rose, bowed deeply, and announced, 'I am at your service, sir.'

'So,' said Max, 'let us examine the possible motive of Mr Blane Levitas. As we know, Mr Levitas is an actor of some universal repute, famed for his attention to absolute realism in his portrayal of a wide range of characters, particularly those of historical significance. It is a well known fact that Mr Levitas's left arm is a prosthetic limb, after he famously had his original arm amputated in order to accurately portray a one-armed character. Like many great actors, Mr Levitas is a larger than life character in his own right, having an outgoing, gregarious, entertaining and, some would say, outrageously flamboyant personality. Alas, like many great actors before him, he is plagued by self doubt, and his extremely extrovert behaviour would be viewed by some as simply a mask to hide his own insecurity, and his periods of

189

exuberant extravagance are, I believe, balanced out by periods of great depression and introversion. It has been established that, prior to Quark's death, Mr Levitas had been an established regular every night in this bar, drinking heavily and holding court with a succession of entertaining stories about his life and career. Following the murder, these sessions ceased immediately, recommencing only a few nights ago. The reason given to me for this was that the murder of the Professor had soured the party atmosphere, that it had become seemingly disrespectful to the late gentleman to behave in this manner while the murderer remained at large. All very commendable. However, this story did not hold to be entirely true when the party behaviour recommenced, as at that time, as is the case at the moment, the identity of the killer had not been revealed. If the reason for the solemnity and sobriety had been exactly what it had been claimed to be, then surely the correct course of action would have been to wait until the murderer had been revealed, apprehended and removed?

'Therefore I had to consider the possibility that there was perhaps more to this behaviour than a simple case of respect for the dead man and, considering this in the context of the establishment of motive, I came to the following possibilities. What if the reason for the cessation of nightly partying was not as a mark of respect, but the onset of a bout of depression for Blane Levitas? This might explain the resumption of drinking prior to any revelation of the murderer, as it could have simply marked the fact that this bout of depression was over and the flamboyant side of his character had re-asserted itself. If we accept this as a possibility, we next have to consider what would have brought on the depression. It could, of course, have been triggered by many factors, indeed some factors which are entirely unrelated to the circumstances which had occurred here on Solauric, but looking at those circumstances there seemed to be two main possibilities. The first is that Mr Levitas was very excited about the opportunity to play the role of such a great historic figure as Samuel Quark, and that when he discovered that the Professor was dead he very quickly worked out that this event would almost certainly result in the postponement and probable recasting of the project, which of course turned out to be the case. Such a realisation could easily have had a disastrous effect on the mental state of a man such as Blane Levitas, and sent him over the edge into a period of abject depression. The second possibility is that this rapid descent into depression was caused by feelings of intense guilt, which would have been the case if he were in fact the killer of Samuel Quark. I have already spoken of Mr Levitas's devotion to realism, and it has long been rumoured that his ultimate goal, the crowning glory of his illustrious career, would be to achieve the ultimate realism and die in character, simply because the nature of the role demanded it. Is it possible, therefore, that it was Blane Levitas who murdered Samuel Quark simply so that he could create the circumstances by which to go out of this universe in a blaze of glory? Perhaps. We shall see.

'Next, we shall examine the killer credentials of Miss Rose Saturn. Miss Saturn was, I am assuming, familiar to you all prior to your trip here to Solauric. I think I am right in stating that she was something of a child star, and that during her transition from child star to a mature actress of some renown, she has rarely been out of the public eye. In recent years, of course, she has been famous not only for her considerable dramatic abilities, but also for her romantic attachment to Mr Blane Levitas, the case against whom we have just reviewed. So why would Rose Saturn desire the death of Samuel Quark? Her attachment to Blane Levitas could be an indicator. Perhaps Professor Quark had raised an objection to being played by Levitas and Rose Saturn killed him before he could insist on having the part re-cast.

Perhaps she had fallen out with Mr Levitas and, knowing him as she does, knew that if Quark were dead then Levitas would be tempted to kill himself in the portrayal of the role, thereby ridding herself of him. Certainly this would go a long way towards explaining the method by which the Professor met his end, as what departure could be easier for Levitas to reconstruct than a single laser blast through the head? Perhaps there are reasons entirely unconnected with Blane Levitas which caused Rose Saturn to commit this murder. She is, as I am sure you have all noticed during your stay here, an incredibly beautiful woman, and it is not beyond the realms of belief that even an elderly gentleman such as Samuel Quark would have had such an irresistible attraction to her that he felt compelled to act upon it. Whether this would have taken such a form as to make Miss Saturn so enraged that she reacted by means of homicide I have my doubts, as I am sure that she has grown accustomed to unwanted attention some time ago and can deal with it without undue concern, but we cannot rule it out completely. So, as you can see, the idea of Rose Saturn in the role of murderer is not without its possibilities. My job is to move from possibilities to probabilities to certainties.'

Max paused, took another sip of his drink then continued, still facing a silent audience.

'Mr and Mrs Farren. Sorry to keep grouping you two together when treating everyone else as individuals, but since you never appear to be apart from each other I have made the assumption that you are either both guilty or both innocent, as it seems that the chances of either of you committing such a crime without the knowledge of the other are minimal. When looking at your personal history and circumstances, there does not, on the face of it, seem to be the slightest connection between yourselves and the late Professor, and nothing which would suggest any overt motive by which you would seek his death. There have been certain events which have occurred since Quark's murder which could, and in fact would, directly connect you to him and to his demise, but, as in the case of the reason for you both being here on Solauric, I believe that these events have transpired without you having any knowledge of their true purpose and therefore cannot serve to incriminate you in any way. There may be facts of which I am unaware that could have given you cause to commit murder, but I do not believe it to be the case. Therefore, I think I can at this point categorically state that Darren and Karen Farren are not the murderers of Professor Samuel Quark.'

The Farrens breathed a huge and audible sigh of collective relief and sat back in their chairs before both breaking out into broad smiles. Much as he was enjoying the drama of the moment, Max felt it unfair to keep the Farren couple entwined in the tension of the unravelling disclosure. They were clearly no more capable of organising and executing a murder plot than they were of selecting two pieces of clothing that did not clash, and he felt that to put their limited mental facilities through the implied suspicion of his revelation process would be tantamount to torture. When he saw their reaction, he knew he had made the right decision. He also knew that declaring two of the audience to be formally absolved of guilt would also increase the pressure on those that remained, as the odds on any of them being named as the killer had suddenly shortened. He sensed this in their faces, with the exception of the face of Blane Levitas, who curiously seemed pleased that he was now in a much more exclusive band of suspects. Once Max had gauged the reaction, he continued.

'To conclude our first grouping over here, we will look at the possible motives of Mr Karl Shernman. As we established earlier on this evening, Karl Shernman likes to win. He likes to, and generally does so, or at least he does as far as his public image goes. Whether he is actually the winner he is portrayed as or is simply masterful in his ability to manipulate the media remains to be seen, but there is one fact of which there is no doubt. That, for all his success, he is and seemingly always will be, second to Jerrand D'Arqueville. It was my contention earlier on this evening that this fact is a constant thorn in the side of Karl Shernman, almost to the point of humiliation. He is deeply envious of Jerrand D'Arqueville, and I believe much of his obsession with self-promotion is as a result of this. He knows that he can never outstrip the wealth accumulation of D'Arqueville so has felt the need to compete with him on a different playing field. D'Arqueville is famous for being a recluse. So what does Karl Shernman do? Well, it seems he goes for the complete opposite. D'Arqueville is a recluse, and reclusiveness in itself breeds suspicion and assumption. People assume that every recluse has something to hide, that they are by their very misanthropic nature, evil. But what evidence do we have to suggest that there is anything evil about Jerrand D'Arqueville? None. None whatsoever. There have never been any criminal charges brought against him. He is a covert supporter of numerous charitable organisations, and has given away considerably more money than that given away cumulatively by the next ten richest people in the universe. No, there is no actual evidence that he is anything other than an extremely generous financial benefactor to millions, who simply prefers to keep his own company.

'But, as I have stated, we have a tendency to demonise those who keep themselves to themselves, and seem to expect the wealthy members of our society to be conspicuous and demonstrative in their charitable giving. It is not enough to give, they have to be seen to be giving. Karl Shernman certainly has a feel for the mood of the public at large, and he saw this as an opportunity to get ahead of his rival, D'Arqueville. He has therefore engaged himself in a relentless saturation of the media with the intent of promoting a kind of personality cult around himself. To a large extent, he has succeeded, as his public persona is one of friend to the people. The public feel they know him. What's more, the public would trust Karl Shernman ten times more than they would trust Jerrand D'Arqueville. The battle for public affection has most certainly been won by Karl Shernman, even if it is a battle in which Jerrand D'Arqueville declines to even take the field. The question is, is that enough? Is that enough to satisfy Karl Shernman's lust for victory? If not, what else could he do? He must have known a long time ago that he could never hope to exceed D'Arqueville in terms of wealth, that as long as D'Arqueville was around then the best he could ever hope for was second place.

'But what if something were to happen to Jerrand D'Arqueville? If something could bring him and his empire crashing down? I am fairly certain from my conversations a few days ago with Karl Shernman that he was doing his best to steer my suspicions firmly in the direction of Jerrand D'Arqueville. The question is, was this simple opportunism following the death of Samuel Quark, or was this the culmination of a plot by Karl Shernman to engineer the murder of the Professor and then incriminate his bitterest rival? Karl Shernman would, of course, be well aware that as a resident of a privately owned planet, Jerrand D'Arqueville would in the event of being found guilty of murder be subject to Space Law rather than Planetary Law and if sentenced to life imprisonment would forfeit all his possessions.'

'You are missing one vital piece of information here, Detective,' said Karl Shernman. 'You are clearly not quite as clever or well researched as you think. I have shareholdings in many of the same companies as D'Arqueville. If he were to be ruined and his empire collapsed, the effect on my own wealth would be disastrous.'

'Sorry to correct you, Mr Shernman,' said Max, 'but I was aware of that fact, and it was for that reason that I concluded that that did not represent an adequate motive for you to kill Professor Quark.'

Karl Shernman rose to speak but Max ignored him completely and moved to face the centre group consisting of Professor Tacitus, Barrington Portent and Sun Gord. Shernman hesitated for a moment, then resumed his seat.

'Professor Tacitus,' said Max, 'you have been of invaluable help to me since I arrived on this planet. Your understanding of historical facts has been vital, and your pleasant company an added bonus.' Horatio Tacitus gave a gentle nod of his head in recognition of the compliment.

'However,' continued Max, 'I have a job to do here and I cannot allow my personal likes or dislikes to cloud the objectivity of my analysis and judgement of the facts. Therefore, Professor Tacitus, I was compelled to consider you in the same light as everyone else here and look at possible motives as to why you may have killed Samuel Quark.' Another nod from Tacitus, but this time more formal.

'Like Samuel Quark, you were an adviser to President Shrube, and on an official standing you were both equals. Science on one side, history on the other, the advice of one serving as counterbalance to the other. Except of course it wasn't really like that at all, was it? You said it yourself, Professor Tacitus. President Shrube was all over Quark, consulting him about anything and everything, whereas your advice was seldom, if ever, sought, and the only reason you were ever invited to these Presidential discussions was to maintain the pretence of balance. The question I had to ask myself, therefore, was what effect this had on you? Did the fact that the President clearly favoured Quark over you grind away at you? Did that feeling intensify year after year until you could stand it no more? Did the fact that Quark seemed

196

to be turning his knowledge into wealth serve to stoke up the fire of hatred within you? Did it all come to a head here on Solauric? Did perhaps the President inform you that for the meeting for which you were here, the meeting that was so important that you had all travelled to Solauric, that was so important that Jerrand D'Arqueville himself was going to attend in person, that at this meeting your presence would not be required, that the President only needed Samuel Quark to accompany him? Did this finally push you over the edge and lead you to kill Quark, to remove that thorn from your side forever?'

Horatio Tacitus sat still, seemingly quite unperturbed. He simply raised his head and said, 'Max, you know that is not true. If I have impressed one thing upon you during our little chats on this planet, it is that I am, above all else, a man of peace.'

'That is so,' said Max, 'and I believe it to be true. I do, however, have to consider the possibility that it is not.'

Max now turned his attention to the Manager of the Hotel Solauric.

'Mr Portent,' he began, 'I would like to be able to say that there are many ways to explain why you might have killed Professor Quark,' (Max paused as an involuntary giggle emerged from Caleb Khorklory standing the other side of the bar behind him) 'but I cannot. You are, for all your bluster, something of a model employee for the Hotel Solauric, as it seems to me that the whole of your behaviour is conducted with the permanent consideration of the preservation of the standards and reputation of this hotel. The only way in which I would have thought you to be implicated in this affair would have been if Samuel Quark had presented some kind of reputational threat to the hotel. If this had been the case, then I have no doubt that your dedication to your employer and to this establishment is such that almost no action, perhaps even including murder, would have been beyond the realms of possibility. However, there is no evidence at all that the Professor ever posed such a threat, and so I concluded it extremely unlikely that you were involved in his death. Granted, your actions on the night itself, when you seemingly condoned the removal of the body, were on the surface suspicious, but I am in no doubt that your actions at that time can be explained in only one way, that your overriding concern was for the preservation of the hotel's image. Besides that, I have been of the impression since I first met you that expecting you to carry out and conceal a murder plot would be like giving a Rubik's cube to a monkey.

'Finally in this group, we have Mr Sun Gord, universe-beating runner extraordinaire. We have already established that Mr Gord's reasons for being here were not as he had stated, and that we believe he was here to see Samuel Quark with a view to procuring either a fresh supply of performance enhancing drugs or, as seems more likely given that this was to be a direct personal meeting, the purchase and perhaps testing of some new undetectable drug developed by Quark's team. The question I had to ask myself here was whether or not such a meeting had taken place, and whether or not any business had been transacted, in short had anything occurred between Gord and Quark which could have led to murder? I think it is safe for me to say that Mr Gord is a deeply paranoid individual. Whether this occurs naturally in his personality or has been brought on by years of drug abuse I cannot tell, but suffice it to say that in my experience characters of this kind need little provocation to kill. If Quark had declined to supply more drugs, or had threatened to stop supply unless a higher price were paid, or perhaps had intimated that there was another athlete willing to pay more, then I believe that Mr Gord, in his current mental state, would have been capable of murder. It may not necessarily have been anything as dramatic as that. I have seen paranoids kill for the most insignificant of reasons. The wrong word, the wrong gesture, the wrong look. All have cost people their lives. Was this the case here? Due primarily to the fact that Mr Gord has not been seen in the hotel during daylight hours since he arrived here, I have no real evidence either way. Nothing to incriminate him, nothing to absolve him.'

Suddenly, Sun Gord made a dash for the door, and was through it and out of the room before anyone could react. The remaining people in the room all turned their eyes from the door towards Max Quadrant, who had calmly leaned up against the bar. From the silence of the bar room they could make out the noise of some kind of physical struggle going on beyond the door, followed by muffled voices, then silence once more. Slowly, the door opened and Sun Gord reappeared, walked across the bar area and slumped back into his seat. Max moved away from the bar and again stood facing his audience.

'As Mr Gord can now testify, I do have some assistance here. A small detachment of Space Police arrived here late this afternoon. I have not involved them in our little gathering as their presence is not necessary for its purpose, but they are stationed outside so if anyone else has ideas of fleeing, then please save your energy. In truth, there is no escape from here anyway, as it is impossible to leave this planet undetected, but I am loathe to spend my time tracking people down in the mountains and foothills of Solauric, so waited until my "insurance policy" was in place before commencing this debate.' Max took a few steps to his right and stood in front of the final group seated by the window.

'So, we come to our last group of gallant guests, President Aldous T. Shrube and his faithful aides. I will start with Mr Edward Broillie, the man responsible for maintaining and enhancing the President's public image.' Broillie rose to speak, but Max quickly raised his hand. 'Mr Broillie, I would rather that you did not contribute to this part of the proceeding, given that each of the people here only has a finite amount of time left in their lives and I for one would prefer not to waste any of it in cryptic and ultimately pointless conversation with you. Suffice it to say, I have met certain people who, to use an old-fashioned term, call a spade a spade. I have met plenty of argumentative types that will call a spade a shovel, and I have even encountered the more cautious variety who will say that spade may be a spade or a shovel. You, Mr Broillie, are most likely to contend that a spade is an implement primarily designed for use by a manual labourer in the process of soil relocation, but which may or may not also be used in an infinite number of other ways for certain unspecified purposes although equally may not be used for anything at all.

'On the night of the Professor's death, Mr Broillie played a significant role in the ensuing proceedings as, with his colleague Mr Joyce, he was responsible for removing the body from the room in which the murder had taken place and relocating said body to the hotel's cold storage area, ostensibly on the grounds of preserving the corpse. Whilst this action did arouse my suspicions that perhaps this was an attempt to destroy evidence, or at least to make the identity of the murderer more problematic to attain, it did not in itself establish or indicate any motive for the perpetration of the crime itself. So, for the purposes of my investigation I largely ignored the events subsequent to the killing and instead concentrated on those that had potentially occurred prior to it; that is, what could possibly have caused Mr Broillie to have reason to commit murder. I will not bore you with my entire thought process in this regard, but the underlying factor that became apparent to me was that, as in the case of Mr Portent, Mr Broillie is, in his own way, totally dedicated to the welfare of his employer, in this instance our President,

Mr Aldous T. Shrube. I came to the conclusion, therefore, that any actions Mr Broillie may have committed were unlikely to have been born out of direct self-interest, but were more likely to have been as an effort to protect the reputation of the President. This possibly explains his actions in the removal of the body. The President's top adviser being murdered on a small planet with only a few people present was never going to reflect well on Mr Shrube, and would certainly not enhance his chances of re-election to the post. There also seems to be a complete absence of any personal reason why Mr Broillie would have wanted Quark dead, so my conclusion here was that one of three things had happened. One, Mr Broillie discovered that some person unknown had killed Quark and he sought to minimise the damage to his employer's reputation and image. Two, Mr Broillie believed the Professor posed some kind of threat to the President, either through something he had done or by something he knew, and he decided to eliminate him before this threat could bear fruit. Three, President Shrube was himself the murderer and Mr Broillie was simply doing what he could to cover it up.'

'This is outrageous!' roared Shrube.

'Mr President,' said Max, 'with all due respect, this is my investigation, not yours. We are on a private planet here, where your jurisdiction is severely limited. I will address you personally very shortly, but in the meantime would ask you to remain quiet.' Shrube was angry. In fact he looked so angry that his blood had gone past boiling point and was starting to evaporate, but he did as he was told.

'Thank you,' said Max. 'If you will permit me to continue, I will move on to the figure of Mr Hal Joyce, Chief Security Adviser to the President. Mr Joyce struck me as an altogether different type of personality to Mr Broillie. While being equally evasive, he evades by brevity rather than by verbosity. My feeling from talking to him was that he also varied from

Mr Broillie in another way, in that I never got from him any great feeling that his overriding sentiment was for the protection of the President. I am not saying that Mr Joyce is in any way in dereliction of his duties as Head of Presidential Security. Far from it. From what I have experienced and researched he does a first-class job. But that is what it is to him, a job. You see, there is a difference here between Mr Joyce and Mr Broillie. A subtle difference, but a significant one. To one man it is his life, to the other his job of work. Mr Joyce was involved with his associate in the removal of Professor Quark's body, but as I stated earlier in the case of Mr Broillie, I paid little attention to this fact in itself in relation to the identity of the murderer. Instead, I came to the conclusion that the same three scenarios which applied in the case of Mr Broillie, being the removal to protect the President's image, the murder itself to eliminate danger to the President, or the cover-up of the murder by the President himself, could apply equally to Mr Joyce. However, because of the difference in character between these two men, I also concluded that in the case of Mr Joyce there was also a fourth possibility.' Max turned back to the bar and downed the remainder of his drink before slowly revolving back round to directly face Shrube.

'And now we come to the last, and some would say most distinguished guest of all, President Aldous T. Shrube. As you all doubtless know, Mr Shrube comes from a very distinguished political family, one which might almost be termed a fledgling dynasty. His father was President some years ago, and I believe that Mr Shrube's eldest son also has ambitions in that direction, so there is the distinct development here of some kind of presidential lineage. But what kind of man is he? Well, Mr Edward Broillie and his colleagues would have us believe that the President is the wisest of the wise, unflappable under pressure, almost god-like in his intelligence and sagacity. Is this true? Well, obviously I speak here from the point of very limited experience, having only been here for a few days and having had direct communication with the President only twice, but I have to say that my impression was that he is a man who, as President of the Universe, is as out of his depth as a centipede wearing lead boots attempting to cross the wild oceans of Centrum T. However, Mr Shrube is not on trial here for his abilities as a competent holder of office. In fact, at this point, he is of course not on trial at all. The purpose of my investigations here relate solely to the identification of the killer of Professor Samuel Quark, and so, despite my reservations as to his ability to decide whether to spread butter or jam on his early morning toast, I have had to limit my considerations and deliberations to possible motives for President Shrube to have been the murderer. We all know at this point that the President was on Solauric to have a meeting with Samuel Quark. We are also reasonably certain that Jerrand D'Arqueville was also scheduled to attend, but did not. It is my supposition that the reason for Quark's murder was some event, or the discovery or awareness of some fact or event, which occurred whilst you were all assembled here awaiting, in some cases, the arrival of D'Arqueville. Why would Shrube have killed Quark? We know that Quark had been becoming increasingly involved with Jerrand D'Arqueville, so perhaps he had informed Mr Shrube that he was to cut his presidential ties going forward and work exclusively for D'Arqueville? This would undoubtedly have represented some kind of loss of face for the President, but enough to commit murder? I think not. If Quark were jumping ship to work for a political rival, that would have been serious and potentially damaging to the President's re-election chances, but still not enough to kill for. But leaving the Presidential service to work for the Richest Man That Ever Lived? That could easily be explained away. After all, who wouldn't go and work for D'Arqueville if he called?

'There is also the question of secrecy. I am sure that, in the course of his advisory work for the President, Professor Quark was privy to certain information of a sensitive and secretive nature, and having such a person walk into the arms of D'Arqueville may have, on the surface, presented something of a problem. But enough of a problem to kill for? Again, I think not. Quark has been working on and off for D'Arqueville for many years, so if he had wanted access to this type of sensitive information and Quark had been prepared to give it, then this would have already happened. Besides, such is the power of Jerrand D'Arqueville that if he wants to know something, he will find out, and I am sure that President Shrube would be as aware of this fact as anyone, and would never be naive enough to think that by killing Quark he would ultimately be depriving D'Arqueville of finding out something he wanted to know. So no, these do not represent likely reasons why Mr Shrube would have killed the Professor, although I could not rule out some sort of "who will rid me of this turbulent Priest?" scenario, whereby for instance Mr Broillie or Mr Joyce took it upon themselves to kill Quark because they misinterpreted something Shrube had said and believed that this drastic action would serve to protect their employer's position.

'I said earlier on that the behaviour of Mr Broillie and Mr Joyce on the night of the murder could be viewed as being highly suspicious, but that there were certain potentially mitigating factors which could explain this behaviour. President Shrube's behaviour on that night was also strange in some ways and is perhaps more difficult to reason. Mr Shrube is not renowned for being a heavy drinker, in fact he is well known for his general temperance, limiting his alcoholic intake to the odd glass of wine with his dinner, so as not to find himself incapacitated should a moment of crisis occur. Very admirable and responsible. However, on this particular night, Mr Shrube sat here at the bar drinking very large glasses of straight vodka. This might be due to the fact that the President was on an isolated planet, millions of miles from anywhere, and felt he was extremely unlikely to be contacted in any kind of official capacity that night, and so took advantage of the rare opportunity to have a few drinks. Possible. But probable? What was also odd was that the President apparently first heard of Quark's death from Caleb Khorklory who was serving drinks behind the bar. This would have been strange in normal circumstances, for a barman to have knowledge of such an event before the President of the Universe, but even stranger when the men engaged in removing the body from the murder scene were aides to the President himself. The timing of the President's actions here is very important as well. When he first arrived in the bar he sat here, at the bar, and, again seemingly out of character, began engaging in casual conversation with the barman. As soon as Caleb makes mention of Quark's murder, he moves away from the bar to take up a solitary position pretty much in the same chair as he is seated in now.

'Now, one explanation of this would be that Shrube comes down here to the bar to relax and have a quiet drink, and being in relaxing mood has a social chat with the barman. In the course of this conversation he hears the bombshell news that his old friend and adviser Samuel Quark has been murdered. Upon hearing this devastating news he orders a stiff drink and retires over here for a period of contemplative solitude, being obviously no longer in the mood for light hearted banter with the barman. All well and good. Except that it most certainly did not happen this way. Shrube had embarked on his vodka drinking spree as soon as he arrived in the bar, not when he heard about the murder. So how about an alternative version of events? Let us suppose for a moment that when he arrived in the bar that night, President Shrube was already aware that Samuel Quark was dead, either because he had been informed of the event, or because he had ordered the murder to be carried out, or because he had actually killed the Professor himself. So, we make this assumption. When he walks into the bar, President Shrube knows that Quark has been murdered. However, for some reason, he does not wish it to be known that he knows. Rather, his whole purpose in coming to the bar alone is to "find out", to be publicly seen to become aware of it for the first time. When he arrives in the bar, he immediately begins chatting with the barman, desperately hoping that he will mention the events that have recently transpired. Despite the enormity of the event itself, the revelation is somewhat delayed, rather ironically by the fact that Caleb assumes that Shrube already knows, by virtue of his not unnatural assumption that if a barman knows something of this magnitude has occurred, then surely the President of the Universe must already know. We note again here that Shrube is already on the large vodkas, indicating quite firmly that he is already troubled by occurrences of which he is still supposedly unaware. Eventually, he manages to get Caleb to mention the killing, at which point he feigns shock and distress and, purpose achieved, he immediately ceases the conversation. This, I would contend, provides the most likely explanation of President Shrube's behaviour. Even if it is true, which I believe it is, it does not prove anything more than, at worst, concealment of knowledge, and probably not even that as, to my knowledge, no one had actually asked the President that evening whether or not he was aware that the Professor had been murdered.

'Ladies and gentlemen, please forgive my digressions. They are not without purpose I assure you, but nevertheless I thank you for indulging me this evening and for giving me your full attention. Due to biological necessity, I must leave you for a short time, but when I return I shall finish this. I will tell you why this murder was committed, and by whom. In the meantime, I suggest that those of you in need of a drink get one, on which subject may I ask Caleb to refill my glass?' Max turned and walked out towards the lavatories. As he passed by the bar, he said quietly to Caleb, 'And put some vodka in this one – plenty.'

# 29

A few minutes later, Max returned to the bar area. The room was silent, and had been so for the time he had been out of the room, save for the odd hushed drinks order. Max walked to the bar, took a sip of his drink, winced slightly at the strength of it, then began once more to address his audience.

'The key to this case was always, in my opinion, motive. As I have outlined here tonight, there are many of you in this room who may have had cause to murder Samuel Quark. But who actually did it? To answer this question, I had to go through all the events which I could conceive that had possibly occurred, and for each one think of a reason why it could not have been the cause of the Professor's death. The nearest analogy I can think of is trying to open a safe when you don't have the combination. You keep trying all the possibilities until eventually, click, you have it. That was my process but rather than go through all the potential motives of each of the possible murderers, meaning all of you, I instead concentrated on the possibilities of what it was that Quark had invented, knowing that if I could establish this, then everything else would fall into place. I tried various scenarios – invention of a new super-weapon, of a new drug, a new food, new lots of things, but none could fully rationalise the events that had taken place. It was then that I began looking through the notes I had made following my conversations with Professor Tacitus, and this got me thinking down a different line altogether. What if Quark had not invented something, but discovered something, or produced some radical new theory just as he did all those years ago with his theories on the infinite nature of the universe? Immediately, I felt certain that this was where the truth was to be found. Everything started to fit together. This type of discovery or theory would indeed be a major event, one that would potentially have an effect on the whole of humanity. This could be the type of thing that someone might be prepared to kill for. I thought about this for a while, and then suddenly I was convinced I had it. Professor Quark had conclusive proof of the existence of the Thorians, and he was killed to protect this secret. The question would be who? Who would kill to protect such a secret?

'OK, let's look at the possibilities. President Shrube? No, certainly not. The President has made defence against the Thorians a central pillar of his administration. Billions upon billions of dollars have been spent on the assembly of huge arsenals of weapons on the assumption of a future conflict with the Thorians. Proof of their existence would make President Shrube a hero, prove that the doubters and cynics were wrong and that he, Aldous T. Shrube, the wisest of the wise, had been right all along. Re-election would be a certainty. So we can rule out President Shrube from this scenario, and by association can also rule out Mr Broillie and Mr Joyce as the President's re-election would almost certainly guarantee their posts for another five years.

'What about Jerrand D'Arqueville? Would this be the kind of secret he would kill to protect? Again, not likely. D'Arqueville has made the larger portion of his huge wealth from the sale of arms. Proof of the Thorians' existence would increase demand for weaponry and further enrich his fortune. Karl Shernman? Well, as he kindly drew our attention to earlier this evening, he has much of his personal fortune invested in D'Arqueville's companies, including the arms manufacturers and developers, so he also could only benefit from the increased Thorian threat, not lose from it. As for the rest of you, I could see no reason at all why any of you would be personally disadvantaged by news of the proven existence of the Thorians becoming public knowledge. So, eventually, I ruled this out as a possibility, but it had changed my thinking and I was sure that I was now getting very close. And then, yes, the tumblers all clicked into place. The reason. The reason why Quark had been killed. I knew what he had discovered. The more I thought about it the more I was certain that I was right. Quark had made the most important discovery in the history of human existence, but had been killed for the same shabby reason that millions before him had been killed. Samuel Quark was murdered for avarice.

'You see, where I went wrong was that when I realised that Quark had been killed because of what he had discovered, I made the mistake of assuming that the murder had been committed to protect this secret, to stop it ever becoming public knowledge. The more I thought about it, the more I realised that I must be mistaken in this assumption. We are reasonably sure that prior to coming to Solauric, Quark paid a visit to the planet of Jerrand D'Arqueville, and it is ninety-nine per cent certain that the purpose of that meeting was for Quark to inform D'Arqueville of his discovery. Such is the nature of this discovery, and its implications for the human race, that even if this had not been the original reason for the meeting it is inconceivable that the Professor would not have relayed it to D'Arqueville during their discussions. We can therefore assume that once Quark arrived on Solauric, D'Arqueville already knew of the discovery. This did of course raise the possibility that D'Arqueville himself had Quark murdered to stop the discovery being revealed, but two things countered against this hypothesis. The first was the fact that D'Arqueville was well aware that Quark worked as part of a large team of scientists, and as such there was a high probability that some of his associates had collaborated on this research, or were at least aware of it. Also, Quark was a scientist, and by their nature scientists record things. They write them down, or dictate them into their computer software via the VisiScreen. It therefore seemed unlikely to me that a man such as D'Arqueville would have thought that he could stop this discovery becoming known simply by killing one man.

'The second point is that D'Arqueville's actions subsequent to his meeting with Quark do not indicate that he was under the impression that the discovery would remain a secret, as he doubtless would have done had he ordered the murder for the express purpose of protecting it. In fact, the very opposite is true. D'Arqueville's actions demonstrate that he was certain that this information would very quickly become public knowledge. It is clear then, that D'Arqueville did not order the death of Samuel Quark to suppress the information in question, and by extension this exonerates everyone else on Solauric from killing the Professor for the same motive, as once D'Arqueville knew the secret it could not possibly be concealed simply by killing Quark. So what was the alternative? If Quark was killed because of what he knew, but not to stop it becoming known, then what was the reason? Only one realistic alternative. He was not killed to stop the discovery being revealed, but to *delay* its revelation.' Max paused for a moment. Still complete silence in the room, an even more intense silence now as the assembled gathering had sensed that the moment had arrived and they scarcely dared to breathe for fear of missing the unveiling. Max Quadrant took a large gulp of his drink, winced again, then continued.

'I referred earlier to the fact that what Quark had discovered was perhaps the single most important discovery in the history of human evolution, and I do not believe that to be an overestimation. I also spoke earlier of my initially favoured theory that he had attained affirmative proof of the Thorian threat, a theory which I eventually concluded could not be true for the reasons which I stated. Now, all of us, I assume, are aware to a greater or lesser degree of the early work of Professor Samuel Quark, and of his theories on the infinite nature of the universe, which made him such a prominent figure early on in his career. While what became known as The Quark Theories became universally accepted, the man himself, being a good scientist, was not content to leave it there. He had to prove that he was right. Not just theory, but proof, absolute proof, that is what the true scientific genius strives for. And so, in all the intervening years between the publication of his original theories and the present, while he was involved in many different projects, he never rested in his pursuit of proof of the infinite nature of the universe. He and his team regularly sent out small probes into the deepest wastelands of space, which sent back information on planets, distances and every conceivable detail on the physical environment through which they travelled. Then, ultimately, after years and years of research and analysis of the information received back from thousands of probes, he found an answer. He found The Answer. And it was not what he expected. What Samuel Quark discovered was not proof of the infinite nature of the universe, but absolute, total, conclusive proof of a finite universe. Finite, as in, "that's it, there is no more". I believe that his earliest probes had effectively sent back messages that they could go no further, that they had reached the end of space. I am sure that he would have at first dismissed this as some kind of anomaly, but gradually as the same information was returned from all parts of space he must have come to realise that what his probes were telling him was true. Space was finite. It had a beginning and it had an end.

'As I mentioned earlier, these probes analysed every planet

as they passed, and so over the years Quark would have built up a massive catalogue database, with information on every known planet in the universe. This would of course have been extremely useful for the government when they were looking for new worlds to colonise, and for people like Jerrand D'Arqueville, who were looking for planets to own for their own private use. But the crucial point comes where Quark discovers that the universe is finite, because at this point his database of every known planet in the universe suddenly becomes a database of every planet in the universe. He knows from the information that has been sent back by his probes that none of these planets show any signs of alien life, so now we not only have proof of a finite universe, we have proof that other life forms do not exist. Ladies and gentlemen, despite being a finite universe, it's still a very big one, and we are the only ones in it.'

Max looked around the room at the faces in front of him as his announcement started to sink in. The looks on their faces absolutely mirrored his own thoughts when the truth had become apparent to him twenty-four hours earlier in his hotel room.

'As I said, to call this the most significant discovery in the history of humanity is not an exaggeration. It answers one of the fundamental questions that man has asked himself from the dawn of civilisation. Are we alone? Well, it seems, the answer is yes. There are no Thorians, no extra-terrestrials, no little green men, nothing. Just us. This discovery will have an effect on every single human being in the universe. It will affect the way we look at the universe around us. It will affect the way we look at ourselves. Psychologically, everyone will be different after they know this fact. But for some people, the effect will go beyond the psychological, and one of these people is Jerrand D'Arqueville.

'Back at Space Detective headquarters on Centrum H, I have a very clever colleague. He is still a young man, but in his chosen specialism he is amongst the very best there is. His specialism is gaining access to other people's computer systems. Such is the demand for these skills that he could by now be a very wealthy man if he chose to work for one of the many organisations who require people with these skills, but fortunately for myself and the other members of the Space Detective Agency, and for the public at large, he is both an inherently honest man and one who values the fight against crime higher than he does the battle for the accumulation of personal wealth. During the course of this investigation, I have been in regular contact with this individual and his assistance has been crucial to its outcome. I am also fortunate to have a son who works in the banking industry, and he too has been invaluable in the provision to me of certain insights and advice as to how things work in that field. I mention these people not just to affirm my gratitude for their assistance, but also as a precursor to demonstrate that what I am about to reveal to you is not mere speculation on my part, but is based on material facts and informed judgement.

'To recap, some people will be more directly affected by the discovery of a finite, human universe than others. Jerrand D'Arqueville knew instantly what the effect would be on him. Remember, for all his varied financial interests, D'Arqueville built his original fortune on the back of the arms trade, and that business still forms a significant part of his empire to this day. Just think for a moment about the effect that Quark's discovery will have on that business. Large-scale armed conflict between humans ended quite some time ago, starting with the formation of the Universal Government, and the massive arms expenditure of recent times, particularly under the Shrube administration, has been justified purely on the grounds of preparation for a potential war against the Thorians or some other as yet unknown malevolent alien race. The internal threat to humanity is minimal, certainly in terms of scale, and now the external threat has been proven to be non-existent. The need to produce large weapons of destruction has vanished in an instant. The effect on the arms trade will be catastrophic. Jerrand D'Arqueville is not a stupid man. He realised this fact as soon as Quark revealed the finite universe to him. He was also aware, of course, that the fact that Quark had told him first gave him a window of opportunity. Once the planned summit meeting on Solauric had ended, the discovery would soon become public knowledge, but until that point he would have an exclusivity of knowledge. Faced with the threat of his holdings in arms development and production companies being almost worthless overnight, he knew he had to sell, but he had to do so without alerting the markets to the fact that something had gone so dreadfully wrong. He therefore set about the process of selling his shares in these companies, not in a mass sale but by transferring small parcels of shares out through his myriad of subsidiary companies, and subsidiaries of those subsidiaries, so that it did not become apparent that the sales all originated with the same person. To do this he needed time, and it was for this reason that he kept delaying his arrival here on Solauric. He knew that once the meeting had concluded, the shares would crash spectacularly, but he also knew that the meeting would not start without him, provided that he was still making an undertaking to attend. His plan was to keep stalling them until he had disposed of his holdings, then turn up for the meeting knowing that he would now be immune from its financial consequences. D'Arqueville did have huge shareholdings in these companies, and of course he could not pass on these types of volumes into the open market without depressing the stock prices, the simple principle of supply and demand dictates that, but he has been clever enough to keep this to a minimum, and on average his actions, despite the massive amounts of shares he has sold, have led to only a twenty to twenty-five per cent drop in value. When you consider that these shares are about to become worthless that is good, if slightly dishonest, business in anyone's book, and it was through these events that I concluded that D'Arqueville had had no intention of killing Quark to protect the secret, nor did he want to kill him to delay the revelation. He didn't need to, as it was within his power to do that himself, simply by stalling his arrival on Solauric. So, all in all, Jerrand D'Arqueville would seem to be in the clear as far as the murder goes. He was not, however, the only person who had a financial interest at stake in the outcome of the Solauric summit.

'Our friend Mr Karl Shernman is famous for the diversity of his business empire. It is commonly accepted that this man can make any company a success. He is, as they say, the Man With The Golden Touch. But how much truth is there in this? Well, my colleagues have, by various means, performed some quite detailed research into the companies in which Mr Shernman has an interest, and their analysis of information which is, how we might say, not generally available to the public, paints a very different picture to that normally on view through the media. The overriding conclusion is that the image of Karl Shernman as a business genius is a complete and utter sham, a gross distortion of the truth, a fraud. Early on in his career, Karl Shernman was very fortunate indeed in that he formed an association with a young man named Jerrand D'Arqueville, who at that time was investing heavily in the weapons business. Shernman at that point had no fortune of his own, but was convinced by D'Arqueville that such an investment was a sure-fire money maker so he borrowed as much as he could possibly raise and took a minor shareholding in some of those companies in which D'Arqueville was investing. It was a gamble, but the most lucrative gamble of all time, as over the next few years his minor shareholdings in these companies became worth

MAX QUADRANT – SPACE DETECTIVE

billions as the arms trade grew and grew to counter the perceived alien threat and, while his wealth was nothing compared to D'Arqueville's, he still became one of the richest men in the universe.

'Whereas many people would have simply thanked their good fortune for this turn of events, this was not the case with Mr Shernman, as his ego would not allow him to attribute this accumulation of wealth to any kind of gambler's luck or the profound insight of another. No, I think he convinced himself that he was a business genius, and it was then that he began to use his massive wealth to take control of other companies and run them his way. The truth, though, as we found out, is that not one of the companies which he took over has been a financial success. In fact, every single one has seen its profits fall since he took over, and the majority have actually fallen to a loss-making position. This has been concealed by propping up these companies' balance sheets by using the large profits from his arms company shareholdings, but the truth is still there all the same. As a business mogul, Karl Shernman is a failure. A failure, but of course an immensely rich one. But rich for how long? The same scenario which faced Jerrand D'Arqueville would also be faced by Karl Shernman, but in Shernman's case the problem was even more severe. If his holdings in arms companies became worthless, his whole empire would come crashing down, as it was the money coming in from these investments which kept all his other ventures solvent. While D'Arqueville faced the possibility of a devaluation in his fortune, Shernman risked losing everything.

'Shortly after D'Arqueville had secretly managed to offload his shares into the marketplace, Shernman began attempting to sell all his shareholdings in weapons related companies. Whether that was because he knew about the finite universe I do not know. I do know that Mr Shernman was in the habit of keeping people under surveillance, and of doing his best to intercept and decode electronic messages, so there is a possibility that he became aware of Quark's discovery in its entirety. Even if he did not know the facts in full, which I suspect from his reaction to my earlier revelation to be true, his people would doubtless have alerted him to the fact that large volumes of shares were being traded in the arms companies in which he had holdings, and I am sure that these same people were clever enough to trace the origin of the sellers back to D'Arqueville. Given the circumstances, it would not have taken a great leap of logic for Karl Shernman to conclude that there was a direct connection between the private meeting between Jerrand D'Arqueville and Samuel Quark and the subsequent offload of the shares, and by simple deduction it would have soon become apparent to Shernman that whatever the Solauric summit was to be about it looked likely that its consequences would be dire for the arms industry. From there, his only reasonable course of action would be to devise a plan by which he could sell his own shares at the minimum loss. But, unlike D'Arqueville, he would be working to a timeframe that was out of his control, and trying to sell in a falling market where presumably anyone who was interested in buying in to arms companies had already done so via the massive sell-off by D'Arqueville. He had to sell quickly, and he had to find someone to sell to.

'When I stated earlier that Darren and Karen Farren were most definitely innocent of the crime, I also stated that not only did they have no motive for killing Quark, but that they were the only guests here who were not actually here for the reason that they thought they were here. I will now explain what I meant by that. Mr Farren, let me ask you a couple of questions. Firstly, I think I am right in saying that of all the guests here you were the last to arrive, and that in fact your coming here was something of a last-minute decision?' Darren Farren opened his mouth and took a breath in preparation to answer, but he was a lifetime too slow.

'That's right,' said Karen, 'we weren't supposed to be coming here at all. We were on holiday on the planet Kucress when Mr Shernman got in contact with us and invited us to join him here. It was very fortunate, really, because Kucress isn't that far away as space travel goes, and he paid for a private spacecraft to bring us here. It was ever so nice of him, it only took us three days to get here, so we didn't even have to go into spacesleep, just came straight here, and I mean Kucress is very nice and all, but, I mean, this is Solauric, isn't it? You can't turn down a chance to come to visit Solauric. It was ever so kind of Mr Shernman to invite us, he's been ever so kind to us since we first met him. Ever so kind.'

'And the purpose of his inviting you here?'

'Just for a holiday. He said he was coming here on a holiday but the place would be full of stuffy politicians and that, and he wanted to see some friendly faces.'

'And since you arrived here, has it just been one big holiday with Karl Shernman?'

'Yes, well apart from the obvious, you know, that man being killed and all that.'

'Nothing else?'

'No.'

'I don't believe that's true, Mrs Farren, and if I could ask you to remain quiet for a moment, I would like your husband to be able to comment. Mr Farren, is it true that your stay here has been comprised solely of recreational pursuits?' Darren Farren made his usual preparations to begin speaking, but was somewhat taken aback by the fact that his wife, currently under the intense glare of Max Quadrant, did not interrupt him.

'Well … yes,' he said eventually. 'I suppose so, it's just been a holiday, although Mr Shernman, who as my wife said has been ever so kind to us, he has been talking a bit of business with us, you know, advising us about what to do with our money.'

'Quite,' said Max, 'and did this advice, perchance, in any way involve buying shares in certain companies connected with the development, manufacture and distribution of weapons?'

Both the Farrens were now starting to look as sheepish as a four-legged animal in a woollen coat standing next to a shepherd, and both seemed reluctant to speak further. Finally, Darren Farren spoke.

'It's not what you think, Detective. He's been ever so kind to us. He said he'd made much of his fortune in this way, and now he wanted someone else to get the same benefits that he had had. I'm sure he didn't mean to do us any harm.'

'I'm afraid you couldn't be more wrong,' said Max. 'Karl Shernman invited you here with the express intention of off-loading on to you his soon to be worthless shares. When it became clear that their sale on the open market would be impossible within the limited timeframe available, he decided to try and sell in one single transaction to the only people he knew who had enough money and, to be frank, who were gullible enough to act as counterparty to such a deal. I am aware that he managed to persuade you to enter into an agreement to buy his shares?' Darren and Karen Farren sat silent, but gently nodded to confirm what Max had said was true.

'Fortunately for you, transactions of this size in shares of listed companies are subject to regulatory approval, and as such I have been able to send word back to my office as to what has transpired here, with the result that the sale will be blocked. Your money is safe. The time period involved here has worked in your favour. Unfortunately, this time period did not work in favour of Samuel Quark, as Karl Shernman became aware that, despite persuading you to buy his shares, this would count for nothing unless the deal were to go through before the announcement of the finite universe was

MAX QUADRANT – SPACE DETECTIVE

made, as this would expose his deception and still give you time to pull out. He was in a race against time, a race which was out of his control. He had no idea when D'Arqueville was going to arrive, the summit take place and the announcement be made. I would imagine that once he became aware that D'Arqueville had completed his sale, he would have suspected that he was on his way here as the reason for his delayed appearance had passed. He may also have suspected that now that D'Arqueville was financially in the clear, he may be desperate to come to Solauric as soon as possible, as he would be aware of Karl Shernman's exposed position and possibly want to use the situation to destroy the man he had for a long time resented as achieving his wealth and fame off the back of his, D'Arqueville's, financial astuteness and vision.

'Faced with this problem, Karl Shernman decided to take dramatic action to gain control of his own destiny. He was in a situation where success or failure was all down to timing. If the sale could go ahead prior to the announcement, he was safe. If not, he would be ruined, probably bankrupt. The only way he could be sure of success was to delay the announcement, and the only way to delay the announcement was to delay the meeting, and he eventually decided that the only certain way to delay the meeting was to cause the death of the main protagonist, Professor Samuel Quark. He knew that this would throw the proposed meeting into disarray, and that with Quark murdered then D'Arqueville would either further postpone his arrival, or perhaps not even come at all. He would also have been aware that a murder on a privately owned planet would require investigation by a Space Detective, and that this would involve a time delay during which all the guests, or suspects as they would then be, would be held here on Solauric until the investigation was complete. He would be hoping that this would allow sufficient time for the necessary regulatory approval to go through in respect of the transfer of ownership of his shareholdings to the Farrens and the deal concluded before the news broke that would render them worthless. And so, it is my conclusion that the man responsible for the death of Professor Samuel Quark is Mr Karl Shernman.'

With a mixture of expressions ranging from shock, incredulity, through to horror, the assembled heads all turned to stare at the famous entrepreneur. For his part, Karl Shernman simply broke into one of his trademark mischievous grins.

'You are forgetting one thing, Detective,' he said. 'On what I believe people of your profession would refer to as the night in question, I was seated here in this very bar with my friends the Farrens, to whom I freely admit I may not have been as overwhelmingly kind to as they perceive, along with Mr Levitas and Miss Saturn. I can assure you that there is definitely only one Karl Shernman, Detective, I have no twin brother. So how do you explain the fact that I am supposed to have killed Quark in his room while sitting here drinking with my friends at the same time?'

'Please do not underestimate me, Mr Shernman,' said Max. 'I have forgotten nothing. I stated that you were the man responsible for the death of Samuel Quark, and that is the case. You do bear the ultimate responsibility. I did not say, however, that you were the person who physically brought about the end of his life. When I realised that you were the person behind this murder, I thought back over our conversations in the light of this knowledge and returned to something that had struck me as strange but which at the time I could not rationally understand or explain. It concerned our conversation out in the garden area, where you had tried, ultimately unsuccessfully, to divert me into believing that Jerrand D'Arqueville was the man behind this crime. That in itself was relatively unremarkable, but what was remarkable about the whole incident was the business with the cigar.

'As I have stated before, Mr Shernman, you do have a slight disadvantage in matters such as these in that being so famous there is an enormous amount of easily available written and pictorial evidence of your life and career. In examining some of this closely, I noted that of all the hundreds, possibly thousands, of pictures of you that I studied, not in a single one of them were you smoking a cigar. Not one of the hundreds of articles that I read about you mentioned you as a cigar smoker, despite the unbelievable amount of trivial details about you which they espouse. In fact several cited you as a vehement opponent of the tobacco industry. At the time, I suspected that this was probably just a typical case of the hypocrisy of famous figures, preaching one thing in public and doing the opposite in private, but in thinking about it again I discovered your true purpose. You are certainly not a regular cigar smoker, in fact I wouldn't be surprised if you had only smoked one cigar in your life before that day, and your abysmal attempts to keep it lit would probably serve as a just testament to that fact. So why attempt to smoke a cigar on that particular occasion? That was the question I asked myself, and the conclusion I came to was that it was born out of a decision made in haste. You walked into the bar with the intention of having a drink and some lunch there, possibly with the intention of trying to talk to me and drop your hints in about D'Arqueville's supposed involvement in the murder, but for some reason when you got in there you decided that you could not remain there. The only option instantly available to you was to go and sit outside, but this might seem strangely unsociable and suspicious for a man of your famously gregarious nature as there was plenty of space available in the bar, so how best to explain and excuse this sudden burst of misanthropy? Easy. Buy a cigar. Everyone knows you cannot smoke it indoors, so you have to go outside. Problem solved. But what was the real reason you were anxious to leave the bar? It certainly wasn't to avoid me as, in actual fact, the opposite was the case, you were anxious to talk to me in order to launch your attempt to incriminate Jerrand D'Arqueville. No, it wasn't to avoid me, it was to avoid someone else, to avoid striking in my mind an association between you and the person I was talking to at the time, a person who was becoming so nervous that he could well have said or done the wrong thing if he was put in the physical presence of the man who was investigating Quark's murder and the man who had ordered the murder itself, the murder that this man had carried out. I am of course talking about President Shrube's Head of Security, Mr Hal Joyce and, while I know this to be true, I am also firmly backed up in this accusation by evidence from my office that shows a recent accreditation from unknown sources into Mr Joyce's bank account amounting to some two million dollars. These amounts were, as I said, received from unknown sources. Unknown to the bank that is, but through my ethical hacker friend we have conclusively established that, while they have passed through a large number of fictitious individuals and various shell companies, the original source of the money is Karl Shernman.

'So, to summarise, Karl Shernman had concluded that the only way to save his financial empire was to kill Samuel Quark. Either to avoid getting his hands dirty with the crime itself, or simply to establish what he believed was a cast iron alibi, he paid two million dollars to Hal Joyce to carry out the killing, and made sure that at the agreed time of the murder he would be conspicuous by his presence here in the bar. Mr Joyce, for his part, shot the Professor through the head with the laser pistol, then as soon as the body was discovered he used the excuse of being Head of Presidential Security – remember Quark was a Presidential Adviser – to return with his associate Mr Broillie and disturb the murder scene sufficiently, he thought, to hamper the investigation, and of course to explain any physical evidence which may have indicated his presence in the Professor's room.

'President Shrube, although not in any way guilty of, or complicit in, this act of murder, I do believe knew of Quark's death at the point he entered this bar on that evening, although I am at present at a loss to determine the source of his information. It is highly unlikely that Mr Joyce would have informed him, since it would have been in his personal interest to keep the news as quiet as possible for as long as possible while he attempted to cover his tracks. Mr Broillie seems to me to be in the habit of telling the President the least information he can possibly get away with, mostly on the grounds that the less he knows the less damage he can cause. This leaves the possibility that Shrube either received the news from outside Solauric, which seems a remote possibility as Jerrand D'Arqueville would seem to be the only one candidate on the outside who would have been that quickly aware of the murder, or alternatively he got the information from someone else in this room. I may never discover the answer to that question, but ultimately it is a mere intellectual annoyance to me rather than an issue which bears any material relevance to the solution of this investigation.

'Ladies and gentlemen, I thank you all for your attention, and will conclude by making the formal announcement that Mr Karl Shernman and Mr Hal Joyce are now under arrest for the murder of Professor Samuel Quark.'

# 30

The next morning, Max Quadrant stood at the reception desk of the Hotel Solauric, bag slung over his shoulder, going through the process of checking out. In honour of his successful solving of the Solauric murder case, Barrington Portent was performing this task personally.

'And remember, Detective Quadrant, you are welcome back at the Hotel Solauric at any time, as our guest. I can, naturally, be assured of your total discretion over the events that have occurred here, once you leave?'

'Mr Portent, that goes without saying. I would like to thank you for your hospitality and for the use of your office during my investigation. It was most helpful. I hope that if I come here again it will be under more pleasant circumstances, but who knows what will happen in the future? Goodbye.'

'Goodbye, Detective.'

Max began to walk out of the main doors towards the spacecraft arrival and departure zone, and the last words he heard as he went through the exit were Portent's.

'... Ah yes, the future, eh? Who knows? There are many ways to explain what might happen in the future ...'

Max neared the departure area, and saw ahead the space cargo ship which he was about to board for the return journey to Centrum H. Another three months in spacesleep, another three months younger than his wife and son. Then he heard a voice coming from behind him.

'Max!' As he turned, he saw Rose Saturn walking quickly

towards him. He stopped, and within a few seconds she was standing facing him.

'Max, I just wanted to say goodbye. And thanks. Thanks for all you've done.'

Max shrugged. 'I got there in the end.'

'Max, you were brilliant!' said Rose. 'It was so dramatic, the way you went through each of us and said why you had thought we might have killed Quark. Was that part of the plan to expose Shernman and Joyce, or was it just to show how clever you are?'

'Bit of both, I suppose. I was sure I had got it right, but you can never be one hundred per cent sure. Sometimes you need to go through that kind of exercise and just watch people's reactions. They can either confirm what you think or cast doubts on your assumptions, and occasionally, as was the case with Karl Shernman, you can get him to fill in some of the grey areas by pretending you know the answers already and just watching his reaction when you reveal them. The other part of it is just to demonstrate a personal theory of mine. You see, I don't separate the universe into murderers and non-murderers, I think anyone can kill. You, me, anyone. It just takes a certain set of circumstances.'

'Well, I can assure you you're wrong there, Max Quadrant,' said Rose, 'I could never kill anyone. And neither could you, not someone who didn't deserve it.'

'Well, there you are,' said Max. 'You're blurring the lines already. First of all I couldn't kill anyone, then I couldn't kill anyone who didn't deserve it. Deserve it in whose opinion? Mine?'

'Oh, I don't know,' said Rose. 'This is a silly conversation to be having when you're about to go. Are you off home?'

'Yes, back to Centrum H for the Millennium celebrations. I think they're going to delay the announcement of the finite universe until after then, so as not to spoil the big party. And you? Are you leaving today?'

'No, not today. Blane and I have a few things to sort out. Thought we'd stay a bit longer. Now that this murder business is all done with we can move on. You see, it's changed us, this enforced stay on Solauric. Before coming here, our life was always so hectic. One of us was usually away working and then when we were together we were usually off somewhere attending premieres and glitzy functions together, or being interviewed or some such thing. So when we were forced to stay here on this isolated planet for three months, it was in some ways the first real serious amount of time we had spent together, and it turns out that away from the acting environment we don't really seem to have much in common at all. So, you know, we thought we'd take a few days when everyone else has gone, and just decide what we are going to do, together or apart.'

'I'm sorry to hear that. I'm sure Blane's a good man at heart.'

'You don't mean that at all, Max,' grinned Rose.

'Perhaps not,' admitted Max. 'Anyway, I'm late already. If they leave without me, I'm stuck here for longer than a few days. It was a great pleasure to meet you, Rose, a very great pleasure, and I'll look out for you. I'm sure you won't be off the screens for too long.'

'Goodbye, Max – who knows, we might meet again some day.'

'Maybe,' said Max. 'But it's unlikely. It's a big universe out there.'

'It's smaller than it was,' said Rose. 'Now that we know there's a beginning and an end, it doesn't seem so big at all. I'm sure we'll meet again. In fact, I know we will.'

Max disappeared through the large aluminium doors of the cargo ship. Rose Saturn stood watching it as it sat inertly in the launch zone.

'I will see you again,' she said out loud. 'Until then, goodbye Max Quadrant, Space Detective.'

# 31

'So, my detective friend did well.'

'Yes, Jerrand, he did very well. Shernman and Joyce have been arrested and are currently being held in custody on board the Space Police vessel here. I think they are shipping them out tomorrow on the long journey to Centrum A, where they are to stand trial for Quark's murder.'

'Is Detective Quadrant accompanying them on this journey?'

'No, he's gone already. I guess his work is done. He'll probably have to attend the trial, I imagine, but that won't happen for quite some time. The case against them seems fairly solid, but with the amount of legal counsel at the disposal of Karl Shernman I wouldn't be surprised if there were some delays in bringing it to court.'

'I think that's a certainty, although things don't always go as planned, or as you might expect them to.'

'Meaning?'

'Meaning just what I say. Things don't always turn out as you expect them to. How did our murderers take to finally being exposed?'

'Joyce had a certain look of resignation about him. He looked exactly like you would expect a man in his position to look. He had seen an opportunity to make some quick, easy money, and now realised that this action had cost him everything and all he could see ahead of him was spending the rest of his life in prison. He looked absolutely devastated.'

'And Karl Shernman?'

'Total opposite, really. On the surface, anyway. He had a look on his face that it was all a big game, that he might have had a temporary set-back, but that he would still win in the end. When he was finally arrested, he was even smiling.'

'And well he might. As you rightly pointed out, he does have access to some very good lawyers. Or at least he does at the moment. When his shares collapse, as they surely will, he may well be bankrupted very soon. By the time the trial comes around, he may not be able to afford the cheapest lawyer in town. Unless, of course, he finds a wealthy benefactor willing to fund his defence.'

'Jerrand, surely you wouldn't?'

'No, no, not me. Certainly not me. I want Karl Shernman to rot in hell, I won't be helping him. But there are some wealthy people out there who do not know Karl Shernman as I know him, who may be willing to help him. Anyway, we are getting ahead of ourselves. Who knows, the trial may not be necessary at all. We have no way of knowing what will happen in the meantime.'

'Jerrand, you know everything. You always know what is going to happen before it happens.'

'I have good sources, that is true. I am pleased with the performance of this Max Quadrant. He is everything I was told he would be. I think I shall definitely make use of him again in the future.'

'And me?'

'Oh yes, always you. You are the one person I can rely on. I will let you know when I need your help again. This is only the first step. The discoveries of my old friend Samuel Quark have forced certain issues for me. There are certain thoughts which have been in my head for some time, and the fact that there are no other life forms in this finite universe of ours has served to crystallise those thoughts into one single idea. I have to consider now the best method to bring about my ultimate goal, but this will involve a series of momentous further steps, and I will very much want you to accompany me on each of those steps. When I am ready to take the next step, I will contact you. Until then, enjoy yourself. As a small token of gratitude for your help, I have deposited a substantial sum of money in your name in the Estrumin Bank, a bank which I also own, so there will be no questions. You are still young. Have some fun. It will be a while until I am ready for the next stage. Until then, goodbye.'

'Goodbye, Uncle Jerrand.'

# 32

It was approaching midnight on the last day of December 2999, and Max Quadrant was sitting at a table in the Uranium restaurant on Centrum H with Chloe and Dan, having just finished their meal.

'That was delicious!' said Chloe.

'Mmmmm ...' agreed Max, although he didn't agree. The table was small, the restaurant packed to suffocation, and the food had been both average and extortionately expensive, but as this was Dan's Millennium treat to his parents, he thought it polite to at least pretend he had enjoyed it.

'It's nearly midnight!' said Chloe. 'Shall we go outside and watch the laserworks?'

'Good idea,' said Dan, and Max followed his wife and son out onto Uranium's small roof terrace overlooking the city centre. Normally the climate of Centrum H was such that at least two extra layers of very warm clothing would be the minimum requirement before venturing outside at midnight, but such was the collective body heat from the masses of people everywhere that they just went out as they were. The roof terrace was packed, but they managed to push and elbow their way over to one of the corners, allowing an almost unimpeded view of the festivities going on below. A giant clock tower especially erected in the city square ticked down to the new Millennium. The sky was filled with the bright lights of the laserworks which made midnight seem like midday. Their eardrums were being continuously assaulted by the giant sonic bombs which accompanied the laserwork show, and all around him Max could feel the bodies of people he didn't know, pushing into him, leaning on him, a mass fusion of their unified laughter and excitement threatening to invade his mind. But the mind of Max Quadrant was not to be invaded on this night. He was thinking about the events he had been a part of on the planet Solauric. He was thinking about his friend Horatio Tacitus, the seemingly endless source of historical knowledge. He was thinking about President Aldous T. Shrube. Would the scandal which would surely erupt when it was revealed that Quark had been murdered by the Head of Presidential Security mean the end to his chances of re-election for a second term? Probably. He was thinking about Jerrand D'Arqueville. What had been D'Arqueville's role in all this? He had been far away on his own planet, but there had been times when Max could almost feel the man's presence on Solauric. He knew very little that was factual about Jerrand D'Arqueville. Rumours were plentiful, hard facts difficult to come by. He knew that, following Quark's initial revelations, D'Arqueville had been acting to protect his own financial position, and that as far as he was concerned the ruin of his old enemy, Karl Shernman, was an added bonus. Aside from protecting his money, what was D'Arqueville's agenda? Was Quark's discovery really just the result of an ongoing project, or was it a specific task he had been set by D'Arqueville? Interesting that Quark had chosen to reveal his discovery to D'Arqueville before all others, including President Shrube. Was the answer to the finite or infinite nature of the universe something that D'Arqueville had needed to know? If so, why? Was he a sinister demon lurking in the wastelands of space plotting some catastrophic act, or was he the great philanthropist who simply chose to keep himself to himself, handing out millions anonymously to those less fortunate without the egotistical need for recognition from society?

He was thinking about Rose Saturn. What was it about her that made her so overwhelmingly magnetic and intriguing? Certainly she was beautiful. Certainly she was charming, warm and amusing. But there was much more to her than that. Much more. She was like a viciously addictive drug. Just a small encounter with her left you instantly wanting more, but the more you got the more you wanted, needed, obsessed over. She had the enigmatic quality of unknown intent. Had she spent so much time with him because she liked him, or because she was using him for some purpose? Why had she been so sure that they would meet again? He had no idea. He just hoped she was right.

He was thinking about Professor Samuel Quark, the man whose greatest discovery had ultimately cost him his life. Never in the history of humanity would the work of one man have such an effect on the psyche of the entire population of the universe. The announcement was scheduled for the following day, the first day of the year 3000. People all across space would wake up feeling rough and just as they were beginning to recover President Shrube would appear on their Visiscreens and break the news that would change everyone forever. The seconds ticked away on the giant tower clock below, the crowds building to a crescendo of excitement. The moment arrived, a huge cheer of elation being comprehensively drowned out by the sonic bombs detonating all around as the sky was suddenly lit from horizon to horizon by an eruption of laserworks. Chloe leant up against him and gently kissed his cheek. Dan grabbed his hand and shook it with the vigour of a man who had drunk too much champagne. Max Quadrant looked out over the City Square. He had his wife and son by his side. There were a hundred or so other diners packed on to the small roof terrace of Uranium. There were at least a hundred thousand in the square below, probably three to four million in the surrounding streets of Centrum H, billions across the universe all joining in this moment of celebration, but he, Max Quadrant, Space Detective, had never felt so alone.

Max Quadrant will return in *Max Quadrant and the Deus Crystal.*

## *Max Quadrant and the Deus Crystal*

Deacon Synapse, brilliant young protégé of the late Professor Samuel Quark, has disappeared and, following pressure from powerful outside sources, Max Quadrant is assigned to investigate. His first step is to go to the planet Tharssadeam, location of the universe's largest secure psychiatric hospital, in order to question inmate Dr Sinnae Mensch, previously chief research partner of Deacon Synapse in their search for the Deus Crystal, a crystal which legend claims will enable the holder to communicate directly with God himself. On the planet Tharssadeam, Max is reunited with Rose Saturn, there to visit former boyfriend Blane Levitas, who has been confined to the mental institution having had a breakdown following a less than flattering review of one of his performances. Together, Max and Rose embark on a journey across space in a search to find out what has become of Deacon Synapse and to discover the truth about the Deus Crystal.